BREATHLESS

BREAKERS HOCKEY #3

ELISE FABER

BREATHLESS
BY ELISE FABER

BREATHLESS
Copyright © 2021 Elise Faber
Print ISBN-13: 978-1-63749-036-5
Ebook ISBN-13: 978-1-63749-035-8
Cover Art by Jena Brignola

BREAKERS HOCKEY SERIES

ONE

Marcel

SHE WAS...INSANE.

That was the only logical explanation.

I'd followed Prudence Hansley, retiree from the NWHL (now renamed the Premiere Hockey Federation, or the PHF) and current Scout and Development Coach for the Breakers, from the rink to this bridge.

And now she was strapping a parachute to her back.

It was late afternoon.

I'd attended the camp she'd been running for the younger players, for those hopefuls who wanted to make the roster, because I was in town and liked to stay in shape, and I tended to get a little tetchy if I wasn't on the ice.

She'd run a tough clinic, put us through our paces, made some good suggestions and corrections, even to me, and then she'd released us. I'd showered. The young guys who'd attended camp all week had gone to do young guy things, and I'd been prepared to go do old guy things—namely, an ice bath, massage, and then getting at least eight hours of sleep—but then as I was leaving, I'd heard Pru take a call that had concern rising in me.

Because the call had been an argument.

Ending with her snapping, "The conditions aren't too dangerous. I'm doing it, and I don't give a fuck what you say."

Obviously, that had prickled every cautious bone in my body.

Because I was a man who was cautious. Who planned and proceeded with care and didn't just dive in.

It had benefitted me in my career.

Prepare. Practice. Prep for every possible outcome.

That was how I'd made it to the NHL.

Because I wasn't the most naturally gifted player, but I worked my ass off, was prepared, and now I was on one of the best teams in the league.

Working with Prudence Hansley.

A fucking goddess, who seemed to thrive on pushing the limits, who lived big and bright, with the constant risk of flaming out.

And who flirted with me. Shamelessly.

I'd spent a lot of time with her (flirting and otherwise) since she was my friend's fiancé's *friend*. Which meant I'd learned a lot about her. She was talented, smart, a great hockey player (whose career had unfortunately ended too early because of a back injury), and...not cautious.

She. Was. Not. Cautious.

Shark diving. Bungee jumping. Climbing mountains. Shaving her head (though she'd apparently done that once in college and had no plans of doing it again because she had a weird-shaped head). The point was that I had heard enough about Pru's adventures to be seriously worried when she yelled she was doing something, even as the person on the other end of the call was clearly advising against it.

So, I'd followed her to a bridge.

A bridge she was standing next to...as she strapped a parachute to her back.

What the actual fuck? I literally could not—could *not!*—believe my eyes.

I popped open my door, stormed across the metal and concrete that was positioned high above a rapidly flowing river.

She glanced up, and though her eyes went wide at my approach, she didn't stop strapping it on. Was she going to jump? Off *this*?

Seriously.

What the fuck was wrong with her?

The woman had a fucking death wish.

I grabbed her arm when she would have stepped over the barrier. "What the fuck are you doing, Pru?"

"None of your fucking business," she snapped, trying to jerk free.

I reached for the buckle of her chute, undid it before she could do something stupider.

Like jump off the fucking bridge.

"Stop," she growled, but was too slow. It was already undone, and I was yanking it down her arms, off her hands.

I'd barely gotten it free when she tried to jerk it out of my grip.

So, I did the only thing I could.

Or maybe, more accurately, the only thing I could think of in that moment.

I launched the chute over the barrier.

Pru gasped and grabbed on to the metal, leaning over the edge. I moved with her, still not convinced she wouldn't do something stupid, like try to jump after it and strap it on mid-air, Black Widow style.

But all she did was watch it sail down into the water deep, deep below.

A splash.

Then Pru spun back and shoved me. Hard. "What the fuck are you doing?"

"Me?" I snapped. "*Me?* I'm not the one who was going to base jump without anyone around after having an argument with a sensible person who said what is *obvious,* and that being that the conditions are too fucking dangerous."

"I—" Her mouth opened and closed. "How the hell would you know what Ted said?"

I rolled my eyes. "It wasn't hard to deduce based on your caterwauling in the hallway at the rink."

"Cat-cat—" She shook her head. "*That* was a private conversation."

"A *loud* private conversation in a public place," I pointed out.

Her chin came up, and her eyes blazed. "I failed to get the memo telling me you have a say over my life," she gritted out.

I didn't. Of course, I didn't.

Which she knew. Which was why she snorted and said smugly, "Exactly."

I reached for her. "Do you have a fucking death wish?"

She batted my hand away.

I reached for her again.

"Don't." A step back as her nostrils flared, but then she spun, took off for her car.

But she didn't get in, didn't start up the engine and drive home.

Instead, she went to the trunk and got out another pack. Another *parachute.*

My temper snapped, and I ripped it out of her hands, tossed *that* over the side of the bridge, and then braced myself because she was going to shove me again.

Which she did.

I captured her hand, ignored the fact that it felt so damned small wrapped in my, even though she wasn't small, she was the *least* small person I knew. "Any more in there?" I growled instead of focusing on that, on how much I liked her flirting, on how much I wished I was a different man, one who could handle all that *not* small. "Because I'll throw those over, too."

"Those are *expensive*," she gritted.

Rage splintered through me. "I don't give a fuck," I snapped. "You want to go base jumping, you do it as safely as possible with spotters or a partner, and you don't do it after someone advises you to not do it today because the conditions are shit."

The wind, already breezy enough to have her ponytail whipping around her face, picked up right then, gusting and silently supporting my assertion.

She plunked her hands on her hips. "I do what I want."

"Yeah." I huffed a rough laugh. "And, apparently, you don't care that you'll hurt people if you die doing something stupid."

Something almost like vulnerability crossed her face. Then her shoulders went straight, her eyes went flinty. "My parents are gone. I don't have siblings. It's just me, relying on *me*, living *my* life." By the time the words were out there, any trace of that vulnerability was gone. All that was left was fire and temper and spunk.

All of which called to me.

None of which described me.

Her lips pressed flat. "So, who's going to be hurt, huh?"

I didn't hesitate. "Hazel. Oliver. The guys. Me."

She blinked. Then clenched her jaw, her words tight. "You

do realize that I'm going to do this, and you won't be able to stop me."

I glanced in her trunk, her back seat, saw there were no more packs. I shrugged. "Today, I did."

More fire. More temper. More spunk that had me wanting to pull her close, to taste all of that *not* small. "So, what," she snapped. "You're going to stalk me?"

Another shrug. "If I have to."

She glared. "You made it pretty fucking clear that you're not interested in me, so why care now? Why press this now? Why *bother?*"

My brows drew down. "Not interested?" I asked, completely aghast.

I'd been lusting after her for months, wanting her since the first time I'd seen her, desperate and dreaming about her from the moment she'd gotten close enough for me to scent her shampoo—something fruity and flowery and fucking intoxicating.

She jabbed a finger into my chest. "*You* turned me down."

I scowled. "You were drunk."

"I asked you out, and you *turned me down.*"

I moved closer. "I repeat. *You were drunk.*" I shook my head. What the hell was wrong with this woman? "I don't fuck women who can't consent, let alone those who can barely stay upright."

That stopped her for a second, and her face lost the hard lines of anger. "You turned me down because I was drunk?"

I huffed out a rough laugh. "Do you need me to say it for a third time?"

Her eyes went wide, and then half her mouth turned up, her body drifting closer. Her mad gone so quickly that I was left with whiplash. "You know," she murmured, dragging her finger down my chest. "This is the most words I've heard you say at once."

On my back foot, all I could do was shrug.

The other half of her mouth tipped up, and her body came flush with mine. Long brown, fruity and flowery-smelling hair, lean and strong curves, a pert nose, and...the most kissable set of lips I'd ever seen. Her breasts brushed my chest, her scent surrounded me. I settled my hands on her hips, brought her just a little bit closer.

"Would you turn me down now?" she asked, dragging that finger a little lower. Toward the waistband of my sweats.

No. I fucking wouldn't.

I would give *anything* to not have to turn her down.

But she knew precisely what she was doing, could probably feel precisely what *she* was doing to me...to my cock.

That lush, kissable mouth curved further. "Would you take me home and fu—"

My fingers tightened, and I might be cautious, might be a planner, but I was also a *man*. And it just so happened that I had planned this very scenario a hundred, a *thousand* times over. "Yeah," I said, covering her hand, bringing it down, pressing it to the hard length of my cock. "I'll take you home, and I'll fuck you, princess." A beat. "But only if you promise to not jump off this bridge."

She frowned. "I—"

Her fingers tightened, her hips canted forward, and I had to grit my teeth so I kept at least a tiny bit of control. "Until whoever was the voice of reason on the other end of that call, telling you today wasn't right"—the wind whipped around us— "says the conditions are good enough for the jump. And then" —I leaned forward, murmured in her ear—"if you still want to do it, you do it."

And I'd be here.

Making sure she was doing it as safely as possible.

Because despite what my ex said, I wasn't the kind of man who clipped someone's wings.

I just wanted the spreading of those wings and the leaping out of nests to happen safely and smartly.

I straightened, watched and waited to see what she would do. Her hazel eyes swirled with emotions—heat, frustration, interest, attraction, annoyance, desire, and more that I couldn't discern.

Then her face went blank.

I braced myself again.

"Okay," she said, shocking the shit out of me as she smiled widely and threw her arms around me. "Take me home and fuck me, Pretty Boy."

TWO

Pru

I WAS in Marcel's car.

Driving to his place, I supposed...

After having left *my* car on the bridge, the keys under the mat since Marcel had plucked them out of my pocket and put them there. That being after he'd pulled out his cell, dialed, and said into the speaker, "I'm calling in my favor. No gossip. Drive Pru's car home. It's parked on the bridge outside of..."

Then he'd relayed quick and efficient directions to our location (and, God, I'd never thought of quick and efficient as being sexy, but when Marcel did it...yeah, my lady parts stood up and cheered my decision to put off my dare deviling and get on with fucking).

He gripped the steering wheel, wide fingers, a dusting of hair on the backs of his hands, his knuckles. Small scars in varying shades of white to pale pink to a bright red line that I knew was the result of an errant skate blade and sixteen stitches the previous season. Strong hands. Capable hands. *Big hands...*

A girl could hope that he'd be *big* everywhere.

"Baby?" I asked, shifting in my seat, dropping my hand onto his thigh (and talk about *big*...yum, nothing like the strong legs of a hockey player).

His hands tightened on the wheel, those knuckles pressing against his skin, going a stark white. He glanced at me with his unusual amber eyes, heat swirling in their depths.

But he didn't say anything.

Just waited for *me* to say what was on my mind.

My mouth twitched. I'd thought the man was totally uninterested in me, thought I'd read the situation loud and clear.

Oh, I'd still flirted.

Because that was my nature.

I didn't quiet myself, no fucking way. I just...didn't cross the line between flirting and creeping.

And I'd firmly put any fantasy of me and Marcel aside.

But now I was in the car with him, orgasms—hopefully—in my future.

With amber eyes hitting mine again, I realized that I'd asked a question...kind of, anyway. Which had me blurting, "What's your favorite position?"

Because I didn't really have a filter, certainly hadn't managed to hold on to one with Marcel—not ever—and because I was genuinely curious as to the answer for this one.

Stillness.

Then, "My favorite position is whatever one I'm fucking you in, princess."

All of the breath squeezed out of my lungs.

My nipples went tingly, pressing against the sports bra I was wearing, the thin cotton abrading the sensitive tips, making them grow hard, sending heat coiling into my abdomen, moisture pooling between my thighs.

"Like that look, princess."

As I was wondering *what* look, those amber eyes returned to the road, but I watched one half of his mouth curve up into a half-moon, giving me the insane urge to kiss the small divot it created, to tongue the dimples I'd admired for months.

So...

I did.

Bracing one hand on the console, using my other hand that was still resting on his thigh to bring me up so my lips could graze his cheek, so my tongue could dip into that tiny crease.

Stubble on my mouth, raising goose bumps on my nape.

He inhaled, and then he lifted one hand off the steering wheel, slipped it between our bodies, dropped it to the side of my neck.

Rough fingertips dragging over my skin, sliding back to bury themselves into my hair.

A gentle tug, the slightest sting on my scalp, lifting my lips away from him.

His eyes blazed when they met mine. "When we get home, princess." He nudged me back into my seat (though he didn't remove my hand from his thigh). His fingers slipped from my hair, drifted across my throat, my collarbone, and then returned to the wheel.

I was on fire.

On. Fucking. Fire.

From some husky words and a few caresses, and I was ready to demand that he pull over the car and fuck me in the back seat...or the front seat...or on the hood...or—

He exited the highway, zipping through the off-ramp and turning right onto a winding street. The sun was starting to go down (another reason Ted had been on me to cancel our jump

—which, considering how things had turned out, I could reasonably say that he may have been right), but it wasn't dark enough yet to hide the mature trees, the leaves beginning to change color, just at the edges. Soon they would be the bright oranges and reds, the yellows and browns. But now they were just a deep green with tinges of color.

I had an insane urge to come back in a month, to see them in the full expanse of fall.

And, hell, maybe I would.

Maybe I'd find some good leaves to use as an imprint—

Crafting. When had my mind swung to crafting from fucking?

Not surprising, I supposed. My mind always swung from place to place. It was how I was wired. If I stopped...

Well, I *couldn't* stop.

Big houses set far back from the street, each with large front doors, well-manicured yards. Each a hell of a lot nicer than my condo, that was for sure. Then again, I hadn't made an NHL player's salary. And there was the fact that I preferred to spend my money on experiences rather than belongings.

Belongings...

Belongings weren't forever. I could hold tight to them, treat them with care, use them to remember...but eventually they broke or wore out and had to be disposed of. My memories, however, and especially those memories tied to the few special belongings I'd kept close and protected...*those* could make sure I never forgot. Never forget that—

Not now.

I sucked in a breath, swallowed hard. *Right.* Not now. Throw up a stop sign, barricade that fucking inroad into my mind, halt—

A warm hand dropped to mine, squeezed tight.

"I can take you home."

Quiet words.

Nice words from a nice man.

But I didn't want him to be nice. I wanted him to be fucking my brains out, to think of me as a fun, flirty chick. And seriously, I needed to have this man's cock inside me, needed to get an orgasm, maybe two, if I was lucky.

So, I needed to get my shit together.

Which meant that I did what I always did—slapped a smile on my face and pressed on. "That's the last thing I want, Pretty Boy," I murmured, squeezing that powerful thigh. "I was just... admiring the tree trunks." Another squeeze to emphasize my approval of his yummy legs.

He snorted but didn't comment further, and I smothered a breath of relief.

I needed this—the release, the penis, the glorious, sweaty night of passion, not only because he was *hot*, but because I really wanted that *quick and efficient* directed at me. A quick, hard fuck that had me entering oblivion.

Especially, since the man had squashed my base-jumping plan.

I made a face.

His gaze zipped to mine again, held for longer than was probably prudent considering he was driving. "You're mad about the parachutes." His eyes returned to the road. "I'll pay for new ones."

"In orgasms?"

That tree trunk he called a thigh flexed, and I nearly moaned.

But then he was turning into a driveway, lifting one strong hand up to press the door clicker, pulling into the garage, hitting the clicker again. The heavy metal panel slid shut, enclosing us inside the dimly lit space as he turned off the engine.

I reached for the handle, intending to get out.

Warm fingers on my arm, the SUV jolting as he slid back his seat, and then I was on top of him, spun in a move I couldn't process, dragged over the console, my thighs straddling his.

His eyes were on fire as they searched my face, and then one half of his mouth tipped up. "In orgasms, princess."

Desire tightened in my middle, scorched through my center—

Then he kissed me.

And I went up in flames.

THREE

Marcel

TOO FAST.

Too fast.

Too—

Fuck it.

I didn't give a shit if it *was* too fast. Because Pru was meeting my tongue stroke for stroke, her hands sliding up my chest, weaving into my hair, holding me against her.

My hands were on her waist, sliding up her sides, drifting along the outsides of her breasts.

She hissed and pressed closer, and I broke the kiss, dragging my mouth down along her neck, nipping at the delicate skin there, inhaling the brisk, clean scent of her and...

Finding my lips dragged back to hers, her tongue in my mouth, and, yeah, I could get on board with kissing her, with going fast, with—

Flicking open the button of her jeans and shoving my hand inside.

Down beneath her underwear, through the curls, and into—

I groaned against her mouth, finding her hot and wet and... *fucking wet.*

"Marcel," she choked when I pressed my thumb to her clit. Not gentle. Not coaxing. She was already a live wire of sensation, rocking against me, her nipples hard even through our layers of clothing, so she didn't need gentle.

And fuck, but I couldn't give gentle, even if she *had* needed it.

Her hips bucked when I circled her entrance, my palm grinding against her clit. "Fuck," she groaned, fingers digging into my shoulder. "Fuck—" Her voice broke when I thrust a finger in deep, curving it forward as I drew it out. Then thrust it back in, along with another.

"That's—" Her head dropped back. "Oh fuck, Marcel, that's—"

Her pussy convulsed around my fingers.

Her moan was loud and long and the best thing I'd ever heard.

Even though my cock ached and my legs were cramped in my seat, space at a premium, hearing her moan, feeling her orgasm around me...it made it all worthwhile.

For about two minutes.

Because then I wanted *more.*

I yanked my hand out of her pants, wound my arm around her waist, shoved open my door. Pru was limp in my arms, but that was okay. I was strong enough to carry her. And I did.

After slamming the door shut, I pinned her against it and kissed the shit out of her.

Which roused her to consciousness, at least enough that she kissed me back and held tight to my shoulders, her legs wrapping around my hips.

Which roused *me*, seriously making me consider shoving down her pants, plunking her onto the hood of my SUV, and *shoving* my dick inside her.

But, alas, I didn't have a condom with me.

Those were inside and—

Hell. I could take a minute, could kiss her, hold her, *touch* her.

I set her on the hood, untangling myself from her grip. She lay back as I climbed onto the bumper and then braced myself over her as I kissed her. No, as I fucked her mouth. And hell, if it wasn't as hot and wet as her pussy had been on my fingers.

More.

Faster.

Now.

I managed to tear my mouth away from hers, jumped down off the hood, ignoring the metal creaking as I moved.

Her pants were open, the patterned cotton of her underwear visible through the spread zipper, and fuck it. I needed to taste her.

Now.

I reached for the waistband of her jeans, dragging her toward me as I tugged them down. Down that lush ass. Down those strong thighs. Down beyond her knees. One boot yanked free and tossed somewhere out of the way. Her jeans dragged off that bared foot—or socked foot, anyway.

But I didn't have time to process that, not when she was shimmying out of her underwear, and that glistening pussy was exposed to my gaze.

Another tug had her ass perched on the edge of the hood.

I spread her thighs, bent, and fucked her with my tongue. Thrusting it inside her, dragging it up to circle her clit, pressing the flat of it to that bundle of nerves.

"Marcel," she gasped, gripping my hair tight, drawing me away from her folds.

"What?" I asked, blowing a stream of air onto her, darting out my tongue when she shivered and didn't push me farther away...or pull me closer.

"Give a girl a second to breathe, would you?" she said, chest heaving, skin flushed.

I smiled. "No, princess. No, I won't give you a second." I bent again...and fucked her with my mouth and fingers.

"Oh, fuck," she breathed. "*Oh fuck.*" She dropped her head back, and I heard it *thunk* against the hood, but she was tough, was a kick-ass, tough-as-nails hockey player, so I didn't stop, didn't make sure she hadn't just given herself a concussion, didn't do anything except press my advantage, to capitalize on the rhythm I'd discovered, to go one step further in providing her with the orgasms I'd promised.

Pru arched against me. "There," she groaned, wrapping her thighs around my shoulders and squeezing me tightly enough that, for a second, I couldn't breathe. "Right there. Oh, God. Yes. Right—"

She cried out my name as she came, and it was the hottest thing I'd ever heard. Hot enough that I found myself not stopping after I'd guided her through her orgasm.

Instead, I kept going, sucking and licking, desperate to imprint the taste of her on my tongue.

Kept going until she stopped me by weaving her fingers into my hair and tugging my face away from her. "Inside," she moaned. "Inside me right now."

I started to scoop her up, to cart her into the house, but she stopped, wove her fingers into my hair and tugged. "Here," she breathed. "Inside *here.*"

"Condom, princess," I said, carrying her toward the door,

turning the knob and pushing it open with my foot. "They're upstairs and—"

She shifted in my arms, tugged up her pants which were hanging off one ankle, shoving her hand into the back pocket, and yanking out a small patterned wallet I'd often seen her with before letting them go again, the denim fluttering through the air like a scarf. "Here," she repeated, gripping the zipper with her teeth and tugging it open. She pulled out a condom with a flourish. "*Here*," she repeated, holding it up as she dropped her wallet and tore open the packet.

Here sounded pretty fucking good.

I plunked her on top of my washing machine, undid my pants, and grabbed the condom from her fingers.

Pushing down my pants, my underwear, rolling the latex down the hard length of my cock.

She spread her legs, wrapping one around my waist and using her heel to draw me close.

Fine by me.

I got *real* close. Then found her entrance, pressed deep, and...my mind blanked out. Tight and hot and...*good*. So fucking good that I forgot about everything except the feel of her gripping me like a vise, her fingernails digging into my shoulders, her hold tightening and keeping me close as I ground into her again and again.

And...again.

"Th-that's—" Her eyes went wide. Her head tilted back again, only this time I was ready for it, reaching a hand up and threading my fingers into her hair, catching her head before it *thunked* back against the cabinet hung above the washer. I brought her close, decided to kiss Pru to prevent her from giving herself a concussion—round two—and kept my hips moving.

Even when we broke for air.

Even when she directed me the entire time.

Faster. Harder. Deeper.

Even when her legs clenched around my waist, drawing me in, when her hand gripped my hair, trying to yank me down.

Even when she tried to take over.

Because I was going to become a professional at making this woman come—not because she'd ground against me and used me like a sex toy, but because I'd discovered every touch that drove her wild. Because I knew how to stroke and kiss her, when to thrust hard and deep and when to pump in slow and steady and—

Right. *There.*

When to do *that.*

Because I wanted to know how to make her scream my name as she came.

Like *that.*

So fucking beautiful, even though I could only see half of her, even though her jeans and underwear were hanging off one foot, one boot still on, both of her socks, her top rucked up around her waist. I hadn't even seen her breasts yet, hadn't tasted them, hadn't been able to feel the hard buds of her nipples against my tongue, hadn't been about to feel them against my palms, my fingers, to suck them deep into my mouth.

So fucking beautiful that my control splintered, that I forgot about thrusting and stroking and touching in the way that would make her come on my cock, and I...let sensation pull *me* under, propel me over that edge.

Pleasure rippled down my spine.

Spiraling through my nerves, making every single muscle tighten, *my* head falling back as I pumped, once, twice, and pressed deep as my orgasm pulsed through me.

And then my knees gave way.

FOUR

Pru

I CAME to sprawled across Marcel's lap, his cock hard and pulsing inside me, sweat covering every inch of my body.

My heart pounded, and I felt like I'd just made a rush up the ice, the puck had taken a bad bounce, and then—legs and lungs screaming—I had to haul ass back into my own zone to protect my goalie and save the game and—

No more.

I didn't get to do that anymore.

Right.

I planted my hand on his chest, went to lift off him, but then got distracted...by that hard and wide chest. Because even through his clothes, it was muscled and yummy and...hell, I brought my other hand up and rested it on his pecs.

Feeling them move beneath my palms in time to his rapid exhalations.

Melting—*me*, not my palms—when his arms were wrapped tightly around me.

I sank into his eyes, those beautiful eyes, falling further because they were glazed, outwardly revealing the pleasure we'd just shared. Not hiding the fact that it had been hot and intense and...had wrecked me. Because I was *wrecked*. Had been totally and completely fucked, per his assertions, and...but the *wrecking* was more than fucking, more than a handful of orgasms. It was deeper. It was—

Panic flickered on the edges of my vision.

Impulsivity and self-preservation encouraged me to gather my clothes and bolt. Well, either that, or stay atop his joystick— literally *joy*stick—and go for another ride because I was already in deep—literally, *ha*—and might as well get my fill.

But before I could clamber off—or well, do some clambering while *on*—Marcel's arm tightened around my waist, and he groaned slightly as he climbed to his feet. While keeping his cock inside me. Because the man was still hard and big and—oh wow—all those little bumps and movements as he walked felt really, *really* good.

"What are—" I began when he eventually stopped, dropping me onto the bed and coming down on top of me, mouth going to my neck and sucking.

"Fucking you," he muttered, lips brushing my skin as he moved down my body, reaching for the hem of my sweatshirt, tugging it and my shirt off, and then my bra was off a moment later, his mouth on my breasts, and—thank God for the stubble on his cheeks and jaw because it felt incredible.

"But we just—"

He sucked my nipple deeply, had me writhing under him. "Yeah," he said, kissing his way over to my other breast. "I've had plenty of time to think about this. Plenty of time to plan."

He glanced up at me, and I got lost in his eyes for a moment.

"Plan?"

His mouth curved into a sexy smile, and I circled back to

quick and efficient (and now added *planner*) to the list. "Yes, princess, *plan*," he murmured, straightening off me and stripping down, pausing to grab a tissue off the nightstand and taking care of the condom.

Then opening the drawer and pulling out more.

Yes.

More.

As in a whole *string* of condoms he flung on the bed next to me before he joined me on top of it, covering me with his gorgeous, sexy body, and dropping his lips to mine, his fingers doing the talking—

At least until I did.

After they'd talked their way between my thighs again, chatted their way up to my clit, conversed me through another orgasm.

"I think I like planning," I gasped as he slid home.

"I think I really, *really* like it."

He grinned.

And then proceeded to fuck me.

And—just for the record—it was fabulous.

***

A WARM ARM over my middle.

A muscular chest pressed to my spine.

And I was planning my exit.

That arm tightened, a husky voice drifted into my ears. "Dinner."

"I was thinking that I should go," I murmured, reaching for the covers.

"Dinner," Marcel repeated.

"I—"

"*Dinner*," he said again, and then his lips found a spot on my jaw that made me shiver. "And then I have more plans."

My mouth fell open. "*More?*"

A smile against my skin. "I'm a planner, princess." He released me, rolled over and grabbed his phone. "Order in? Or do you want me to cook for you?"

I'd just closed my mouth, but his questions—or rather, his second one—had my jaw dropping open. Because I'd known zero men who cooked. Well, zero men who cooked after they'd already slept with me, zero who offered to cook for me after they'd gotten their orgasm—or *orgasms*.

Well, he did say he had more plans, so there was that.

But *that* contradicted my typical experience. Which was that my hinting at my exit was usually trailed by them finding my jeans for me. And my bra. And panties. And practically shoving my shoes onto my feet.

"What would you cook?" I asked.

One broad shoulder lifted, fell. "Whatever you want."

"What—" I blinked, rolled over, both because I was getting a crick in my neck and because I needed to see the man's expression straight on. "Whatever I want?" I asked, raising a brow.

"Got a full fridge," he said. "What are you hungry for?"

"I—"

He smoothed back my hair.

Smoothed. Back. My. Hair.

"What are you feeling like? Pasta? Chicken? Pizza? Burgers? Tacos? Maybe something different. Breakfast? Strawberry waffles—"

I clamped my hand over his mouth. "Too many choices, Pretty Boy."

A dart of his tongue against my palm before he peeled my fingers away. "Waffles, burgers, or tacos?"

"Tacos?"

His mouth curved. His eyes flicked down...yes, down between my legs, and I found myself biting back a grin. "I can make tacos."

"With—" I cut myself off before I could make the innuendo cross the *ew* line. "How about waffles?" I asked.

Fingers dancing up my thighs. "Okay," he murmured, and I watched as something incredible happened. His fingers weren't the only thing dancing. His eyes danced with humor, and they were so pretty that it actually took my breath away. Then he added, "With cream."

I froze. Found myself giggling. "Ew," I muttered. But that didn't stop my giggling.

He bopped me on the nose. "Not yours, princess," he said, "not yours."

"I—"

A nip of my bottom lip. "Waffles," he proclaimed. "With strawberries." A beat, his mouth curving upward. "And cream." He wrapped his fingers around my waist, tugged us both out of bed, bent and snagged his T-shirt from the floor. He tugged it over my head, bent again and yanked on his sweats (no underwear and giving me a glimpse of his glorious—*glorious!*—hockey player's ass, because seriously hockey players—myself included, thank you very much—had the best asses).

Then he strode from the room, pausing at the threshold, glancing back at me, saying again, "Waffles."

Then he was gone.

And...then, for perhaps the first time in my life, I followed.

I should be planning my exit.

Calling a rideshare.

Giving him the space that this one-night stand called for.

Fucking. Maybe a few hours of sleep. Then zipping out before the sun rose.

But the sun was fully up. We'd had waffles. We'd had cream...on the crunchy, fluffy breakfast food...and then Marcel had had *mine*.

Then we'd showered.

And...more creaming.

Then I'd been sore and exhausted, every muscle in my body fatigued because I hadn't had that hard of a workout since...well, since *ever*. Not in my playing days. Not in my college days. Marcel had kicked my ass. Thoroughly.

In the best way.

Now we were on his couch. I was wearing a pair of his boxers and his tank—which was really just an excuse for my boobs to try to play peekaboo—or maybe I should call it peeka*boob*. One, because it was Marcel's, it was so big it practically hung off my torso (and I wasn't a small woman—I had broad shoulders, big thighs, could deadlift more than a few of the men I'd known over the years). But second, tank tops were one of those things that the universe had inflicted on women. *Want to be cool while you slept or lounged? Try one of these! Want to also nearly poke your own eye out with your tittie? Sign up for a Tank Top Deluxe!*

Okay.

I was losing it.

Probably because I'd been orgasmed into oblivion.

Maybe also because I'd been stuffed full of waffles and strawberries and whipped cream that came from a container and that he'd whipped up and added powdered sugar to until it was fluffy nirvana, and not a squirt bottle—something I'd never had outside of a fancy restaurant.

But mostly because after all the orgasms, the food, Marcel

had carried me into his fabulous shower, set me on the counter next to the sink—after he'd laid down a towel to protect my ass from the cold countertop—turned on the taps of that fabulous shower, adjusting and waiting until the temperature was just right. Or at least that was what he appeared to be doing since he would put his hand in, feel the water, turn a knob, put his hand back in, turn the other knob, and rinse and repeat, until he'd appeared satisfied, turning back to me and lifting me back up into his arms.

This was something I didn't normally allow.

Because I was strong and had been taking care of myself for a long, long time.

I could walk into the shower. Hell, for that matter, I could walk from the bedroom to the bathroom on my own two feet, thank you very much.

But...circling back to orgasms.

And the fact that the man had melted my brain with them.

Even then my clit had a heartbeat, felt bruised enough that the thought of anyone touching it in the next millennium made me shudder.

(Also, I knew that Marcel, with his quiet but somehow still confident and capable hands—or fingers...or tongue—could convince me to let that clit take another beating...and enjoy that assault in the process).

But mostly, I ignored the fact that I could walk on my own two feet because it felt nice to be held against Marcel's chest.

Well, that and because I was in an orgasm fog and my legs felt like jelly, even though they were strong.

And then the hot water hit me, sluicing over my skin, warming and loosening stiff muscles I hadn't even realized I had.

It felt so good that I didn't protest when he sidled in and stole half the stream.

There was enough to share.

And his body felt amazing against mine, especially when he took a bit of my weight without a word of protest.

And I forgot about exit strategies and orgasms.

I forgot about moving to the next thing as quickly as possible so that I didn't *remember*.

I just stood under that shower, the warm water pouring over me, strong arms around me, and for the first time in nearly twenty years, I just was.

FIVE

Marcel

I HAD HER.

For a few moments, I had her.

When she'd been in my bed, a softness having crept over her face, together in the shower, her body under that hot water. So I'd filed those clues of Pru away to use later.

Storing it with every piece of knowledge I'd gleaned about her since she'd first sidled up to me at CeCe's the previous year.

Untouchable because I'd been nursing a broken heart, because my head was in a place where I wasn't receptive to any female at that moment.

But also...reverting to quiet because I hadn't known what to do with *that* female.

One who was brash and strong and unequivocally herself and...who didn't play games.

She wanted me.

She'd made that clear.

It was as simple as that. And after four years of Marissa's

shit, of never knowing which way was up—was this a trick? Did she say something and mean something else? Was this some test I was inevitably going to fail and feel like a total fucking loser for?

And then feel like even more of a loser because who let someone else make them feel some way?

I was in charge of my own destiny.

Yeah, other people were along for the ride, other people whose feelings and needs I had to consider, but...ultimately it was my life, my shot at happiness.

And I only got one chance at it.

Thanks to Hazel and a room full of porcelain (and the permission to shatter it all) for teaching me that particular life lesson.

So, I'd made up my mind to take the next opportunity that she gave me, and I thought, grinning to myself, it had worked out so well it had nearly killed me.

Death by Pru.

I'd sign up for that any day of the week.

She sighed and cuddled closer, the lean strength of her pressed tightly to my side.

I wrapped my arms around her, let my eyes slide closed.

I WOKE SLOWLY, body on fire.

My bed...was empty.

Jasmine on the sheets, a brown hair on my pillow.

A quiet house.

"Fuck," I muttered, tossing the covers back and moving with a groan to my dresser. I yanked on a pair of sweats, poked my head into the bathroom, just in case Pru was seeing to business rather than having cut and run—

Something I shouldn't care about, considering that was the definition of a one-night stand, which was clearly what she'd been angling toward.

Considering I'd had to orgasm her into staying the night.

I splashed some water on my face, reached for the towel to dry it...and that was when I saw it.

A note.

Thanks for the great night.
Have to get on the ice.
See you around, Pretty Boy
-Pru

Disappointment coiled through me, but I knew it was for the best. One night. Explosive chemistry. Enough orgasms that my dick felt broken. Enjoying her body. And then call it good.

Of course, I'd like to enjoy her body for a little longer. Hers was *incredible*—lithe curves, an ass I could grip with both hands, breasts that were small but perky as hell, along with the sexiest nipples I'd ever had the pleasure of tasting.

If she'd stayed, I would have attempted to revive my dick in order to have another day with her—and I had no doubt I would have succeeded.

Better she hadn't.

I liked Pru.

I'd spent much of the last six months wondering what it would be like to have her.

Now I had.

And while it was as fantastic as my mind had made it out to be, there was truth to the statement of too much of a good thing. Pru was good. Good enough that I felt the itch to have more, to

have more than one night, more, more, *more*. To keep her close.
To convince her to stay...maybe forever.

Panic shot down my spine so violently that my knees shook,
that I needed to brace myself on the vanity, fingers clenching
the granite.

I couldn't do that, couldn't *risk* that.

I planned. I prepared. I didn't slice out my heart and offer it
up on a platter to a woman who I'd had to pleasure practically
into unconsciousness to get her to sleep in my bed.

Well, orgasms along with waffles...

Whipped cream on lush lips.

More whipped cream...on a different set of lush lips.

Pru naked on my kitchen table, a waffle in the maker,
burned to oblivion as I'd tasted that cream, tasted *her* cream,
tasted—

"Fucking hell, man," I muttered. "Get your shit together."

I glanced up, stared at my reflection...and sighed.

Luckily, I'd had plenty of practice at that.

THE SHARP TRILL of the whistle made me wince...and then
unwittingly jerk to attention.

Even though I was one of the helpers and had my own
whistle clipped to the top of my glove.

I couldn't help it.

My brain was attuned to the sweet, *sweet* sound of the
whistle—and prepared to skate extra drills for punishment.

Though, in fairness, I hadn't been punished with skating
drills for near on a decade.

Though, in truth, that shit stuck with a man.

Especially when the coach had made it his mission to
make me as miserable as possible. Gotta love men trying to

make everyone around them feel like shit. Such a special skill.

So even though the whistle made my nerves prickle, my body jump to awareness, I'd had years of tamping down that reaction as well. I slapped on a smile, started to skate to center ice, where Oliver James was standing, ready to give his orders.

Oliver, who shouldn't even be up on two skates after all that had happened to him a little more than a year before—an illegal hit, broken bones, surgery, infection, and finally...losing his leg.

Oliver, who'd somehow overcome that, and while he wouldn't be playing professional hockey again, had picked up a spot in a rec sled hockey league and now...was coaching tiny little girls with sparkling pink stickers on their helmets, others with ribbons in their hair, some with fierce expressions and absolutely *no glitter*, all of whom resembled marshmallows as pads were strapped to their limbs, jerseys tugged over their heads.

And they skated with no fear.

Flying across the ice and wiping out at regular intervals, crashing into the boards and each other and popping back up... maybe even faster than I could.

"Let's go, Coach Marcel!" Hannah cried, skating up to me and grabbing my hand, drawing me forward. "We can't be the slowest!"

"We can't?" I teased, dragging my edges, making her work a little to bring me toward center ice.

"No, we have to be"—a grunt, her tiny legs bending, her skates digging into the ice—"*first!*" Another grunt, a strong pull, and then I let up on my edge, scooped her up under her armpits, and sailed us toward center ice, stopping an inch from Oliver.

And spraying my former teammate with ice in the process.

Oliver's lips pressed flat, and he lifted a brow.

Hannah giggled.

The brow lowered, the lips turned up into a smile.

"All right, girls," he said, "listen up." And then he began describing the stations they would have at practice, but they were young and little and squirmy, so Oliver did it in a way that was smart as hell. Naming all the drills with funny names (The Duck, Squirrel's Nuts, Sharks, Banana Tag, Unicorn's Horn, and Quack-Quack).

The last he assigned to me.

Because...it was hell.

And *that* was payback for the whole spraying my former teammate with ice thing.

But I took my licks...and my group of six girls to my corner of the ice. A quick refresher of the drill that was a modified version of Duck, Duck, Goose and ringette, adding in a tiny net that went up to around my shin.

It should be fun.

And, for the girls, it was.

For the coach in charge of the station? It was hell.

I skated my ass off, chasing the girls since I was the Goose, yelling "Quack! Quack! Quack!" at the top of my lungs, and then chasing down the ring when it invariably sailed wide because the net was tiny and they were still learning how to shoot.

And then doing it all over again. For seven straight minutes.

Which shouldn't seem like very long, considering it was... *seven* minutes. But straight skating and dodging and yelling and puck (or ring) shagging, and it was exhausting. And then doing it all over again. Times six for each group that made their way through my station. Because the whistle barely blew before I was sucking in air trying to catch my breath (while trying to not look like I was sucking wind because I was a fucking professional hockey player and chasing around a bunch of girls shouldn't tire me out) and the next group was on me.

And I was the "Goose" again.

And running down rings, skating after girls (who Ollie clearly did a good job with considering they had great basics and speed, along with never-ending energy).

More whistles. More goosing.

More—

I was lying on the ice, pretending to be messing around, but really fucking wiped when...the cold ass shower of snow covered me from head to toe.

"Fuck," I muttered, expecting to see Oliver having sought payback as I swiped ice out of my eyes and sat up.

"I did it!" Hannah cheered before whipping around on her skates and sprinting away, stopping at full speed and showering the boards (thankfully this time) with snow.

She whooped, and despite having spent the last hour working her butt off, continued sprinting and stopping and showering snow around. One part mischief. Ten parts sheer determination. Add in a perfect (and yeah, look, I was a freaking hockey player, not a mathematician) combination of skill and competitiveness and grit.

That one was going to make it.

I wasn't sure in what (though she showed promise in this sport, obviously), but in whatever she put her mind to.

Guaranteed.

"She's something else." Oliver's quiet voice came as I finally summoned the strength to push up my skates and begin cleaning up my station.

One of the perks of the big leagues—I didn't often have to clear the ice.

But it felt good to do something that brought me back.

Before things had gotten so fucking complicated.

"Yeah," I said, scooping up a ring. "I'm not sure if she's going to be the next president or knock Brit Plantain out of her spot as top woman in the league."

Oliver smiled. "Maybe both."

I grinned back. "*Definitely* both."

We laughed then Ollie thanked me for helping.

"Happy to," I said. "Won't be able to do much once the season really picks up, so it's fun to be with the girls now."

"Even if they run you ragged?"

"Even if my asshole of a friend puts me on *Quack-Quack* duty."

"You deserved it," Oliver muttered. "Snow showers?" He shook his head and then jutted a chin in Hannah's direction, who was now perfecting the snow technique, spraying it high enough that it was reaching the glass. "You gave that one the key to the kingdom, and now I'm going to be dealing with that the entire season."

I dropped the rings into a bucket. "It's a necessary skill."

Oliver's brows lifted. "How is *that* a necessary skill?"

"Because it's fucking fun," I said, my voice dropping, "and if these girls get nothing else, then they should get that *this*"—I threw an arm out, encompassing the rink, the skaters readying to get off the ice, the pucks and sticks and goals, the *sport* on a whole—"is fun."

Silence. Then a grin, wide enough that it reminded me of the man my friend had been before his injury. "You know what?"

I just looked at him, my *what* unspoken.

"You're right."

And then Oliver took off, faster than it seemed possible considering the man only had one leg (and a kick-ass prosthesis that gave him an awesome amount of mobility). Add that in with his own grit and persistence, and Oliver was more skilled than most players could hope to be.

He whipped across the ice.

And...then he gave Hannah a snow shower that made her shriek and attack and chase Ollie.

Chaos erupted and more players joined in.

Tag and snow showers ensued.

And...it was fun as hell.

SIX

Pru

I LOOKED AT THE BRIDGE.

At the water below, saw for the first time the rocks and trees standing up like huge toothpicks—ready to slice through my parachute (or body parts)— and rocked back on my heels.

The chute was packed, prepped and checked and folded, ready and waiting at my feet.

All I had to do was strap it on, climb over the guardrail, and...go.

But...

I wondered if the rush was worth it.

If I'd *even* get the rush. Because I'd been searching for that feeling for a long time, and it was getting harder and harder to find.

The fear.

The terror.

The clenching of my stomach. The twisting of my heart. The knotting of my intestines. The painful muscle-tightening.

The nausea. The *oh shit-oh fuck-oh shit-oh fuck* litany as I sought to *feel*.

Alive.

More.

Something. Anything.

But though that terror might grip me for a few moments, though I might feel alive and scared and like my *alive* was going to be gone in the blink of an eye, it never lasted.

A flash in a pan.

A moment of crystalline sensation, and then I was back to *this.*

Searching. Constantly searching for the next thing. Constantly looking forward, hoping that the next moment would bring the clarity, the *feeling* I craved.

That I'd lost.

That I'd...never get back.

Except, strawberry waffles and fingers gently brushing back my bangs. Strong fingers gripping my arm, tugging my body to his.

A parachute sailing over this railing.

Another.

And one more at my feet.

Not strapped to my body. Not heavy on my shoulders as I climbed over the heavy steel barrier. Not whipping open when I pulled the cord, just on the razor-sharp line of too late.

Never too late.

But close.

So close that the terror would grip me, that I'd *feel.*

A hand, rough and calloused but oh so careful as he soaped up my body. A plate sliding in front of me with a kiss to my temple.

Affection. Given without thought.

And...

But it didn't surprise me that Marcel had *that*. That he would give *that* so easily. Of course, he gave good boyfriend. He was nice and funny and sweet and shy. He'd had his heart broken by the fucking bitch of an ex of his, and he *still* gave it, still managed to make our hookup seem like more than just… well, more than just fucking.

I just—

Didn't do that.

Why? Why didn't I do that? Why didn't I do *boyfriends* or give good girlfriend?

Because…no one had ever made me feel.

Not like Marcel had with the temple kisses and gentle fingers brushing back my bangs, not with strawberry waffles and innuendos about cream and a plate in front of me encouraging me to eat before it got cold, before his own food was ready, before…

The breeze slid over my skin, kissed my nape, dusted my collarbones, danced along my exposed forearms.

It didn't touch my temple.

Didn't brush back my bangs.

Didn't…give good boyfriend.

So I did what I did best.

I stopped thinking.

I *acted*.

I—

Picked up the parachute and launched it over the railing.

Walked back to my car.

Got in and drove.

———

A bag of food at my side, growing colder by the second.

The scent of fried food filled my nose, and not particularly in a good way.

But I couldn't make strawberry waffles, had never learned how to make cookies. Didn't have a signature dish.

I had a tweaky back that meant I couldn't deal with the grind of a full hockey season any longer, a belly (and arteries) that had consumed far too many curly fries in my twenty-odd years, and a body that was used to the cold.

Even though the sun had set and Marcel's house was empty.

Even though a chill was settling into my bones in a way that made it nearly impossible to ignore.

Even though—

Lights flashed down the street, and although it was dark enough that the SUV just looked like any other SUV, I knew—*knew!*—that it was Marcel driving toward me.

I felt it in the heavy *thump* of my heart. Felt it in the butterflies fluttering around my stomach (when I was definitely not a butterfly or fluttering type of woman). I felt it in the tingle down my spine, the prickle in my skin.

I *felt* it.

Felt.

Him.

Better than the terror of seeing a Great White swimming toward me, larger than a car, teeth bigger than my thumb, the sense that the ocean was a mysterious depth of horror with more things in it that could kill me than I could begin to imagine. Better than my lungs and back screaming as I finished a shift, but not giving a damn because my team had scored and we were going to win, and winning was *fucking* life. It was better than my boots slipping on a narrow trail, losing my balance, thinking that I was going over the cliff on my right, and yet somehow managing to not.

Life.

The man was life.

Or he could be *my* life.

And...my eyes prickled.

Because it all finally made sense.

But I didn't cry. Not when my team made the finals and lost. Not when we won the next season. Not when I made it to the top of Kilimanjaro. Not when those thumb-sized teeth came way too close for comfort and we'd been jerked out of the broken shark cage.

Marcel driving up after I'd sat on his porch for an hour?

That had tears forming in my eyes.

I blinked them back. *Of course.* Because I was Prudence Hansley (which, in case anyone was wondering, meant that I was a total badass, and badasses didn't cry).

Standing, I snagged the bag and moved toward the garage, toward the car pulling into the driveway.

Marcel—no surprise—was in the driver's seat.

And so fucking pretty. Not just his face, either, which was an artist's rendering of smooth lines and rugged features. After our night together, I knew it really was a shame that he wasn't in underwear ads (he *was* profiled in watch and sportswear commercials and one cologne ad, however). The world should be able to appreciate all the beauty of his body, and him on a billboard in just his skivvies would do that.

Fifty feet wide. Cars driving by, probably causing accidents because everyone would want that body in their home, in their bed.

My fingertips clenched slightly at the thought.

Or maybe no underwear. Maybe just for me.

Because I wanted first dibs. Wanted *all* the dibs.

I'd made it down the walk that led to the driveway at the

same time that the car paused to wait for the garage door to open.

The window whirred down.

And I got all that pretty unobscured by glass.

Marcel and the smooth lines of his face, the stubble on his jaw that begged to be kissed. Something I hadn't done nearly enough during our night together. Something I was definitely going to remedy that night. When he'd said he was going to fuck me, he had. He'd lived up to the promise. He'd fucked me senseless.

But I hadn't gotten my fill, my taste.

Tonight, I was going to do that.

After I wooed him with chicken nuggies and curly fries.

I moved to the car.

"Pru," he said softly, something odd creeping into his expression, "What are you doing here?"

The soft should have clued me in.

The soft should have made me stop and realize.

But I was *feeling*—and cue the meme from *The Sound of Music* with Julie Andrews spinning in the open field. I was *feeling!* And it was fabulous.

Until it wasn't.

Because he'd used that soft with me during our night together, over waffles and temple kissing and smoothing back my bangs and soaping me up in the shower.

But he didn't use it with me in real life.

No one did.

"I"—I held up the bag, smiled widely, still feeling, still *so fucking stupid*—"brought you dinner," I said. "It's not waffles, but…"

And then I saw.

I. *Saw.*

The bag dropped.

My lids slid closed. Just for a second. Just for long enough for me to practically feel the steel doors slamming shut around me. One after another. *Thunk. Thunk. Thunk.* Muffling the feeling. Muffling the living. Muffling everything until I felt numb again.

I'd thought...

"Pru."

"Right," I said, chipper as always. "More for me." I laughed. And I'd had years, *decades* of living with that muffle, enough that it was easy for my laugh to sound natural, enough that I knew my smile was. My eyes went to the female in the front seat.

Petite and beautiful. A pound of makeup and hair styled in a way I knew I'd never *ever* master.

Big boobs with loads of cleavage that was displayed fully because the little of her shirt that I could see was that it *was* little, as in made of very *little* fabric.

Nothing like me.

Right.

I got it.

A wave, my smile staying firmly in place. Because...practice. Because...another steel door was slamming down, this one heavier, enough that I practically felt the reverberation vibrating through me as it hit the concrete encasing my feet, my shins, my knees.

I was a bunker.

Locked down and secure.

Rivets tightening to keep everything in place.

"Have fun tonight," I said.

The door popped, but I was already turning away. "Pru."

"See you around, Pretty Boy."

We'd had our one night. We'd had our fun. And now he was done.

I got it.

Had had decades to get it.

Warm fingers on my arm, a tight grip on my biceps that threatened to have parachutes and strawberry waffles and temple kisses slam through that steel.

I detached herself. "Bye, Marcel."

And then I was out.

SEVEN

Marcel

I WALKED INTO THE RINK, bag slung over my shoulder.

It had been six weeks since I'd seen Pru.

Literally six weeks since I'd laid eyes on her.

Because she'd finished her training camp sessions and then had gone off on an extended vacation, getting her adrenaline days in before the season picked up.

This was from Hazel.

How the psychologist couldn't recognize that her best friend was running away from life, I didn't know, but I supposed she hadn't seen the light go out in Pru's eyes.

Replaced with different light.

With the mask she'd put on for the rest of the world to see.

I would have never known the difference, never *seen* the difference had I not been the one to bring that difference around.

With a woman who didn't matter.

A pretty girl who'd been hanging out at the rink, who'd flirted and blinked long, false lashes at me, and I'd thought...

Why the fuck not?

I was single.

I could do this, could take what was freely offered.

Then Pru. A bag of food in her hand and light in her eyes. We hadn't made any promises. Hell, she'd left my bed before I'd been awake, sneaking out like it was a one-night stand.

See you around, Pretty Boy.

Except, I hadn't.

Because of that extended vacation. Which was three weeks long, during which she had apparently done all sorts of dangerous things because Hazel had recounted them with awe, so proud of her friend for bungee jumping, spelunking, cliff diving, and helping to build houses in Africa—which, the last I could see being proud of. The former three, knowing what I knew about the bridge and parachute and base jumping had sent more than a sliver of fear down my spine.

Pru had gone straight into scouting trips (more info from Hazel, offered during our weekly night out at a local bar).

Now...she was walking down the hall toward me, her nose in a tablet.

She looked beautiful. Tanned from her vacation, her brown hair streaked with lines of blond that spoke of plenty of time in the sun. Lean curves and lithe body clad in a Breakers sweatshirt and navy sweats.

Strong thighs wrapped around me.

Breasts to my chest.

Fingers digging into my shoulders—

I stopped.

Processed what I hadn't before.

That being the cast on her left arm.

Almost hidden by the sweatshirt covering her down to her

wrist, a slender strip of black fiberglass poking out beneath it, crossing over her palm when she lifted it to push her bangs back.

"What the fuck?" I snapped.

She stopped, glanced up at me.

Not far because she was a tall woman, but I was taller, and that meant it took a moment for her eyes to hit mine. I told myself this was because I *was* taller, but I knew it was because she didn't want to look at me.

Because I'd brought some girl home when she'd brought me dinner.

Because I'd hurt her.

And I didn't realize that I would miss her dancing eyes, her teasing expression, the flirting...didn't realize I would miss *Pru*.

Until it was gone.

Until she was gone.

"Hey, Marcel," she said, and if I didn't know better, I would say that her tone was completely normal. But I *did* know better. And that meant I heard and felt the distance.

And I fucking hated it.

I stepped forward, grabbed her uninjured arm, and drew—okay *tugged* her into one of the empty meeting rooms lining the hall. Usually, the guys used them to phone their families, if the front office staff didn't need them, because it gave us guys privacy to unleash all our "I love you"s, and "It's okay, baby"s, and whatever other sweet talk might be necessary that we hoped our teammates wouldn't give us shit for.

It didn't matter.

Shit was given, always. Because that was hockey. Because that was the Breakers—now that we'd cut out the poison on the team and found a way to move forward that made everyone happier and the team gelling in a way that meant we'd won the Cup (twice, thank you very much).

But shit given or not, the rooms did offer a modicum of privacy.

So, I tugged Pru by her uninjured arm (this required me scooping the iPad out of her hands so it didn't hit the deck when she tried to jerk out of my hold) into the nearest empty room and slammed the door.

Then stood in front of it.

Because seriously, *what the fuck?*

She glanced around the space, back at me, then seemed to realize that I wasn't going to move until she gave me some fucking answers. This was probably because I had leaned back against the door and crossed my arms.

She was a badass hockey player.

But I was bigger. And stronger. *And* I had two functional arms.

"What?" she asked.

I lifted my brows but didn't repeat my question from earlier.

She sighed. "What the fuck isn't a question, you know that, right?"

I just lifted my brows higher.

"Okay, fine. It *is* a question," she muttered, propping herself on the edge of the conference table. "But it's not a question that gives me anything."

I waited.

She sighed again. "I'm guessing you're referring to this?" She held up her arm.

I just held her gaze.

Her lips pressed flat. Then she pulled out her phone and began tapping at the screen.

"What are you doing?"

"I have a meeting with Luc," she said. "I'm telling him I'm going to be late."

Shit.

Luc was Luc Masterson. GM of the Breakers and boss to us both.

I heard the little *whoosh* of a text message being sent.

She kept typing.

"What are you doing now?" I asked, and I didn't miss that my sharp tone had morphed into curiosity. Probably because this woman always kept me guessing...like showing up after pulling a walk-of-shame with dinner and a smile that I'd all but destroyed.

Because I'd brought a woman home.

Never mind that I'd taken her back to *her* home about two seconds after Pru had driven away.

Any desire I had—and maybe I was a douche to say that it had been minimal—had fled. Carrie was a gorgeous girl. One that looked and acted a lot like Marissa (especially after I'd hit the clicker to close my garage door and began backing out of the driveway—and yes, I knew that I had Pru's appearance to thank for me not being an idiot and going further down that path).

So yeah, Carrie and Marissa were pretty. But they were also high maintenance, and their nice was a thin layer of paint slapped over a thick layer of bitch.

I knew better.

I'd been trying to prove to myself that I hadn't been disappointed to wake up and find Pru gone. That it was better for both of us to have gotten it out of our system.

I just...liked her.

Liked the slender curves and lean strength. Liked the way she was so big, how her personality always seemed to fill the room. Happy and chipper and a hard worker.

And good on her skates and with the puck and with the guys.

She...fit.

A hell of lot more than a Marissa or a Carrie or a—

Whoosh.

"Texting Oliver," she said.

I frowned. "Why?"

"Because the meeting is with him, too."

She slipped her phone into the pocket of her sweats and crossed her arms—or well, started to anyway. The uninjured one made it all the way across. The casted one started to move then halted, and I didn't miss the wince on her face.

"Which was it?" I asked, instead of acknowledging that I was an asshole for keeping her from her work, from making her late to a meeting with both of her bosses. A meeting—I glanced down, studied what was on the screen of the tablet, saw notes and a PowerPoint presentation at the ready—which she'd be presenting.

"Which is what?"

I scowled.

She slid back on the table, letting her legs swing, her feet drifting back and forth, back and forth just above the carpet. One of her brows lifted. "I know you're a man of few words, but you're going to have to be more specific, Marcel."

Marcel.

Not Pretty Boy.

Not rude. Not snapping. Not angry.

Just...clear.

I hated it.

I still needed to know. "Which one of your 'adventures'"—yes, I was a dumbass who did air quotes—"broke your arm?"

The other brow joined the first, and for a second, I thought she wasn't going to answer.

Then the outside of her mouth quirked up, revealing an adorable curve that was shaped like a backwards C (a curve I'd kissed). "The *adventure*," she said dryly, "of me trying to navigate my condo's stairs during the freak cold snap last week."

My mouth fell open, and I pushed off the door. "Stairs?" I growled, prowling toward her. "Are you telling me that you fell down a fucking flight of stairs a couple of days ago and you're at work?" A beat. "*Today?*"

That cold snap had been last week, yes.

But it had been last *Friday* and today was Monday. So, she'd fallen down a flight of stairs three days before and was working that morning and—

"Yes," she said. "And it wasn't a flight of stairs. It was a few steps. Concrete ones I've already paid to have covered in non-slip so I won't go skating again when winter actually comes."

"How many is a few?"

I'd started to calm down because taking care of the concrete was smart and responsible, and hell if my dick didn't like smart and responsible (almost as much as it liked imprudent and risky, I was realizing), but then her gaze darted away, and another wave of anger washed over me. "*Pru,*" I warned.

"A few," she began, "is a—"

I gripped her chin, turned her head so she was forced to look at me. "How many?"

"A few—"

I leaned in, was surrounded in jasmine and woman and *Pru.*

My cock twitched.

"How. Many?" I gritted, ignoring it.

"Eight."

My fingers convulsed. She winced, and I quickly released her, smoothing my thumb over her chin in apology, staying close. "Eight steps?" I asked, having sucked in a breath and releasing it slowly, striving for calm, *desperate* for calm. "*Eight?*"

Okay.

That was less calm and more bellow.

But...baby steps.

And fuck, don't say steps. Don't think steps. Don't—

Fingers on my jaw. Not soft like Marissa's had been. Nor like Carrie's. They were calloused. A little rough. All Pru.

So...perfect.

"I'm fine," she said quietly. "I should have known better. But it's so freaking early, and—"

"The Arctic air mass," I finished, just as quietly, when she broke off.

"The fucking Arctic air mass," she agreed. "Took me by surprise. But eight weeks in this bad boy, and I'll be good." She stepped back, reached deep into her pocket, and pulled out a silver Sharpie. "Wanna sign my cast?"

Distance.

Careful, smart distance. *Planned* distance.

But I wasn't feeling careful, wasn't feeling planning or being smart.

I was feeling *Pru*.

"Pru," I murmured, stepping closer, smoothing back her hair, her bangs, the little pieces that always seemed to fall forward out of her ponytail and get into her eyes. "I want—"

To go back.

To not have brought Carrie to my place.

To have been in a position to take Pru up on her offer of dinner.

"Silver or gold Sharpie?" she asked, pulling out another pen.

"I don't want to sign—"

"No?" she said, shoving the markers away. "Well then, I've got to get on it. Luc's schedule is slammed today, and he squeezed Oliver and me in." She began edging toward the door.

I should let her go. I *should.*

But...there was something in her eyes, in that night we'd spent together, in her frame, in my heart. Aw, fuck. It was all of that. But it was my heart.

My heart was involved. My heart was in deep.

My heart—

Was currently thudding against my rib cage threatening to propel me into a full-blown panic attack.

"I need to go," she said.

"I don't want you to," I blurted. Fuck the panic attack, the pulse hammering in my veins. Short of someone cutting out my tongue, I couldn't have stopped those words from flying out of my mouth. "I want you to—"

"You know I liked your cock," she said lightly, cutting me off and patting my chest condescendingly. That burned, but I couldn't say that I didn't deserve it. "But once was enough for me." She brushed past me, reached for the doorknob.

Words stoppered up in my throat. Then they came out.

And they weren't helpful.

"It was three times."

A shuttering in her eyes. A curve in her lips that was so damned natural it was a blatant facsimile. "Three times was enough."

She slipped through the door.

It *clicked* closed behind her.

Softly.

Finally.

EIGHT

Pru

I PAUSED against the closed door.

But only for a heartbeat.

A. Heart. Beat.

Mine was thundering in my chest, squeezing tightly and rapidly, shooting blood through my body, to my face, which I was sure was bright red.

Then I took a deep breath, released it slowly.

Because I knew that three times wasn't enough.

Not nearly.

But I also knew myself, my life.

So, three times...it would *have* to be enough.

———

HAZEL RAPPED her knuckles on the frame of my open door.

"Hey," I said, coming in when I nodded. "How are you feeling?"

My heart?

Or my dumbass broken wrist?

"Like hell," I said.

Because it was an answer that fit both questions. Look at me go.

Hazel winced, her expression concerned. "I'm sorry, honey. Why don't you knock off early?"

I shook my head. Knock off early and be trapped in my tiny condo with my own thoughts? I stifled a shudder. Sweet Jesus. That was a nightmare I did *not* need. "I've got a few more things to get sorted before the regular season starts next week. I wouldn't be able to relax if I knocked off early."

"Push through. Get it done." Hazel nodded, and then because my friend was all self-aware and responsible and mature and shit, she added, "Then take a break." Her pale brown (but not hazel because that would be too convenient) eyes sparkled. "So long as you promise that break will hit you before you burn out."

This time I didn't hold back my shudder. "I could do with less talk of *breaks*."

Hazel's expression went chagrined. "Shit. I didn't mean—"

And great, now I was making my friend feel bad. I tossed the pen I'd been writing with on my desk (thankful again that it was my left wrist that was broken and that I was a righty), and stood up, crossing around the boring block of wood and two chairs that came standard with all the Breakers support staff's offices.

They did the job.

And I wasn't much for decorating, so the whole space was standard. Unlike Hazel's office—she had used her decorating budget down to a penny—but also Hazel's office was the place the guys went to unpack, to reconfigure their mental state. They needed a nice space. So maybe mine wasn't nice. But it *was* clean and organized, and I had a little cactus Hazel had bought for me—it was still alive, mostly because it required very little watering.

"I know," I said, grabbing Hazel's hands with mine.

This being somewhat clumsy because my left one was in that fucking cast.

"I just..." I still heard the sound of the bones breaking when I had stupidly put it down to brace myself, and my body won the tug of war—or slam, or whatever. I'd gotten hurt plenty of times in hockey. Hell, my back was fucked and would probably be for the rest of my life, those disks compressed and herniated and never to be whole again.

A stack of jelly donuts with some of the filling squeezed out.

There was no fixing the squished baked goods.

No fixing my back.

No going back.

Managing. I just had to manage it.

Another thing to put on my list. Fun times.

"It was scary," I said, instead of telling Hazel that. "Along with feeling like an idiot, because I should have been paying attention."

"You were rushing because I gave you a hard time about running late."

"Rightfully so since Late is my middle name."

Hazel smiled, releasing our hands and pulling me into a hug. "I know for a fact that your middle name is Temperance."

"Because my parents had a cruel sense of humor."

"Because they"—Hazel pulled back, lips twitching—"had no idea their little angel would be a terror."

"Or a devil." A shrug. "My middle name should have been Satan."

"You're going to be struck down on the spot," Hazel warned me.

"If that was the case, I would have been struck down years ago."

Brown eyes on mine. Brown eyes that saw too much. Mostly because we'd known each other for too damned long.

"I know why you weren't paying attention," Hazel murmured. "And I know why this time right now is hard for you. Which"—she slung an arm around my shoulder, squeezed as she guided us around the desk and nudged me into my seat— "is why I'm going to let you distract yourself with work."

Thank God. Because it was the anniversary of my parents' deaths.

Because, broken bones aside, it all felt raw and fresh and painful...even though it had happened far too many years before. Even though my heart and mind and emotions were supposedly coated in steel.

"However—"

I groaned.

Hazel ignored me and kept talking. "I'm going to demand your presence this Thursday for unhealthy cheese night at CeCe's. With hurricanes. And Oliver on call to drive our drunk asses home."

Alcohol.

Dairy, mostly in the fried variety.

It sounded perfect.

"You're on," I said.

"Damn right I am." A kiss to my cheek. "No pain meds on Thursday because we're not mixing prescription pain killers and booze."

I hadn't even bothered to fill the script.

I knew too many people who were hooked on oxy to risk dealing with my pain with anything stronger than ibuprofen.

Even though it had been offered to me plenty often.

Nope. No, thank you.

"You're on," I said again instead of giving Hazel my rundown of the pharmaceutical industry and its various faults. They had plenty. Hazel knew this. I knew this. We'd watched enough documentaries and yelled to each other about the injustices of the companies getting off by paying settlements (fucking settlements that didn't begin to cover the cost of their culpability or excuse their role or make up for the lives ruined) without having to admit guilt.

But I digressed.

And maybe needed to cool it on Netflix for a bit.

"Thursday," I said, focusing. "Cheese. Fried, preferably. *All* the alcohol. And ranting about some social injustice or another."

A hand on my shoulder. "You know your parents would be proud of you."

That was the crux of it.

They would be.

And it made everything harder.

Luckily, I didn't have to delve into that with Hazel. Because conveniently there was a tall, dark, and handsome man striding by my open door.

"Hey, Sexy Pants," I called, making Hazel jerk and straighten, her lips twitching when she saw exactly who was in the hallway. "Your girl here is tired," I said. "You'd better take her home."

Oliver's eyes flared, and he bustled into the room. "You're tired, baby?" he asked, concern in his voice. *Too* much concern. He studied Hazel's face and then whipped off his jacket, wrapped it around her. "We need to get you home. Right now." He began coaxing her toward the door.

I took a moment to process.

Because, yeah, Oliver was protective. But he wasn't like this. He knew Hazel could handle her own shit, knew Haze had her own mind and let her use it, especially after her douche of an ex had treated her like shit and tried to gaslight her and... was just a total asshole all around.

So, Oliver cared. He watched out for her.

But he didn't take one look at his woman's eyes and begin bustling her home.

And it clicked.

"Are you guys going to have a shotgun wedding?" I asked before Oliver managed to get Hazel into the hall and doing it loud because Hazel was protesting that she wasn't tired, that she was fine, and that he just needed to relax.

They both stopped, glanced back.

"Umm," Hazel began. Earring fiddling. Pink on her cheeks.

I gasped. "You promised me hurricanes!"

"Umm," she said again, darting a look toward Oliver and then back to me. "I was going to make mine virgin."

"It's *all* alcohol."

"No, it's not. It has...orange juice." She nibbled on her bottom lip. "And maybe like grenadine or something."

It was more question than statement. And I knew the feeling. Because I didn't know what was in the drink either. Just that it had a lot of booze and very little juice, and it tasted yummy. "So, you're having orange juice." I cut my eyes to Oliver, who was all but itching with impatience to get his woman home, even though I had been fibbing about the tired part. "Which means we won't need Sexy Pants to be designated driver."

Haze stuck out her bottom lip. "We will."

"Why?"

More pout. "Because I'll be cheese drunk." A beat. "And orange juice drunk."

I laughed and crossed around the desk for a second time. Only on this occasion, it wasn't to comfort my best friend. It was to hug her tight (and to hell with the twinge in my arm because the healing bones really didn't like tight squeezes). And it was to whisper in Hazel's ear, "I'm so happy for you, babe."

Haze squeezed me back (more to helling with the twinges). "Thanks, honey."

"I love you."

"I love you, too."

My friend's voice was watery. My eyes were dry, but despite my whole steel doors and walls and concrete between myself and the rest of the world, I was feeling *this*. Because Hazel was good and kind and amazing, and because Oliver was equally as awesome. They'd both had shit heaped on them, and they both deserved every single bit of happiness.

I straightened. "I get to be a godmother, right?"

Hazel blinked then grinned widely. "Damn right you are." Another hug. A whisper just for my ears. "I can't think of anyone I'd rather have."

I leaned back, smiled mischievously. "Because I'll take them to do all the fun things?"

Hazel nodded, tugged my ponytail. "Exactly."

Oliver groaned.

"What?" I asked innocently, straightening again and letting him have the space to get his arms around his woman by leaning back against my desk. No surprise, Oliver moved right in, straightening the jacket he'd put around Hazel, even though it was quite warm in my office.

"I'm thinking about the kinds of things you consider *fun*," he muttered.

I grinned, couldn't resist pushing his buttons. "Are you worried I'm going to take a toddler shark diving or something?"

Oliver shuddered. "That's not remotely funny."

My smile didn't fade. "I'd definitely wait until they were eighteen." A tap of my finger to my chin. "Maybe sixteen—"

"Pru," Hazel warned, but her eyes were twinkling.

"Bye, Haze," I said, waving them off as I sank down into my chair, pulling open my laptop. "I need to Google high-risk activities for babies."

Oliver groaned.

Hazel rolled her eyes and gave me a finger wave.

They left.

I did some Googling...but it definitely wasn't of the high-risk activity variety. It was right down the baby gear rabbit hole.

Onesies and a cute little wave-patterned blanket, a bunny that was sort of cute, sort of creepy and would fit in perfectly with Oliver's Fugler (a truly ugly stuffed animal—as it was designed to be that way by the manufacturer, complete with fake plastic teeth, tighty-whities, and maniacal eyes) named Mac that he'd won in a team challenge. I also picked up some pregnancy support things. Not that I knew what it was like to be pregnant, but they were highly rated to help with the boobs and the stomach and the nausea and apparently constipation (because God, seriously, the universe had to make it harder on pregnant women aside from the whole pushing out a water-melon from a lemon thing?).

I bought *all* the things.

I spent too much money.

So much that I'd need to cancel my snowshoeing weekend up in Banff that December.

But, for once, I didn't care that I might miss out on an adventure.

Not one bit.

Because my friend was happy. And that was enough for me.

It had always been enough.

NINE

Marcel

THE CRACK OF A STICK.

Stinging on my palms.

"Jesus," I muttered, stilling the puck and pulling one of my hands out of its glove, shaking it, and then repeating the process with the other. "Do you need to put that much sauce on it?" I called to Conner Smith—Smitty—who was laughing his ass off at me.

Rightfully so, because I was whining and complaining about sore palms.

But also...damn, the big man had a hell of an arm.

Or arms. Or an entire tree-trunked-size body that he could put into motion to fire the puck across the ice at warp speed.

The fucker had won the All-Star competition for hardest shot the previous season.

And there was a reason for it.

That reason also being why my palms were stinging like motherfuckers.

"Yes, I do!" Conner called back. "Get those gloves on, princess! Another one is incoming."

That moniker reminded me of another princess. One currently sporting a cast and driving me slowly insane.

I'd seen her in the halls.

She was perfectly polite.

Polite.

Pru.

No *Pretty Boy*. No shameless flirting. Just polite and professional, and I fucking hated it.

But I didn't have much time to focus on that, not with Smitty lobbing another puck at me.

Lobbing was the wrong word.

He was launching it, cruise-missile style, at me.

Which, despite my bitching, was what Conner would do in the game, and since I had asked Smitty to do me a favor so I could practice my tipping, launching was what needed to happen.

Even if it made my hands sting.

Wah-wah.

I knew.

The puck came flying, about a foot off the ground, just like we'd talked about. High enough to sail over stick blades in front of the net, low enough that it would hopefully avoid the bodies holding those sticks. Though, that wasn't always, or even often, the case. A player could hope, though, and sometimes the hockey gods were kind and it got through...and sometimes the gods were fickle for their opponents, and it bounced off every shin guard, ass, and/or helmet on the way in. Those were the best...when they happened to the other team.

A puck bouncing this way and that on Marty, our goalie, wasn't ideal.

Anyway, I digressed.

And stopped doing so only a fraction of a second soon enough.

Getting my stick in position, tilting the blade, timing the flick of the latter at...just...the...right...time.

Ping.

"Fuck," I muttered.

Or not *exactly* at the right time. The puck glanced off the crossbar and bounced out...out meaning that it bounced right off the back of my helmet.

"Ow," I muttered again, lifting the head protection and rubbing my skull, which was now stinging way worse than my palms had.

Smitty meanwhile had been—what did the cool kids call it nowadays? Oh right. Conner had been *unalived.* And was currently laying on the ice, busting up, his laughter echoing around the rink.

Because the man was a giant and also had giant, roaring laughter.

Of course, I did.

Also, thank fuck the rink was empty, Conner and me having snuck onto the ice before we flew out that night for the team's final preseason game.

The real shit would start Saturday.

And I, for one (okay, I along with the rest of the team), couldn't be more excited. Two killer seasons. Winning the Cup back-to-back, but more importantly, winning it for Oliver's last season. Being able to bring it home for the man who was the heart of the team.

That had meant everything.

A rap on the glass.

Speaking of the devil, Oliver was standing by the boards, wearing a suit...and a huge grin on his face.

Well, a huge grin on the part of his face that I could see.

Because the rapping was actually pounding. As in, Oliver was bent double and slapping his palm against the glass as he absolutely lost it.

"You're on your own with Hannah," I shouted, loud enough that Ollie had to have heard it.

Proving me right, Oliver straightened, still grinning like the motherfucking Cheshire cat and held up his phone. "Totally worth it," he shouted back. "Especially since I got it all on video. From whining about sore hands to head shot. Oh, my God"—he bent again—"this is solid gold shit. Fucking hell. The open net was *too* open!"

Smitty's booming laugh got louder.

I was about to *unalive* them both.

And then resurrect them, only to *unalive* them both a second time. Just for good measure.

"You'd better share that video," Conner called, pushing up to sitting, snow all along the length of his back. He wasn't wearing pads—just skates and gloves and a helmet—and I hoped amongst all hope (and threw a prayer to the hockey gods) that the snow soaked right through his navy tracksuit and froze Smitty's balls off.

Probably wouldn't work anyway.

The man was a mountain, and mountains never seemed to be fazed by snow or cold.

But, mountain or not, the lack of pads meant that I—who was wearing a full set, since I was standing on the receiving end of the mountain man's All-Star powerful shot—couldn't fire the puck back, bean it off Conner's ass (or thick *ass* skull).

Instead, I had to contend with glaring.

And shouting, "You'd better not share that shit!"

Oliver held up his cell. "Already in the group chat."

"Shit," I muttered, hanging my head, knowing that the damage had been done, that the messages had to already be piling up, that by the time I hit the showers, it would be *everywhere*.

Oh, the shit that would be given.

"I hate you!" I yelled, straightening my helmet, jerking my stick at Conner, indicating that he get his dumb ass off the ice and get the fuck back to work.

But that indicating didn't mean that I didn't hear the gasp.

Hear Hazel—who was the absolute shit, in the *absolute* best way—exclaim, "You can't hate my man. He's awesomesauce."

"Oh, sweet Jesus," Smitty grumbled (which was less grumble and more rumbling, as in rumble that easily reached the couple cozying up to each other on the other side of the glass), "please, tell me you didn't use the word awesomesauce."

"Sure did," she called back. "Because my Oliver is the bestest and most *awesomesauce* man on the planet."

Conner's lips twitched.

Deciding to ignore the fuckers giving me a hard time and take advantage of the break (see, planning was good for *some* things), I shagged some pucks, skated them back up to Conner at the blue line.

I'd just turned away when Oliver called, "You just wish you had a girl who said you were *awesomesauce*."

Amusement faded from Smitty's face as I pushed up, began fussing with the pucks, a flicker of dark sliding across my friend's face. *Fuck.* It was gone so quickly that I barely caught it. But he was quiet, I paid attention, and so I did see it. Recognized it because I'd been through it myself. Because Marissa had torn me into shreds, broken my heart. And because I'd been paying attention to Pru, who was good at hiding what had torn *her* into shreds.

Like called to like.

Pru hid hers well.

Conner tried to, but his personality was bigger. It lacked

finesse, and while he might put on a good front, he was hurting too much for that to be truly effective.

Especially for a man who'd been through the same thing.

For a man who made it my job to pay the fuck attention when the people I cared about were hurting.

Which was why I decided to do something about it.

"Hey," I snapped, dumping a few more pucks in the pile before skating back to the net. "I want to get this shit done, lazy ass. Shoot already and try not to hit me in the head again."

"I'll remind you," Smitty rumbled, "that your shitty tip was responsible for the head injury!"

I lifted my stick, glared at Oliver, who was showing Hazel something on his phone (no doubt the recording he'd shared with the fucking world), and then returned my glare to Conner, yelling back, "Lies!"

"Luckily," Smitty said, winding up. "It's all on video!"

He fired.

I was—*luckily*—ready. I positioned. I flicked.

And this time, the puck went into the net instead of crashing into the back of my head.

TEN

Pru

WALKER KNOCKED on my office door.

The kid was a lot of good things, punctual included.

"Hey, Pru," he said. "Is this still a good time?"

I nodded. "Of course, bud. What's up?"

He held up an iPad. "I wanted to see if you had time to go over some of the video from the game."

He was *such* a good kid.

My kid. Well, not mine, and not really a kid. He was nineteen and fresh out of juniors, but he was mine in a way that meant I felt possessive and proud. It was my scouting that had gotten him a chance with the Breakers.

Of course, it was his skill and effort and energy that was going to earn him a permanent spot on the team.

But he was going to run himself ragged if he kept up like this.

I didn't mind him touching base with me after training camp, or a tough practice, or a game, but he was going to drive himself crazy if he continued to be so cerebral about something that was instinctual, that could go bad if he overthought it.

He needed to not worry about messing up so much.

He *needed* to play.

"I do," I told him. "Of course, I do."

A nod, his broad form crossing the room and sinking down into the chair in front of my desk.

"But I'm not going to."

His brows pulled together. "I—what?"

I pushed out of my chair, crossed around my desk, and leaned against the edge. "I'm not going to go over any more video with you." My lips curved. "For the moment, anyway." I nudged his foot with my own. "Because you're doing fine. You're doing *great*. Now"—another nudge—"*now* you need to breathe and relax and *play*, bud."

"I—"

"And trust me when I say that I will come and talk to you if I need to. That there will be plenty of video for you to go over this season, that the other coaches and I will *definitely* have things for you to improve and work on, but that right now, you need to play, bud."

He opened his mouth.

"You need to *play*."

"I—"

"Play," I repeated.

His shoulders dropped, a breath slipped out from between his lips.

Then he looked up, smiled. "I can do that."

I nudged his foot one more time. "Damn straight you can."

"You know your mom's not going to be mad," I said into the phone, Hazel having spent the last fifteen minutes in worried jabbering over the wedding and how her mom was going to flip because there would be some deviation from The Plan.

Yes.

The Plan.

The Reids were taking their daughter's wedding plans *very* seriously.

I loved that for Hazel.

I *didn't* love this worry.

"Your mom has already been asking about grandbabies," I reminded her.

"But *after* the wedding. They're supposed to come *after* the wedding."

I adjusted my cell so I could keep opening boxes of baby gear. It was challenging with one good arm, but I was determined—and living the one functional arm life for the next six weeks—so there was no use complaining about it. I just braced with my casted arm and hacked away at the packing tape with my good one as I unearthed the gifts.

Thankfully, I'd bought gift bags.

Because wrapping paper would have been too much.

I sucked at wrapping presents in the first place and add in my being down an arm and I'd be gifting Hazel with presents that looked like they'd gone five rounds with a blender.

Good times.

Snorting to myself because baby stuff was both so tiny and so expensive (and also so...worth it because I couldn't wait to see Hazel's face when she opened all the things), I asked, "Are you going to pop a kid out on the altar?"

Hazel made a noise—disgust, shock, anger. No, probably shock. I was good at shocking my friend. "No," she said when she'd recovered. "I'm not due until February."

"That's months away from October. Relax. You'll be fine."

"I just—"

"Make your mom ridiculously happy."

"My dad," she began.

"I think your dad knows you've had sex."

Another noise, this one of the shushing variety. "Don't say that. I'm just his...I don't know. Virginal innocent daughter."

I froze.

Then busted up laughing. "Already the pregnancy hormones are rotting your brain."

"And *already* you're not funny," Hazel muttered grumpily. "See if I take you out for fried cheese."

"Oh, you'll take me."

"No, ma'am."

I opened the last box. "Yes, ma'am, because I'm the only one who will feed your fried cheese addiction."

Silence. Then, "You're addicted, too."

"Damn right I am."

Hazel giggled. "We're being ridiculous, aren't we?"

I wasn't sure about the *we're* part of that statement, but Hazel was hormonal and pregnant and not that far out from a wedding (just over two weeks now). She was allowed to be a little nutty. So I merely said, "Yup. We sure are." I finished stacking the baby items into the box. I'd find some time to make it look all nice and floofy (if that was a technical term) in the gift bags I'd bought, fluffing up the tissue paper and pretending that I was good at wrapping.

Not that it made a difference since it always got crushed in transit, and the first thing someone did when they opened the gift was to take it out and ruin any good floof.

But I didn't make the gift-wrapping rules.

I just...threw money at the situation and perpetuated them.

Good times.

"You know your mom is going to love to add some event to the wedding to surprise all the guests with the baby."

"Like a signature list of mock-tails?"

"I was thinking more like jumping out of a giant cake wearing only a diaper."

"You're not funny."

Except Hazel was giggling like a fiend.

"So why are you laughing?"

"I..." More laughter. "Don't." A breath. "Know."

"Hormones and happiness," I teased. "The perfect combination."

Hazel giggled for a few more seconds before she got herself together. "You're still not funny."

"I love you, too."

A beat. "You know, you could have happy, too." Bless Hazel's heart for not mentioning hormones.

"I *am* happy."

The beat was longer this time. "Are you?"

"Don't, Haze."

My friend sighed, was quiet for a long time. Then her voice went deliberately light. "You know how it is, honey. I just want you to have what I have."

And I knew that would never happen.

It just...wouldn't. That wasn't me being dramatic or ridiculous or spending my time pretending to be an ostrich. I...didn't have the capacity to be in a relationship like Hazel did.

"I know," I said. "And I love you for it. But I *am* happy, babe. I got to play hockey for a long time, at a high level. I have a job I really dig, and I get to be in the same city again as my best friend."

Hazel sniffed, hormones at work again.

"Plus, I'm going to be the best godmother ever. Especially, when I tell the little gal or guy that I found that I can get them scuba certified at eight." I grinned. "Shark diving at eight. I dig it."

"I'm never going to tell Oliver that you said that."

I settled back on the couch with a smile. "My work here is done." A beat. "Well, maybe after I pack mule that kid up Everest."

Hazel giggled. "You're going to be the best godmother ever."

"Damn right I am."

"AND THEN," I said, waving a cheese stick like it was a sword, "I told her that I was going to rip out my laces and choke her with them."

Hazel gasped. "You didn't."

I nodded. "I totally lost my cool. I mean, first, it would take way too long to try to unlace my skates. I like them tight and my shin guards lay on top of them. Then there's the hockey socks and the tape—"

"*That's* the problem you have with what you told me?"

Another nod. "Well, it was totally ridiculous. I'd never get the laces out fast enough to choke her, and then I'd be trying to skate after her one-footed and—"

Hazel giggled.

"Illogical, see?" More giggling. "So anyway. I was suspended for three games." I shrugged. "Funny story, the refs generally don't like it when you threaten people on your own team."

"Did they give you a penalty?"

"Luckily," I said, "no. Or not one to my team anyway. Once the coaches separated us, I got kicked to the locker room, and Margarite had to go home with her parents—"

"Seriously?"

"Well, they were in the stands, and they couldn't exactly send her to the opposing team's room."

Hazel swiped the cheese stick from my fingers, dunking it in ranch and taking a huge bite. Probably because she'd gotten tired of me gesturing with it.

But oddly, cheese sticks were excellent oration assistance devices.

"You knew that, didn't you?"

"Knew that they'd send that piece of trash Margarite home with her piece of trash parents?"

Hazel nodded.

I smiled. "Yeah." I snagged another cheese stick, took a bite of this one, not that it would stop Hazel (who normally could eat for two on these nights, but with that baby cooking in the oven, was eating for more like *twenty*-two). But at least I'd get a taste before my friend stole it from me. "Coach had heard what she said to Katie, what she called her, so even though Coach didn't approve of me threatening to choke out—and then grabbing her in a headlock and yanking her jersey up and over her cage"—so *fucking* satisfying, by the way, because Margarite was a troll—"he knew why I'd done what I'd done."

"So, you didn't get punished." A beat. "Besides the suspension from the league."

I laughed. "Oh no, I *got* punished. Besides the suspension, I had to do community service at the rink."

Hazel's eyes got wide.

"I was the public skate moderator." I shuddered, for real for once. Because it had been...torture.

"That must have been bad."

"Take what you're imagining and then multiply it by middle school kids being dumbasses, high school kids being dumbasses, add in other kids trying to get laid, and in the middle of all that a bunch of elementary school kids and families just trying to have fun."

"That sounds..."

"Like torture?"

Hazel grinned. "Like the perfect punishment for a player who threatened to choke her teammate with her laces."

I snagged the plate of nachos our waitress, Julie, set down before Hazel could get her pregnant mitts into it. "It was justified!"

"But is violence ever justified?"

I glared. "So asks the woman who punched out her ex?"

"He assaulted me."

"Margarite did the same, just because it wasn't physical doesn't mean it wasn't an assault on Katie," I grumbled.

And then wished I hadn't.

Because Hazel was clearly teasing me. She was definitely on my (and Katie's) side, and my grumbling made her go pale, her lips parting with what was no doubt going to be an apology.

"Don't apologize," I said quickly. "I know you were just teasing."

"I—" Hazel clamped her mouth shut.

"Seriously. *Don't.* It's okay. I'm still just salty over all those public skates I had to patrol," I said, reaching for another chip.

Except, my chip-reaching was aborted mid-reach, my *—ol* in *patrol* extended to *ooool*—when Hazel jumped up out of her seat, her hand going to her mouth as she sprinted away from the table.

"Haze—" I started to reach for her.

She was gone, sprinting down the hall.

"What the..." I whispered, staring in shock for one moment before I grabbed both of our purses and waved at the server, indicating I would be right back.

Luckily, Julie knew us, knew Hazel and I wouldn't stiff her, because that was all the time I spent before chasing after Hazel, turning down the hall and finding it empty. Thankfully, there were only two locations to go. One, the alley behind CeCe's, and two, the bathrooms.

The latter of which I had to walk by to reach the former.

And walking by was all it took for me to understand.

Because coming from the women's restroom was the sound of a poltergeist.

A.K.A. the sound of a pregnant woman losing every single bit of fried cheese she'd consumed that evening (and that was no small amount).

I pushed in through the door, saw Hazel bent over the toilet, stall wide open.

I moved to the sink and wet a paper towel, tugging my ponytail holder out of my hair since Hazel's was down. I finger-combed my friend's hair back, swept it up into a quick messy bun, and then rested the wet paper towel on Hazel's neck.

The poor thing was still retching—and seriously, did this bring me back to my college days—so I simply knelt as close as I could in the small stall and gently rubbed Hazel's back.

Hazel, who barely one hour before had proclaimed she was one of the lucky ones.

Because she hadn't gotten morning sickness.

Well, it wasn't morning.

But it sure as shit was sickness.

I kept one hand rubbing, used the other to thumb out a text to Oliver, telling him to get his ass here to get his woman home.

Ten seconds later—no joke, *ten seconds* later—he said he would be right there.

I knew *right there* would be *right there.*

Because he was probably right around the corner, worrying about his pregnant fiancé and playing Neanderthal.

She mine. She carry my baby. Me must be near to protect.

I wouldn't have thought Oliver had the alpha gene in him, but I was glad that Hazel had it on her side. And extra glad it meant that Hazel wouldn't have to cool her heels feeling sick and miserable because I couldn't drive her home.

Two hurricanes ago, I could have.

Now, I wasn't drunk, but I wouldn't get behind the wheel of a car.

"I think I'm done," Hazel croaked a moment later, sitting back on her heels, starting to rise.

I flushed the toilet but put a hand on my friend's arm, moved the cool paper towel to Hazel's forehead. "Stay there for a minute," I ordered. "I'm going to get you some water to rinse out your mouth."

Hazel nodded.

I pushed up, reached the door right as it opened.

Julie stood on the other side, a glass in her hand, stirring the clear liquid with a spoon. "Flat Sprite," she said softly. "Helped me when I was pregnant and sick all the time."

"How'd—"

Julie smiled and shook her head, her blond ponytail bouncing. "Only time I've seen her not drink. Coupled with the pale rush to the bathroom." One shoulder lifted and dropped. "I knew." She pulled the spoon out, extended the glass.

"You're a goddess," I whispered, taking it.

Julie waved a hand, dismissing the compliment. "If you give me your card, I can charge you guys out."

I nodded, pulling out my wallet and extracting my credit card. "Thanks, Jules."

"Any time."

She disappeared through the door, and I barely had Hazel on her feet and sipping the flat Sprite when the wooden panel swung open so quickly that it slammed into the opposite wall, making us both jump and Sprite slosh over the rim of the glass.

I snagged the cup from Hazel's hands.

And just in time.

Because Oliver rushed forward, cupping Hazel's cheeks, his voice soft but intense, his gaze searching hers.

I didn't hear all he said, mainly because I'd stepped away to dump the soda down the drain and to give them some privacy.

Hazel's voice was weak, and clearly, she felt terrible.

So, it didn't surprise me that Oliver was bustling her to the door with nary a look back.

He loved her. He was worried about her.

He was temple kisses and waffles and smoothing back bangs with Hazel.

"Pru?"

I glanced up from the sink, where I'd been—for some reason—rinsing the glass, met Oliver's eyes. "Thanks," he said.

"Anything for her," I said softly.

Pale blue eyes went intense, but he didn't say anything else, just nodded and with his arm around Hazel's waist, began walking her out.

ELEVEN

Marcel

I'D TRAILED Oliver when he took one look at his phone and
tore out of the sports bar like a defenseman was back-checking
him on a breakaway.

Without a word.

Just shoving out of his seat and sprinting out onto the
sidewalk.

Luckily, I'd seen Oliver turn right, toward CeCe's. Our
usual haunt and the spot we were banned from that evening
because Hazel and Pru were having a night out.

Worry clenched my stomach, but I took a minute to throw
enough cash on the table to cover our tab. Because the last thing
the team needed was to have two of our players—even if one
was a former one, he was still part of the organization—dine
and dash.

Second, our server had been cool.

The kid didn't deserve to not have a good tip.

So, I took a hot second to make sure both instances were

covered. Then I grabbed both my and Oliver's jackets and headed out into the night, the cool evening immediately penetrating the bared skin of my arms.

Ignoring that, I moved toward CeCe's, made it to the main dining room just in time to see Oliver with his arm around Hazel, who looked like death, she was so drawn and pale. They walked toward me, and I stepped back quickly to open the door, holding it wide for them. "What's wrong?" I asked when they were out on the sidewalk.

Good God, she looked worse up close.

Hazel's eyes met mine, and she smiled weakly. "Funny story," she whispered, "I might not have morning sickness, but I sure as shit have the evening version."

Oliver's arm tightened as he tugged her toward the car parked on the street, half a block up.

I followed them, and it took me a moment to process her statement.

Then I did.

Then I grinned, though it was a grin that quickly smothered when Oliver caught me smiling and growled.

"It's okay," Hazel murmured, patting my chest. "*I'm* okay. I just...apparently I can't have cheese"—she gagged—"nights."

"No cheese nights," Oliver snapped, even as he gently rubbed her arm when she gagged again. "Not ever again."

"I like cheese"—another retch—"nights."

"No more ch—"

"Maybe we should cut out mention of the C-word?" I said, moving forward and opening the passenger door when Oliver bleeped the locks. "Just for tonight?"

Hazel smiled at me, the cool air seemingly beginning to revive her.

Well, *that* and eliminating the mention of everything that began with ch- and ended with -eese.

"Good idea," she said. "No C-word."

Oliver ignored us, scooping her up and setting her on the seat before reaching over her and buckling her in. He started to straighten then stopped, cupped her jaw, and rested his forehead against hers. "I'm sorry, baby."

I took a step back, feeling like a voyeur.

Especially when Hazel covered his hand with her own and then said softly, "I'm not." She smiled. "Means our baby is healthy."

A gentle expression that I had never seen on my friend's face before. Then he leaned in to kiss Hazel.

"Babe," she said, turning away slightly. "I just lost a lot of ch—" She cut herself off. "A lot of the C-word. No kissing without me brushing my teeth first."

"I don't care," Oliver said, though it was rough and still more of a growl, his protective instincts at full alert.

"*I* care—"

Oliver kissed her anyway.

It wasn't short.

It wasn't sweet.

It was long and deep and with plenty of tongue—and by plenty, I meant *plenty*. I got that from the short glimpse I caught before I spun away, waved a hand over my shoulder, and said, "I'll see you guys—"

Pru walked out of CeCe's, two coats, two purses in her arms.

She glanced both ways, hesitated when she saw me, her face going carefully neutral. Fuck, I hated that. Hated her looking at me like that.

I wanted the flirt.

I wanted the hope that had been in her pretty eyes as she'd held a bag up, before I'd rolled down my window and revealed Carrie.

I wanted—

Her shoulders went straight, and she strode toward us, walking right past me with a simple, "Hey." Shoving between the open door and her friend, interrupting the long and deep kiss like she'd seen it all before and it didn't faze her.

And maybe it didn't.

Hazel was her best friend, after all, and Hazel came with Oliver, and PDAs were in no short supply with those two.

She plunked one of the purses down at Hazel's feet, knocking Oliver back a step, but doing it in a way I could tell was gentle and in control and totally aware that she didn't want to make him lose his balance—especially when that balance wasn't what it once was. So, it was careful and pushy and planned out, and I could appreciate all that *careful and planned out.*

Even though it didn't seem like it was Pru.

Because it *was* her.

Because even though she cultivated all that im*pru*dence, she was still smart, still mindful.

Hazel's trance broken, Oliver stepped back and rounded the hood of his car, barely stopping to grab his jacket from me before he got into the driver's seat and buckled in. But I hardly paid my friend any attention. Not when Pru was smoothing Hazel's coat over her front, handing her a to-go cup of some drink.

"Courtesy of Julie," she said quietly, and though I strained to hear the rest of her words, the traffic and the wind drowned them out.

I did hear them exchange goodbyes, though.

And the sound of the door closing, the engine starting up.

I moved up next to Pru as Oliver drove away, standing in silence until they'd disappeared, knowing I should say something, anything, and yet knowing that none of my planning had brought me any clarity for this particular situation.

Pru didn't seem to have that problem.

She just tugged her phone out, said, "Night," and started walking away.

Was a good *twenty feet* away before I got my dumb ass moving.

"Wait," I called. "Pru, wait!"

She didn't stop, not even as she shrugged into her jacket, her cell in one hand. Nope. She just gripped that phone like the fucking magician she was, popping it out from the sleeve like she was making a bouquet of flowers appear out of thin air. Heels clicking on the sidewalk, pulling her hair out from beneath the collar of her coat without seeming to miss a beat.

Certainly, she didn't drop her phone.

Nope, that sucker was gripped tight, and it took me a moment to—well, it took me a moment to catch up to her long strides, several more to stop staring at the lean lines of her legs, the curve of her ass.

Pretty.

So damned pretty.

Without the makeup, the stilettos.

In the heeled boots that wrapped around strong calves, stopping just beneath her knees. In the plain jeans (no crystals on the pockets, no strategically torn holes in the thighs, at the knees). In a simple black peacoat that nipped at her slender waist.

Then I realized what she was doing on her phone.

Calling a fucking *Lyft*.

What the fuck all? My car was half a block away. She didn't need to wait for a car, get into one with a stranger. I'd drive her home and—

I stopped thinking.

Somehow stopped thinking for once (and I wasn't even naked).

I snatched her phone, force-quit the app, and shoved it in my pocket.

Conveniently, this coincided with us reaching my car.

I snagged the door handle—thank the hockey gods for the auto unlock door variety—and wrapped an arm around her waist. This was made easier because she was spinning to face me, probably to yell at me because I'd snagged her cell. But I navigated a spin, opening the door, tucking her inside, and slamming the metal panel shut in a move that was—thank *you* very much—very fucking smooth.

And probably something I would never be able to replicate again.

But I'd learned how to appreciate the victories I received.

So, I just hauled ass around the front of my car, got in, (and locked the doors in case she decided to do some tucking and rolling). Then I started up the engine, pulled away from the curb.

She was sputtering.

Furious noises emerging from her throat, forming sounds that weren't quite sentences. Hell, they were barely words at all.

Just like a kitten growling at a dog it spotted.

Which was a sentiment I wasn't going to share.

Because I wanted to live. Because I liked my balls where they were. Because...

"What the fuck are you doing?" she snapped.

Ah. There were her words.

"I'm taking you home."

Not that I knew exactly where her home was. I *did* know, because Hazel had mentioned it once, that she had a condo in the neighborhood next to my own.

So, I'd start there.

And I thumbed a text discreetly (and yes, illegally) to Hazel, asking for Pru's address.

A buzz in response a few seconds later.

I checked the screen at a red light, memorized the address—thanks for more thinking, or at least, thank the fates for a brain that was able to memorize shit easily.

Usually, it was plays on the ice.

Tonight it was to process an address, to memorize it, to mentally map it out. And yeah, then I clicked the address, pulled up the directions...because for all the mental planning, an actual map was still better.

All while Pru sputtered.

Then found her words again.

"Pull over right now," she growled, "and let me the fuck out of this car."

I glanced behind me, changed lanes. "Nope."

Silence.

A long, tense quiet.

Then, "What do you mean *nope?*"

"I mean," I said, "that I'm driving you home. You're not calling a fucking car. You're getting home in *my* car. And while I'm getting you home, we're going to talk."

Silence.

This time it was long and tense. *This* time it was furious, filled with absolute rage, fury that was palpable, burning my skin. I glanced down, half surprised to find that my neck and arm weren't filled with blisters from that glare.

And long.

I couldn't forget that.

Which reminded me that I probably needed to be the one to get the talking portion of the events underway.

Which...wasn't my strong suit, as pretty much anyone who interacted with me for more than five minutes knew.

Still, it wasn't like Pru was going to jump in and fill the silence.

And anyway, there was some shit that I needed to straighten out.

"I didn't sleep with her."

I kept my eyes on the road. One, because I had to, or I'd risk crashing the car. Two, because I was a coward and didn't want to see her face.

But still, she didn't say anything.

So I found myself blabbering on. "The girl who was in the car with me. I—" I swallowed hard, cleared my throat. "It wasn't like that."

She snorted.

"Okay," I admitted. "It *was* like that," I said. "You'd gone. It felt...not good. I was at the rink, she was there, I'd never—" I sighed. "I was with Marissa from high school. I don't—haven't ever done a one-night stand. I—" Fuck, this was embarrassing. "I've slept with a grand total of four women, you included. Carrie *not*."

A beat.

"*Four?*"

It was aghast.

An aghast question.

"I—" I started to tell her that I'd been loyal to Marissa, that I'd only slept with two women in the last year and that was after the requisite three to five dates—and I'd been with them for a few *more* dates before I'd broken things off.

Because it hadn't been right.

Because...they hadn't been Pru.

"How in the hell do you fuck like *that?*"

TWELVE

Pru

FOUR.

Four!

That wasn't the most pertinent part of this conversation, nor the thing I should be focusing on (hello, the man practically kidnapping me off the street), but...*four!*

He'd slept with four women.

And one of them was me.

Which brought me to my previous question or statement or treatise or...whatever—

How did a man like him, a man with serious skills, serious *fucking*—literally—skills fuck like *that?*

It had been mind-blowing.

He'd been intuitive. He'd brought tricks I'd never heard or felt or seen and—

"I plan," he said, his soft voice rumbling through the car. "I plan and I plot and I prepare." His eyes flashed back to mine before returning to the road, and the twinkle of amusement in their depths was...chef's kiss.

Words I hated.

Words I *loved.*

"And then I take care of business."

It should have been cheesy, but rumbling down my spine, dipping in between my thighs...that sentiment had heat curling through my middle, melting through steel, creating a tiny mouse-sized opening in those walls.

"This is where you give me shit for a bad line," he murmured.

Enough for amusement to join the heat in curling through the opening, in wrapping its tendrils around me, in pulling me up and up and *up* until I slammed through the surface of a wave or a pool or a lake. One second beneath the muffled, heavy liquid. The next exposed to the air, sounds assaulting me, feelings sloshing this way and that through my middle.

"You didn't sleep with her?"

His mouth, or the half of it that I could see, anyway, had been curved up. My question made it go flat.

And then he was pulling off the road, shifting to the shoulder of a street, I realized, that was very close to my place. He turned in his seat, extended a hand, and I could practically feel the brush of his fingers on my jaw, the roughened tips, the way they would stroke over my skin, slip up and push my bangs back.

I shivered in anticipation.

His hand dropped, rested on the console.

Disappointment wove its way into that mouse hole, corroded and ate away at the metal until it was more...of a mole hole? No, they weren't much bigger than mice, right? Okay, so a study in vermin sizes wasn't my specialty, but I knew that rats were bigger. So, a rat hole? No. That didn't seem big enough, unless they were of the New York City variety. Hmm. I had it. That freaking hole was now large enough to fit a badger.

Yup, a badger-sized hole. Jagged edges and rusted through, perfect for an ill-tempered critter.

Because that's what it was. Feisty and persistent and—

Dangerous.

As in, this was a dangerous game I was playing.

And, as always, the moment a speck of danger was present, I wanted to dive the fuck in.

I didn't have the self-preservation gene—

Lie, my inner voice said.

I was good at ignoring that voice. Really good at it.

That's what came from decades of practice.

"No, princess," he said, and I had been so distracted by that ignoring and the urge to live trial by fire, to jump headfirst, to allow danger to wash over me so that I could *feel,* it took me a minute to rewind my brain.

Past badger-sized holes.

Past freakishly large NYC rat-sized entrances.

Past mouse-sized ones.

To the question I'd asked.

About *Carrie.* Ugh. Even her name was better. And for fuck's sake, was I seriously going to allow jealousy to trail into that badger-sized hole, to make itself at home with longing and danger and disappointment and...a swirling of too many emotions? So many that my first instinct was to clamp a panel over the hole?

No.

Because my next...

My *next* was to dive the fuck in.

Because *princess* and temple kisses and waffles and bang stroking.

"Good," I murmured, spinning in my seat and grabbing his

face, kissing the shit out of him. Tongue into his mouth, lips moving on his, even though he'd gone very still. Even though my actions couldn't possibly be on his list of expected Pru behaviors and responses.

That was what had me continuing to kiss him, even though he wasn't kissing me back.

Because I knew I'd short-circuited all that planning DNA inside Marcel's brain, and he needed a moment to catch up.

And then he didn't.

And then he *really fucking didn't*.

His hands brushed mine away, knocking them aside as effortlessly as a feather, and he leaned forward, wove one into my hair, which was down for once since Hazel still had my ponytail holder and I hadn't bothered to look in my purse for another one. Fingertips pressing into my scalp, lacing tightly through the strands, enough so that the slight pinch added to my pleasure. Then his other hand got involved in the party, dropping to my side.

Click.

My belt was unbuckled.

A jerk, and my body was bent over the console, my breasts colliding with his chest in a way that had my nipples doing a happy little dance.

And then *he* was kissing *me*.

Oh boy, was the man kissing me.

Deep and wet and long. No sense of hurry. Just a sense of... coming home.

His strength bracketing mine, holding me close as he explored.

As though he had all the time in the world.

And I fucking loved it.

Then he was slowing our kiss, setting me back in my seat, tugging my seat belt over me, latching it closed.

Pulling back onto the road.

I sat there, lips tingling (and cue my pervy gameshow announcer to ask, "Which set?"—muahaha), and he drove... unerringly to my condo.

My eyes went wide when he pulled into my guest spot—that, at least, I knew was easy to see, considering my car was well-known among the team...mostly because it was a clunker of the worst sort. Ugly gold paint (with sparkles! And I was about as far away from a sparkle girl as it came). Rust spots on the wheel wells, a broken passenger door handle. Windows that stayed up in all seasons because if they went down...they stayed down.

That was why Hazel and Oliver had picked me up.

Because my friend had been on me to get a new car for *years*.

But Biscuit did her job. She got me to work and back. She was big and heavy and didn't skid on icy or snowy roads.

Plus, Biscuit had been with me for a long time.

Too long, according to Haze.

I didn't care. That behemoth was mine, and mine alone, and I was driving Biscuit until the day she croaked her final, smoggy breath.

Then he parked, and the car fell silent, and...I remembered the steel and badger holes and emotions and—

Look.

I wasn't proud of it.

But my daredevil, dive right in self had a moment of panic, okay?

"Well," I said, going for breezy but knowing it didn't sound the least bit lighthearted. It was a croak, not unlike what Biscuit would make. "I'd say thanks for the ride...if only you hadn't kidnapped me into taking it."

He reached for me. "Princess—"

Danger, danger...had me hesitating.

But eventually self-preservation kicked in, and I popped the handle. I liked danger, sure. But I didn't like it destroying me.

And Marcel...well, he had the potential to do that.

I dodged that warm, large, pleasure-bringing hand, and pushed open the door, unfolded from the inside of the car, and did it in a way that had me high-tailing it for the stairs—

"Forget something?"

I halted on the bottom tread.

Didn't turn around, because I knew immediately what I didn't have. My freaking purse! This is why I hated carrying the things. I'd rather shove a narrow wallet into my pocket and call it a day.

But my keys and my wallet were in the evil leather thing. Not to mention he still had my cell in his pocket.

Grr.

Marcel didn't fill the silence, and neither did I. Which was why I heard him bleep the locks of his car, heard the quiet tread of his steps as he moved toward me.

Then felt his presence at my left shoulder.

My fingers clenched into fists.

This was fine for those on my right hand, my left clench-ing...well, that had me hissing out a pained breath.

"Easy, princess," he murmured, stepping closer, brushing aside the hair trailing down my nape. Lips pressing there.

I shivered.

He straightened. "Let's get you inside." Another murmur and done so close to my ear that I found myself melting, leaning back against him slightly.

I didn't lean.

I didn't melt.

I *did*...for this man.

A nudge had me moving up...up those eight stairs (with their newly applied non-slip epoxy).

"Just saying," he said, still soft, though this time it was more growl than murmur, "you and I are going to have a talk about these steps later."

I went stiff, refroze all that melting.

But then his warm chest was pressing against my back, coaxing me forward toward my door. His pelvis brushed my ass, and...a puddle, all over again.

Arms wrapping around me, bringing my purse in front of me, and reaching in for the keys. He extracted the set, held them up for me, stayed close as I fumbled through the ring, finally found the right one.

Only to have him take the set from me when I started to extend them toward the lock.

Warm breath on my nape. Strength surrounding me, making me feel small and petite (when I wasn't), but most of all, making me feel...safe, protected, cared for.

An elephant-sized hole in my steel.

Oh fuck.

The door opened.

Marcel nudged me through.

Fear and terror. Living and exhilaration. Longing. Desire. I spun in his arms, beyond ready to say fuck it all and to get the man inside me, to take him any way he would come, would take *me*, would—

His gaze drifted over my shoulder.

His brows pulled together.

Fury dipped and danced across the pretty planes of his face.

Then his beautiful amber-brown eyes were on mine, but

they weren't soft or gentle, or even hot and blazing with need for me.

They were cold and flinty.

Like stone.

"What the fuck, Prudence?"

THIRTEEN

Marcel

NO WONDER she hadn't wanted me to drive her back to her apartment.

No fucking wonder.

Baby shit lined every corner of the room.

Clothes and toys and some weird seat-looking thing. Different shaped pillows were piled onto the couch, a stack of diapers on the coffee table, and...it had been just over eight weeks since we'd slept together.

Her brows pulled together. "Don't take that tone with me."

I stepped closer, bent my head. "*What. The. Fuck. Prudence?*"

Take that tone and ramp it the fuck up.

Because seriously, *What the fuck?*

"You want to explain to me why you've gone from nice guy to asshole?" she snapped.

I stuck out an arm. "Seriously?" I shot it to the side, indicating the room, the copious amount of baby shit. "It's like the baby section from Target exploded in here."

"Okaaay," she muttered, shaking her head. "So, I got a little carried away. Big deal. I canceled my trip to Banff for snow-shoeing to pay for it. I probably shouldn't go, anyway. Last year was a bad avalanche season—"

She was pregnant with my baby and talking about casually traipsing through the snow...snow that might slide the fuck off a mountain and bury her the *fuck* alive.

I lost my mind.

"No," I snapped, reaching for her. "No more *adventures*. No more *danger*." I snagged her shoulders, held her in front of me, barely resisting the urge to shake some sense into her. "For once in your goddamned life, princess, you're going to be smart. You're going to be careful. You're going—"

"I'm smart," she declared, lifting her chin. "I like adventures, but I'm not stupid about them."

I scoffed. "Right. Because *this*"—another wave to the room of baby shit, the room she'd clearly had no intention of telling me about—"is *smart?*"

She flinched, but her chin lifted. "I can afford it." Her voice had grown small. "Life is about making adjustments and priori-tizing. I did that so I could—"

"Buy stupid shit?"

This bought me another flinch, one that finally got through the fog of my anger. And just like always, on the rare times my temper got the best of me, all that rage faded, and horror dawned. Not quickly enough, though. She jerked out of my hold, strode to the door.

And I'd have to be an idiot to miss that her hands were shaking, that her skin had gone pale, that hurt was written into the lines of her body, the fluidity of her movements.

Fuck.

I was an asshole.

I opened my mouth to apologize, but she beat me to the talking portion of events.

"*You're* going to leave," she said. "And we're never going to be anything more than polite acquaintances." A beat. "Not ever again."

"Pru," I whispered.

"Not. Ever. Again."

I moved toward her, extended a hand to cup her cheek, dropping it to my side when she jerked away from it. "You're having my baby," I said. "We have to be more than acquaintances. We—"

"*What?*"

The aghast question did more than cut me off. It stoppered any words, excuses, apologies up in the back of my throat.

Her hazel eyes flared.

She shook her head, shoulders slumping slightly, pink edging into her cheeks, thank fuck. But then that pink went red, and she jabbed a finger into my chest. *Hard.* "You're a goddamned idiot, you know that, right?" Another jab, and I wrapped my arms around her waist, drew her near enough to close and lock the door behind her. Something she luckily didn't notice, probably because she was still jabbing at my chest. "Aside from the fact that I *can't* have kids"—a flash of pain in her eyes—"as in, *can't* have them in a way that's permanent and not some dumbass doctor saying that I have a weird shaped uterus or something." It was my turn to flinch. "I *can't have* kids. As in, this"—she waved a hand at her torso—"body will *never* carry a baby." Her palms came to my chest, shoved. "And, even *not* knowing that, dumbass, who is the one person we both know who's pregnant, who was puking her guts up at CeCe's and needed *Oliver* to come in and take her home? Huh? *Huh?*"

I *was* a dumbass. Of course, I was a *dumbass.*

Hazel.

God, I'd *just* seen her, looking pale and sick, talking about evening sickness and gagging over all mentions of cheese.

Pru was her friend. Her *best* friend.

Of course, she'd go a little crazy setting Hazel up.

She was still shoving at me, but I kept my hands at her waist, held her close. "You canceled one of your adventures so that you could buy Hazel baby shit."

"It's not *shit*," she snapped. "It's important baby equipment." She shoved hard enough that she rocked me back onto my heels, and I had to loosen my hold so we both didn't go down. Then she moved toward the door again.

I took a different tack, moving toward the gear and holding up a onesie emblazoned with *Milk Drunk* on the front. "This is *important baby equipment?*"

She scowled. "Kid needs clothes, doesn't it?"

"Yeah, princess," I said softly. "Hazel's baby needs clothes." I held up a contraption with straps and Velcro, and God, was that a bra? "And this?"

"And Hazel is going to carry my future godchild," Pru muttered. "She needs to be comfortable, too. That's for nursing"—her expression flattened—"I mean, I don't know if she's going to try to nurse, but she's Hazel, so I'm sure she will, and that's supposed to hold the baby close for nursing and skin-to-skin time and catch any milk that might—"

She cut herself off with a sharp shake of her head.

Then she unlocked the door, pulled it wide. "Go home, Marcel."

"I'm sorry, princess."

She froze.

"I misunderstood."

Still playing statue. I moved toward her, couldn't turn

away from the naked pain in her eyes, even though she tried to turn away, tried to avert her gaze. Fingers on her jaw, her cheek, brushing back the hair that always seemed to get in her face. "I really am sorry I was an asshole," I said, waiting until her eyes hit mine again, still pained and twisted, but warmth on the edges. "I'm usually a pretty even-keeled guy, but my temper occasionally gets the best of me. And I can be a royal dick."

Lids sliding closed.

A step back, but she was already practically against the door, her step bringing her flush. So, I didn't hesitate to step in, to bring *myself* flush. "I'm sorry, baby," I whispered. "*Really.*"

She held my eyes.

For long enough that it felt as though my soul had been presented at the pearly gates and I was waiting for approval to be allowed through that barrier and into heaven.

Then she nodded. "Apology accepted."

My mouth tried to curve—because who said that? And because, coincidentally, I didn't miss that she hadn't mentioned I was forgiven.

Apology accepted.

Forgiveness still out of reach.

Not that I expected different. Not that I *deserved* different.

So, I'd just add this to my list of things I was seeking her forgiveness for—Carrie, asshole behavior—and asked, gentle as I could, "Why can't you have babies, princess?"

Steel curtains slammed down.

The pain disappeared, emptiness taking its place. "Go home, Marcel," she whispered, shoving me hard.

But I'd braced.

I'd seen the blankness appear, the barriers being erected.

I was prepared for her withdrawal.

So, I braced, bent, scooped her up, and then kicked the door shut before I started for the couch, dumping her on it before going back to the door, throwing the lock.

She was struggling to her feet when I made it back to the couch.

Which made it easier to heft her up, toss her over my shoulder, and walk down the hall.

Onto the mattress, dropping down on top of her.

"Why, princess?" I asked, bringing my face close to hers, near enough to smell her shampoo, to scent the jasmine on her skin. I made a mental note to do some snooping, to find out if it was a perfume or lotion, and then to buy a bottle of whatever it was to keep at my place.

Her neck arched, taking her eyes away from me, making my own latch onto the tendons standing out in sharp relief on her throat, calling to my mouth, my teeth, my lips, my—

I'd bent and traced my tongue along one before the thought even manifested in my mind.

She shivered.

But still didn't look at me.

"Why?" I repeated.

Every muscle in her body went taut, and I braced again, braced to be thrown off. I was cornering a scared animal, knew I'd deserve whatever hurt she tossed my way.

But I needn't have.

Because her body going taut wasn't in preparation to unleash on me.

At least not physically.

Her words...her words, on the other hand...they eviscerated me.

"They shot me," she whispered. "After they shot my parents, they shot me."

That was so far from what I'd expected her to say—and my mind had been conjuring some pretty scary shit along the lines of cancer and life-threatening illnesses—that I was stunned silent.

And silent, her words kept coming.

Robotic. Cold. Bare facts recited.

All the while, my mind was spinning. I'd seen her naked, seen every line of her body. Bullets and surgery would mean scars. I hadn't noticed any scars, any—*fuck*, any bullet wounds.

"My parents were missionaries. We were in South America"—her throat worked, those tendons going tight again—"I can't actually remember which country. I was young, and we were always traveling, always moving on to the next place. And then we were stopped, our car blocked from going forward. We were forced out onto the side of the road. They demanded money—"

A thread of emotion in her voice.

One that was gone just as quickly as it appeared.

"Well, no surprise, we didn't have much, didn't have enough to satisfy them." She paused, paused for long enough that I was tempted to speak.

Luckily, the words stayed lodged in my throat.

Because after that pause, she continued talking.

"Then the local police showed up. The guys who'd stopped us panicked. They shot my parents, shot me—"

More silence.

More of her throat working.

"They were gone. The police got me to the hospital. But the bullet I'd taken had bounced around my insides. I lost three feet of small intestine, my uterus, one of my ovaries, my cervix, and my spleen." Her neck relaxed, those empty eyes on mine. "So, no babies for me," she told me. "And no surprise pregnancies." A sick, facsimile smile of her normal variety. "Lucky you."

FOURTEEN

Pru

THE STEEL WAS DOWN.

My shields were safe. I even cracked a joke.

But the badger—or, wait, elephant-sized hole had been plastered over with subpar metal. It was bowing and buckling under the strain of the past.

The fear.

The noise.

The blood.

The heat and humidity. The smelly man pressing his hands onto my stomach as his partner drove us down the mountain, drove us to the small local hospital.

Ripe, bitter body odor.

In my nose.

In my soul.

Because that man had saved my life. Both of them had, and I had never seen him again. Never heard his voice again, whispering to me in Spanish, telling me to hold on, and that I was safe, and that I would be okay.

And all the while, I'd cried for my parents.

To come help me. To wake up. To be okay.

Even though I'd known they wouldn't be. Not left on the side of the road like that—never mind that they had been dead before they'd hit the ground.

I'd left them. *I'd* left them and—

They were gone.

So, I made sure I'd never had people again to leave. Except...Hazel had ruined that, hadn't she? And Beth, the other member of our trio, though she was so busy with her job in New York City that we hardly talked anymore.

But when we did, it was like pulling on an old pair of worn jeans.

Super comfy, perfect fit. Easy to move in.

Beth *fit* us. Even with her fancy clothes and heels and super important job at a charity helping kids get involved in organized sports.

I had ties.

But I'd been purposeful in keeping them slender.

Until Hazel had approached me at OSU, asking to interview me for her thesis. I was down for supporting mental health in sports, especially under the pressure cooker of being a student-athlete—which, don't get me started, was more athlete-student since coaches all but owned their players, and academics had been less important to them than wins or goals on the scoreboard.

Hazel had come with Beth, and they'd both gotten close.

But for me, as much as I liked Beth, Hazel was my person. My *one* person that I'd risk strengthening my ties to. Because Hazel was awesome and sweet and could out-stubborn me on a good day. Because Hazel wouldn't put up with me erecting distance between us.

But also because Hazel was the type of person who didn't put strings on her caring.

If I wanted to disappear for six months, Hazel would be right there waiting for me to glide into home with stories of my adventures.

Friendship. Easy friendship.

Friendship that had grown and strengthened over the last year, until I didn't want to disappear for six months. Because I liked Baltimore, liked my friend, liked my job. Liked that connection—even if I wanted to pretend to be good on my own.

Maybe it was less pretend and more...self-preservation?

Either way.

I was here. With strong ties to Hazel and the team. And now my best friend was having a baby.

Why did that make me imagine I was a giant from the cartoon of *Jack and the Beanstalk*, knocked to the ground, tied down with heavy ropes and huge stakes to keep me in place?

Probably because it felt like the truth.

And also, probably because...it was okay.

"You would have made gorgeous babies, princess."

Soft words.

Soft words that made my throat go tight and my eyes lock onto the ceiling. I'd had plenty of time to grieve for that loss. It was just...maybe Marcel was the first person who'd ever made me want to consider what it might be like to have the ability to *make* babies.

And that...made the grief fresh, had it bouncing around inside my steel walls, ramming itself against the animal-shaped (I'd lost track of which one) hole, desperate to escape.

I clenched my jaw, didn't let it.

I'd learned to be strong in a hail of gunfire, had tempered that strength with the help of my awesome godmother, who I'd had for five wonderful years. A godmother who made certain I was protected and safe and didn't end up in the system—instead, I had landed in an expensive boarding school, taken up hockey, fallen *in love* (and I meant *in love*) with the sport. Which meant, I'd worked my ass off, gotten a scholarship, and then had been lucky enough to play division one hockey, to join the professional women's league, and to play a few more years there.

Now I worked for one of the best NHL teams in the league.

I was fucking lucky.

So, I might try to lock it down, might revel in the numbness, but the one thing I definitely felt was gratitude.

For a man with strong body odor and strong hands, for a surgeon at a small hospital in the middle of nowhere, for a godmother who'd made certain provisions were in place to look after me.

So that brought me to twenty-six, lucky as hell, and not dwelling on the past.

Living big and free and—

Fingers on my jaw, lips on my temple.

And I was beginning to wonder if all my living big and free was actually that. Or was it a cage, a net that had ensnared me, protecting and preventing me from being hurt.

But also from...*feeling* big.

"Waffles," I murmured.

Marcel lifted his head, amber eyes layered with confusion. "What's that, princess?"

"I—" And, sweet Jesus, my voice broke.

He started to push off me. "Are you hungry?" he asked gently. "Because I can make—"

He was offering to cook, to make *waffles* for me.

Fuck.

Fuck.

Tears burned the backs of my eyes. "Off," I ordered, squirming beneath him. "Get off, Marcel. Right now."

But his weight didn't shift, his hand came to my jaw. "What's the matter, Pru?"

What was the matter?

What was *the matter?!*

Everything.

Every single *fucking* thing.

"Princess—"

He smoothed back my bangs.

And...I lost it.

Tears, tears I didn't think I could cry any longer, slid free from my eyes, a sob burst out of my chest and—

I cried.

Marcel rolled, flipping us onto our sides, curling his arms around me, one hand weaving into my hair, the other clamping down onto my hip, drawing my body flush to his, my face into his throat as I sobbed and sputtered and generally just lost my shit.

No, not generally.

Absolutely.

So *absolutely* lost my shit. Was near hysterical, only able to recognize that in a distant part of my mind. Because the rest was wrapped up in memories, in emotions, in—

Lips on my temple, arms holding me close.

Gentle words of reassurance, not telling me to stop crying, but instead saying that he was there, to let it out, that he had me.

He. Had. Me.

No one. None had *had* me.

Not for fifteen years.

And I didn't know what to do with that, so I just let Marcel hold me, to press his lips to my temple, to whisper his soft words, to hold me close.

Until the tears stopped coming.

Until embarrassment hit me *hard.*

And I meant *fucking hard.*

The tension began in my toes, showing off that vulnerability, creeping up my calves, my shins and thighs. It hit my stomach, spread across my chest.

"Marissa cheated on me with Mark Shelby."

"I—" The word was rasped out—and promptly cut off—because I knew that. Because it was something that not only Hazel had shared, but was common knowledge among the organization and one of the reasons Shelby had been released from the Breakers (the others being copious and widespread because it was common knowledge Shelby was not just an asshole, but also a criminal, since he'd been prosecuted and found guilty and was currently residing in a six-by-eight cell after the illegal hit that had injured and ultimately ended Oliver's career...and taken his leg).

"She was my future. I'd had it all planned out—"

I sucked in a breath.

"*We'd* had it all planned out. The house. Marriage. Pets. Kids. A future bumming around in an RV when I retired and our kids were old enough." His fingers contracted lightly, tensing against my scalp. "Stupid, huh? Twenty-four and thinking I had it all figured out."

I got it then.

Understood what he was giving me, knew that it was because he'd cottoned on to my embarrassment.

And he'd given it. Freely.

So, I found I could give it, too. Just as freely.

"It's not stupid," I said. "You wanted something. You put things in place to get it."

"It's stupid if the person you're planning them with isn't on the same page."

"Marissa was a troll," I said, pushing up on his chest, on the mattress, shifting so that my legs were tucked beneath me and I was staring down at him.

For all of a second.

Because Marcel didn't let go of my hair, and when I sat up, he followed me, curling close, tugging me into his lap, so my back rested against his chest. His fingers slid through my hair, stroking low and gently. "It's stupid when you ignore it being wrong, just because you have *plans*."

"I'm somewhat scarred by you referring to *plans* like it's a dirty four-letter word," I said. "That doesn't fit with the picture of Marcel I have in my mind."

He chuckled, his warm breath brushing the back of my neck and making me shiver.

"Marcel?" I asked.

His fingers trailed through my hair, down my spine. "Hmm?"

"Want to help me wrap some baby presents?"

He stilled.

Then he burst out laughing.

It was the best sound in the world, even though it blasted right through that elephant-sized hole. Even though it exposed me to the light.

Because the light was Marcel.

FIFTEEN

Marcel

I TRIED NOT TO STARE.

I was failing.

But Pru...she was fucking beautiful, standing next to Hazel at the altar.

Wearing a pale blue dress, holding her friend's bouquet. Another woman stood at her elbow. Redheaded, pretty, tiny, and curvy, unequivocally gorgeous.

But she didn't hold a candle when it came to Pru.

I was staring and I knew it. I just didn't give a fuck. Or maybe, I couldn't find the strength to look away.

Especially when she surreptitiously wiped away a tear.

Tough, badass Pru with a soft spot? *That* struck home.

Not fair.

I already knew she had a soft spot. I'd seen a glimmer of it at my house with the food, the night after we were together. I'd seen it with the extra time she spent with Walker, settling the young player into his role on the team. I'd seen it when she called Marissa a troll and got upset for me. I'd seen it...

A lot.

In her story, her past, how hard she worked.

In her tears and how she'd buzzed around the last few days, making sure that Hazel and Oliver had as much off their plates as possible so they could focus on enjoying their wedding even with them having the gall to plan such an event during the hockey season.

(Not that they'd had much of a choice, what with Hazel's parents—cough, Hazel's *mother*—having all sorts of grand wedding plans).

The point was that Pru was sweet beneath all that steel.

I liked her. A *whole* fucking lot.

And as she smiled, tears down her cheeks as her friend kissed the man she loved, as the night wore on and she continued buzzing, making sure everything went off without a hitch—from the cake cutting, to the toasts, to keeping herself on the dance floor, encouraging a bunch of recalcitrant hockey players onto that floor, and when I finally cornered her, managing to steal a slow dance, I told her so.

To which, her response was a shrug. "It's Hazel's night."

All the explanation that was needed. At least according to her.

At least according to *me*.

Because I got it now. I saw her, saw Pru, saw behind the carefully constructed walls.

And everything that I'd gotten a glimpse of? I liked it.

So much that I wanted more.

I WAS on the team plane.

Conner was next to me.

Watching the tip video...because he was cackling, loud enough to shake the plane.

Sighing, I pulled out my cell, brought up the group text, and saw why. Some joker—Raph, probably, because he had an affinity for both tech and pranks—had photoshopped me and my head jerking from the puck fucking crashing into it, into a video of a pop concert, timing the bop of my head with the catchy tune.

The tune that was playing everywhere.

When would the fucking video die?

It had been weeks.

"Fucking hell," I muttered, flicking the video and spinning in my seat to glare at Raph.

Who gave me a smirk and blew a kiss.

The tune played again—this time loud enough that I heard it through Smitty's earbuds, and then I heard it somewhere else on the plane.

"Kill me now," I muttered.

An elbow. "*Unalive* you now."

"You're not funny."

"That's not what Pru said last night when we went to dinner. She—"

I didn't hear the rest of the statement, not when I was fighting the haze of fury that washed over me as my possessive caveman tendencies took over. I'd known she had a business dinner with Conner, wanting to go over some information about a few prospects he'd played with in the minors.

But that didn't mean I liked hearing about the woman I had already begun to think of as mine, going out with one of my friends.

Especially when Smitty added, "Then she held my hand

and told me I was the prettiest boy around. She'd totally do me, sweet piece of ass like that—"

If I'd been in my right frame of mind—that *not* being the frame of mind that had red creeping into the edges of my vision —I would have recognized that Conner was just being an asshole and trying to get a rise out of me because no one would ever describe the mountain that was known as Smitty as a pretty—*prettiest*—boy.

But I was in full caveman mode.

Which meant that I swiveled in my seat, gripped the lapel of Smitty's ugly ass suit (the man had a thing for plaid—wild and *ugly* plaid), and growled, "Don't finish that *fucking* sentence."

Conner wasn't the least bit scared.

Circling back to mountain.

I might be six foot and almost two hundred pounds. But that wasn't big, not by hockey player standards. Certainly, not by mountain standards (which, for those who were curious was, six-six and two hundred and thirty pounds).

Smitty could crush me.

There was no doubt.

But Conner was completely nonplussed—as he often was, unless The Mountain's temper was pushed too far...then avalanche, and Smitty could unleash the world of hurt. Luckily for the rest of the hockey-playing world (and humanity), Smitty didn't lose his cool very often.

Free and loose in most things—teasing and pushing the envelope with locker room talk, getting naked *all the fucking time*, and often saying stupid shit.

But he was aware of his size.

And controlled it.

He also had that mostly-sleeping temper.

Thankfully, that temper stayed sleeping when he brushed

my hand off his suit and grinned, fist-pumping and booming (because, fuck, when *didn't* the man boom?), "I knew it! I fucking *knew* that you were into Pru." A beat. A rumbling chuckle. "Into Pru. Ha. That rhymes. You into Pru."

I dropped my head onto my tray table, *thunked* it twice.

Because the plane had gone silent.

I could have heard a pin drop. Well, okay, I heard the engines, but the background noise of conversation, of the drink cart moving up and down the aisles, the occasional thrum of bass or a movie echoing out through someone's headphones... those were all gone.

Because the team, the coaches, the support staff...they were all listening in.

"Fuck. My. Life," I muttered.

The Breakers were a professional family. A hockey team, a business, an organization that was worth millions of dollars, yes. But we were also close, had worked hard to build bonds after Shelby had so thoroughly destroyed them.

We cared about each other.

Which meant we were nosy as fuck about each other's lives and tried our fucking darnedest (yes, for some fucking reason— fuck my life again—I was saying darnedest) to get involved.

Minding your own business?

No. That didn't exist for the Breakers.

We were full-on nosy bastards.

And now the entire team and support staff and coaches knew that I was into Pru.

The only saving grace I had at that moment was that Pru wasn't on this road trip.

Because almost as soon as the silence fell, it broke, that poppy song Raph had photoshopped me into blaring from somewhere near the back of the plane, my phone pinging with a text that said—

> M into Pru. Pass it on.

Sweet Christ.

I was surrounded by children.

My cell buzzed again, this time from a message sent privately to me.

From Hazel, who'd clearly seen the message, probably because Oliver was still on the train and had passed the gossip along.

It was a gift certificate to Wreck It, the rage room she'd taken me to the previous season, the one I was addicted to and where I went to work out shit. The one that helped me control my temper.

Another buzz.

> Date night? ;)

Sweet Christ times two.

My cell vibrated one more time.

> She'd go to her death bed with this, but Pru loves irises and would melt if a man brought her some.

Another second passed before my phone buzzed again.

> Like, for example, if said man brought her a bouquet of them and took her on a date.

My fingers moved on my phone's screen.

> To a place she could destroy shit?

A beat. Another message came through.

Pru likes to live on the edge...but she's still a
girl. Dinner AND the rage room would be
perfect.

I bit back a grin.

Pocketed my phone.

Ignored Smitty still yammering on about "You into Pru"
and playing that fucking photoshopped video on repeat. I
thought about what she had given me the night in her apartment the week before, how we'd laughed as we wrapped (me
neatly, her clumsily—which she blamed on the cast, but which
I knew was definitely a Pru-thing and not because of a Pru's-
arm-is-broken thing) the giant pile of presents she'd bought for
Hazel and Oliver. I thought about the way she'd melted into me
when I'd brushed a kiss to her temple and said goodnight.

I thought of the tears and the steel plates that surrounded
her, about the shark diving and the trip to Banff for snowshoeing, and the way she'd smiled up at me when I'd tucked a lock
of hair behind her ear.

She wasn't Marissa.

She was more, so much fucking more that she had the
potential to break me in a way that my ex never had...and we
hadn't even gone on a single date yet.

And...I didn't care.

Instead, I pulled up the notes app on my phone...and I got
to planning.

SIXTEEN

Pru

THE KNOCK at my office door had me tearing my eyes off the screen that was currently showing the Breakers' game.

This one was against Boston, who always had a strong roster and had become a big rival.

Of course, it was also the beginning of the season, so the game wasn't as intense as it might be during the lead-up to the playoffs later in the year. But the guys were out there, working hard, building on their chemistry and working through kinks in the system.

The preseason had mostly been for *my* crew, for those that I took through training camp, for the few who had the chance to make the starting roster—or, at the very least, be on a rotation to play occasionally with the team. Sometimes they scratched and another player took their spot. Sometimes they played with the Breakers' minor league affiliate. Sometimes they played a stretch of quite a few games in a row.

And sometimes they made the roster. Permanently.

Like Walker had a chance to do.

Raw skill. Speed. Strength. Already gelling with the team during practices, the preseason games, and now during the beginning of the season.

So my gaze should be glued to Walker when he was on the ice, watching the player I'd scouted kick ass.

But Walker was on a line with Marcel...so no surprise, I'd been glued to Marcel's lean strength, his speed, his confidence with the puck and along the boards and in the offensive zone that had grown over the last few years, instead of focusing on Walker, on the player I'd scouted, and I'd be doing a victory lap over (because Walker was a *fantastic* fit with the team) him being on the top line.

But I only had eyes for Marcel.

Because he was smart.

So *fucking* smart.

Because...he planned.

My lips twitched as I looked up and saw Hazel in the doorway.

Quickly, I stood up, crossed to my friend (it helped that there was a whistle and Marcel's line went for a change, so my reptilian brain that wanted to watch every single one of his strides relaxed). "Everything okay?" I asked.

Hazel could have bought stock in paleness, and more in nausea, unfortunately. Nausea that ended up with vomiting... and not just in the evening.

I had walked in on my friend just before lunchtime, losing the remains of her breakfast into the trash can. Luckily, I had stocked up that morning. I'd zipped back to my office, grabbed the ginger ale, the ginger candies, the ginger lollipops that were supposedly specially formulated for nauseated pregnant women, along with the pack of saltines and Sprite I'd stashed in my desk drawer, and returned in time to snag the trash and dispose of it after she was done, before returning to offer my friend the various remedies.

The lollipops were foul apparently.

The ginger ale made her gag.

The candies were meh.

But Julie's recommendation of flat Sprite had done the trick. Along with a half-dozen of the saltines.

I vowed to stock up...and had texted Oliver, advising him of the new information.

I knew the man was going to hit up Costco and fill their pantry with copious amounts of the two items.

Now, Hazel wasn't vomiting, but she looked tired and pale, and it was late and—

"What's going on with Marcel?" she asked.

Swinging for the fences, knocking that ball right toward my head, leaving me tongue-tied and on my back foot and—

Hell, one second, I'd been considering remedies for morning (or evening, or afternoon, or *whenever*) sickness. The next, my friend had fixed me with a piercing stare that locked my knees, glued my feet to the carpet, and had me blurting, "I really like him."

Hazel's mouth dropped open.

And...she gagged.

"Hold on," she stammered, running past me and lurching toward my trash can, throwing up into the black plastic bag that lined the bin. "This"—retch—"is *not*"—retch—"a sign of how I feel about you and Marcel—"

Retch.

Fuck.

I moved toward the drawer, extracted a can of Sprite, pouring it into an empty coffee mug (clean and kept there for this purpose, thankfully), pulled out the plastic spoon I'd stolen from the break room, and got to stirring, getting the bubbles out like the pro I was becoming.

I set it on the edge of the desk, grabbed a handful of crackers and set them on a tissue—because I didn't have napkins—though they *were* on my Hazel-puking-all-hours-of-the-day grocery list.

Then I settled Hazel into a chair, put the vomit-filled trash can by the door, and returned to give Haze the drink and snack.

"It's not about you and—"

"Shut up and eat and drink," I ordered. "You can tell me all about the rest of your nutty thoughts after you get some sugar back into your system."

"I'm fine—"

"Do I *need* to call Oliver?"

Hazel narrowed her eyes. But she picked up the mug of Sprite and drank a little, nibbled on one of the crackers.

Meanwhile, I—knowing that Marcel would be proud of me for my planning—had scouted out all the nearby big trash cans earlier *and* had made friends with Mary, who was the head of the cleaning staff. I now had the code to the cleaning supply closet *and* an entire roll of small trash bags to replace those that Hazel was using with regularity.

I tied the filled bag, dumped it in one of the large cans, and returned to the office—and my Hazel Drawer, pulling out a fresh sack, slapping it into the trash can, and then sitting in the seat opposite my friend.

Hazel had eaten three crackers and drank half the Sprite.

She also looked like she'd sold her stock in pale.

At least for the moment.

"Better," I said.

"You know I'm going to lose my shit eventually with all this fussing that you and Oliver have got going."

I lifted my hands. "I'm just abiding by my godmother duties."

"And Oliver?" Hazel grumbled.

"He loves you."

That was explanation enough.

It was also enough to make Hazel's face soften. "He does, doesn't he?" she murmured, sipping the soda.

"Yes," I agreed.

Which was why I'd sent him a text while on trash duty in the hall.

And knew he'd be there in less than five minutes.

Not because I—*cough*—wanted to avoid discussing Marcel. Of course not. I would never be so underhanded as to avoid discussing my feelings with my best friend.

"You know I'm going to sic Beth on you," Hazel muttered.

"I don't know what you're talking about."

"Marcel," Hazel said, like his name was explanation enough.

And, I supposed, it *was* explanation enough.

I liked him. I had been vulnerable with him and hadn't freaked—and *he* hadn't freaked. He'd just offered up hair stroking and gentle words and—

"He gives me temple kisses," I whispered.

Hazel's face softened, clearly knowing *exactly* what I was saying and what I *wasn't*. Because I wasn't the type of woman who'd ever let anyone show me that kind of affection—Hazel and Beth, aside. Mostly because they'd brow-beaten me into accepting it.

Well, that, and continuing to offer it, even though I had treated it like they were offering me a live cobra every time they tried to give it.

But Hazel and Beth aside, I didn't let a man give it to me. That went against my strings.

It was why my number was a hell of a lot bigger than four. Because pleasure and affection didn't mix, not without creating ties that could destroy me. So, for me, pleasure had been totally separate. Orgasms okay.

Bang stroking, strawberry waffles, temple kisses firmly *the fuck* off the table.

So, for me to admit that Marcel gave them to me, that I accepted him giving them to me and...well, Hazel knew *exactly* how big that was.

"Oh, honey," Hazel whispered, her eyes going glassy with tears.

"Don't," I ordered, and fuck, but it was like my own tears the night in my condo with Marcel had made it impossible for me to board up that opening, to lock down my tears. Because my throat went tight, my vision watery.

Hazel sniffed.

"I said, *don't*," I croaked.

"I can't help it," Hazel said, her voice totally choked up. "Fucking pregnancy hormones."

I laughed and then sniffed—a sob catching in my lungs. "I'm fucking terrified."

Hazel's tears had escaped. I felt my own sliding down my cheeks.

I'd lost it completely.

And found that I couldn't care...or not *too* much, anyway. Not when Hazel was reaching for my hands and clasping them tightly.

"I'm so happy you have temple kisses."

I grinned through my tears. "I've lost it, haven't I?"

"The barbed wire and steel to keep the world at bay?" Hazel grinned back. "God, I hope so."

"All that steel and concrete and barbed wire didn't make

one fucking bit of difference when it came to you, though, did it?" I asked dryly.

Hazel's smile widened. "Of course not."

"It's always the quiet ones who are the most stubborn."

"Is that from experience?" Hazel teased. "Or because Marcel can out-stubborn you, too?"

I swatted Hazel's arm. "You're the worst."

"You've"—Hazel leaned in, hugged me tight—"got temple kisses."

"And waffles and pushing my bangs back and—" My voice broke.

Hazel sniffed again. "Fuck, Pru."

"It's the pregnancy hormones," I said sagely, leaning back slightly, watery smile meeting Hazel's.

"Then what's *your* excuse?" Hazel accused.

"It's in the water?"

Hazel froze. And then we both started laughing and crying, trying to get control of ourselves...which was seeming more impossible by the moment. But finally, I sucked in a breath, released it slowly. "Okay. *Okay.*"

Hazel nodded, did some breathing of her own. "Okay," she agreed.

Then we were staring into each other's eyes, silent tears dripping down our cheeks, saying all the things with our gazes that we couldn't say aloud (at least on my side, because I damned well knew without Hazel having made that initial little grasshopper hole in my walls all those years before that Marcel would have never been able to blast his way through), when I heard, "Jesus fucking Christ."

And turned to see Oliver in the door.

"Don't tell me *you're* pregnant," he accused

I felt my lips curve. That reminder should be painful, my joking about it should be, too. Especially with everything so open, so vulnerable after decades of me pushing it down, pretending it didn't matter. But...I had Hazel and tears dripping down my cheeks. The numb was gone. Things weren't muffled anymore.

My head was above the waves. My ears were unplugged.

I'd spent that night the week before wrapping baby gifts for my best friend with a man who'd lost his cool and apologized, who'd owned up to being wrong. Who wanted to look after me, who hadn't run from my baggage, even though it was big.

Who'd teased me about my wrapping abilities and had pretended to accept my excuse of the cast—even though he clearly knew that was a lie.

Who'd tucked my bangs back and hugged me tightly at my door when I'd yawned, making me promise to save the rest of the wrapping for after the wedding and when he got back from the team's road trip...and came over...and brought me dinner.

Who'd brushed a kiss to my lips, my temple, my nose, and my forehead.

Then had walked down my stairs, muttering about getting someone to install new treads because the non-stick epoxy wasn't good enough for me.

Then had stopped at the bottom, turned around, and ordered me to close and lock the door...and then to get my ass in bed.

An order I'd accepted.

Because *I'd* ordered that he text me as soon as he was in bed (since he'd pushily made us exchange numbers earlier in our wrapping extravaganza—not that I'd minded that order either).

And he had.

In bed. Now sleep, princess.

And I'd texted back,

> You too, Pretty Boy.

And *then* he'd sent a kissy emoji.

A big, burly hockey player had sent me a kissy emoji...and I'd liked it. Liked it so much that I'd sent back heart eyes with a giant smile on my face, all while hugging my cell tight to my chest.

Ridiculous.

I didn't care.

Because he'd stared at me during the wedding with warmth in his eyes, held me gently when we slow danced to a song that would be engrained in my soul. Because he'd texted me while he was on the road and called me when he went to bed, his husky voice talking to me about everything and nothing.

Because I was finally less worried about what I didn't have, what I *never* would have, and was more focused on all the good I *did* have.

It was enough.

It was more than I'd ever hoped for.

And it was just the beginning.

SEVENTEEN

Marcel

MY DOORBELL RANG.

It was...I winced at the time on the clock.

Early.

Fucking early.

The flight back was after the game last night. Which meant that it had been late, and that I'd gotten *in* late, and because I had my usual post-game adrenaline rush, I hadn't gone to bed until *late*.

Because I could sleep in.

No practice.

No optional skate.

Just another game that evening.

And someone was now knocking on my door, having stopped with the doorbell, and I was going to *unalive* them if it wasn't a fucking emergency.

Or if it was Smitty showing up, trying to be a pain in the ass.

Groaning, I rolled out of bed, stumbled down the hall, down the stairs, and yanked open the front door.

"Oh, thank you, Jesus," Pru said, her gaze dipping down and then back up.

I went from half asleep and grumpy as fuck to still grumpy but realizing I was wearing only a pair of boxer briefs and recognizing the need in Pru's eyes, that need making my already hard morning wood even harder. In a second—in a *fucking* second—blood from any of the unnecessary organs of my body (i.e. my brain) headed straight for my cock.

Since it was too early for words, since I still had all that grumpy, even though part of me—a *lot* of me—liked the appreciation Pru was showing for my body, I just snaked an arm forward, wrapped it around her waist, and yanked her body to mine.

A heft had her up over my shoulder, my mouth curving into an amused smile when she squealed in a way that was very much not tough hockey player, fearless adventure seeker.

It was female.

As in, *my* female.

"Put me down," she sputtered.

"Hurting you?" I asked.

"I..."

"Pru?" I asked, flicking the lock. "Am I *hurting* you?" Her broken arm hadn't seemed to slow her down at all, but she still had a *broken arm.*

"I—" A breath, her voice going husky. "No, you're not hurting me."

"Good." I spun and took the stairs, walked down the hall, and into my bedroom.

I set her on the mattress, collapsed behind her, wrapping her tightly in my arms. My cock was aching, but I was exhausted, so I tugged the blankets up and over us, held her close, and ordered her to, "Sleep."

She went still.

Very still.

"I didn't realize I'd wake you," she murmured, so quietly I could barely hear the words, having to strain to do so, especially with the haze of sleep drifting up and over me again.

"Late night," I grunted.

"I'm sorry," she whispered.

"Don't care," I grunted again, squeezing my arms, indicating nonverbally that I liked her in them—even if it was a hellish hour of the morning. "Sleep," I ordered again.

I thought she would keep talking, that the part of her personality that never seemed to stop was just going to go, to *keep* going, spinning like a top that magically never slowed, never hit the surface it was rotating on.

But...she settled.

Burrowed into me, rolling into my chest, her face going to my neck, one arm slipping between us to rest over my heart, her other winding around my waist.

And she went still again, her breathing slow and even...and I was exhausted.

That slow and even coaxed me under.

SUNLIGHT PEEKED in through the edges of my blackout shades the next time I was aware of opening my eyes.

My bed was empty, and for a moment, I thought I'd dreamed Pru showing up.

But the scent of jasmine lingered in the air, and the pillow next to my had a dent in it.

And then there was...The Feeling.

That sensation of not being alone, of settling, of *feeling* like I was home. Yes, I was in *my* home, the place I'd bought after Marissa, wanting a fresh start, a fresh place to begin again.

But it had always felt a bit off.

Except that one night, now more than two months ago.

Pru.

It was all Pru.

Because she was home.

And in *my* home, and...shit. *Shit.* I'd ignored her to get some sleep when she came to me for the second time, giving me a gift, opening up, and I'd taken her to bed. In a literal way. As in, to my bed where I'd collapsed and—

A crash came from downstairs.

And I realized I'd better cool it on the spiraling and go track down the woman who'd shown up on my doorstep at a godawful hour.

I yanked the covers back, rolled out of bed, and hit the stairs, my nose confused from the moment I stepped out into the hall and began descending them. The scent filling the space seemed both familiar and oddly off and—

Another crash.

A soft, feminine curse (the tone, not the curse, because that was a hockey-worthy one).

I turned the corner into the kitchen...and promptly realized what the problem was.

She was fighting with my waffle maker.

The one that made kick-ass waffles, but also the one with the fancy—and tricky—lock. The one that would spew half-cooked batter everywhere if that lock was not engaged, and the one that—for some godawful reason—if the user managed to *get* engaged, was super tricky to get unlocked.

I should probably invest in one of those ones that with a spin of the handle it clicked into place and cooked.

But I liked *my* maker.

And I couldn't lie and say I hated watching Pru's ass as she bent her face near it, cursing up a storm before trying to coax it to work for her.

"Come on, baby," she murmured. "Just do it for me. One time is all I ask. Just be quiet and don't wake Marcel while you —" She broke off, grunting quietly as she fought with the waffle maker again.

That got my eyes off her ass, got them drifting around the kitchen, noting the sink that was full of dishes, the flour on the counter, the bowls of batter on the counter next to her...and the two empty plates.

How long had she been at this?

Long enough to have waffle batter splattered in her hair.

I was a man who liked organization, who valued cleanliness and order, but I found myself grinning, not giving a shit about the mess, nor a fuck about Pru showing up on my porch when I hadn't gotten my pregame uninterrupted chunk of sleep.

I cared that she'd showed.

That she'd nuzzled into my throat, wrapped her arm around my waist.

I cared that she was making me waffles...

Or trying to, anyway.

"Gah!" she exclaimed, still quiet, still trying to not wake me —the consideration of that sent a bolt of warmth through my heart. "Will. You. *Just.* Wor—"

I hadn't processed I was moving, not until my arms were around her, my lips at her ear, "Like this, princess," I murmured, grabbing her hands, guiding them through the proper unlock process. The waffle maker popped open, and I was right about the source of the *off* smell from earlier—that being poor, defenseless, tortured waffles. But I didn't give a fuck about the waffles, defenseless or otherwise. Not when I was pressed to Pru's back, her ass, my arms full of lean, strong woman. Not when I had jasmine in my nose.

Not when she was there.

My lips found the lobe of her ear, nibbled gently. "Waffles?" I said softly, leaning forward to brush my jaw along hers.

Probably giving her stubble burn, but she didn't seem to mind, relaxing into me, and I was like a fucking cat, wanting to roll in her scent, to rub mine along every inch of her. Yes, it was caveman and possessive and probably over the top. But my little scene on the plane with Smitty proved just how possessive and over the top and caveman I was feeling about one Prudence Hansley.

In deep and not giving a damn.

"I was trying to make you breakfast," she whispered. "Or... well, lunch, at this point."

My gaze flicked from the windows to the clock on the microwave. It was one in the afternoon...which meant I couldn't have waffles.

I needed to have my normal pregame meal.

Late lunch and an early dinner. All the healthy shit that would fuel my body during the game. That didn't include refined flour and sugar. It *did* include lean protein (chicken), greens (broccoli, spinach, and the occasional treat of kale), some complex carbs (brown rice or quinoa or barley).

"Princess," I began.

She went stiff, and I felt her start to retreat, that steel to bolt itself back into place.

Then it halted.

She relaxed.

"You have a game tonight," she said softly. "You can't eat shit."

I pressed my lips to her temple. She settled back against me. "No, babe, I can't."

"Right," she whispered. "I'll—um—" Her gaze slid from in front of us to the side, presumably taking in the mess she'd made of the space. "I'll just...clean up."

"Or," I said, prying her hands from the waffle maker and flipping off the switch, "you can help me with my pregame warm-up."

She spun in my hold, giving me her front, probably not missing for a second that my dick was hard. Not that she could have missed it jabbing her in the ass when I'd sidled close. I digressed, and I was doing all that digressing because her brown eyes were warm, her ponytail a little askew, her cheeks pink, her mouth curving.

"I said it before," she murmured, "but it's worth mentioning again. Oh, thank you, Jesus." She ran a hand down my chest, down my bared torso, her fingers dancing across my abs, stopping just above the waistband of my boxer briefs.

"Like what you see?" I asked gruffly.

Gruff mainly because those fingers had dipped *beneath* the waistband of my boxer briefs and had wrapped around the hard length of my erection.

Tightly.

Stroking.

Dropping to her knees.

EIGHTEEN

Pru

I BARELY GOT my lips around the head of his cock before I was off my knees, a rough hand dipping into my jeans, wide fingers spearing into the wet heat of me.

"Oh fuck," I breathed, my head falling back, his fingers delving deep.

Marcel's other hand was busy, yanking up my sweatshirt, nearly tearing out my ponytail when he dragged the material over my head. But the sharp little bites of my hair pulling did nothing to temper my need.

No. That tug on my scalp inflamed it.

I wanted more, wanted his fingers plunging into the strands, winding them around his fingers, tugging my head back, his mouth sucking at my throat hard enough to mark me.

And like the fucking god he was, Marcel did that the moment my shirt hit the tile.

Bra off. Mouth sucking at my neck, nibbling gently, nipping sharply, soothing the sting with his tongue.

Fingers—wet from the slick heat of me, sliding out from my pussy, gliding over my clit, moving out of my underwear.

I began to protest.

He shoved down my sweats, my panties in one sharp movement.

My protest died on my tongue.

"Hang on, princess," he ordered gruffly, wrapping one of my legs around his hips, bending and spinning and lifting me onto the edge of the counter. Away from the hot waffle maker, but not away from the mess I'd made. Something toppled onto the floor, cold snaked across my ass.

I squeaked...and then groaned.

Because his boxer briefs hit the tile, and he was pressing into me, a hot glide, a burning stretch of internal muscles.

I wrapped my other leg around him, locked my ankles together, and then...held on.

Because that was the only thing I could do.

That hot glide turned into a rough pound, deep, grinding thrusts that pinned me between the squared edge of the granite and his body. It was hard—*both* were hard—and not exactly comfortable, that counter digging into my ass, but then his hands were there, cupping my cheeks, and he was moving, rolling his hips, taking me deep and fast and *oh so good*.

My hands found his shoulders, the cast bumping his head, not that he seemed to feel it, hell *I* couldn't feel the injury, not even when I dug the fingernails of both hands into his hard lats.

Because he'd found my mouth, thrust his tongue deep, and...I was there.

Already.

With just him grinding into me.

With just that perfect movement, that perfection of pressure on my clit. With his big, rough hands on my ass, his mouth taking mine.

My orgasm was barreling toward me like a meteor toward Earth in a bad science fiction film.

Too fast. Too pat. Too soon. Too *perfect*.

And then I stopped caring about *toos*.

Because it was on me, grabbing me by the ankle, yanking me beneath the surface of the water, drowning me in sensation, numbing the reality around me. Halting my hearing, my eyesight, my breathing as pleasure tore me absolutely asunder.

Too much.

It threatened to keep me under forever.

To keep me in the depths for all eternity.

I felt his movements speed, the pace increasing, the thrusts growing harder, drawing out my pleasure—that *drowning-too much* pleasure—then losing their rhythm, coming in fits and bursts as he groaned and toppled over with me.

And I was still drowning, still beneath the surface.

Then his lips released mine, a mouth found my temple, brushed lightly, drifted to my ear. "Breathe, princess." An order, albeit a soft, gentle one.

I obeyed, sucking in a breath that was jagged and jerky and *hurt*.

But then I was there, awake and alert, numbness gone...and I thought that it might be gone forever. Because when I opened my eyes and breathed, my ears working, dropping back into my body that had just been riddled with sensation, I saw Marcel's eyes.

The amber depths were twinkling and gentle.

And I *felt*.

So big, so intensely, that adrenaline ricocheted through my body, the world lit up in technicolor. I felt the memory stamp itself on my brain.

The stubble on his cheeks.

The flash of white teeth.

His mussed hair, swollen mouth. The feel of him hard and pulsing inside me. Hands still on my ass, still protecting me from the squared edge of the counter.

The warmth flowing through me.

"I think I unalived you," he teased, bending and pressing his lips to my throat.

My lungs still hurt, I was breathing so hard, but the smile on his face when he straightened, the liquid heat flowing through me from the simple touch of his mouth to my skin, had me want to tease him back. "I *think*," I said, dropping further into my body, able to feel the cool slide of liquid between my cheeks, realized it wasn't his cum, but the result of a tipped over bowl of batter, "you made a bigger mess than I did."

His gaze left mine, glancing around, no doubt taking in the mess—made worse by our "pregame workout"—and then it flew back, colliding with mine, and he grinned. Huge.

So big that I felt the actual impact of it land in my belly, an arrow slicing through flesh, but not hurting. Warming me from the inside out.

"Wanna know the best part of making a mess, princess?" he asked silkily.

His cock was still hard inside me, his fingers had been gripping my ass, but now they were drifting in, gliding up and down.

I shivered, shook my head.

"It's even more fun to clean it up."

"I don't think—" My words were lost on a squeak as he tossed me over his shoulder and started from the room, skidding slightly on the spilled batter.

But he was a hockey player.

He navigated slick surfaces—*heh*—like a pro.

And this was no different.

He paused to wipe one foot then the other on the kitchen rug, and then kept moving.

"We've got to stop meeting like this," I told his ass—glorious because...hockey players had the *best* asses, and I could say that, *mean* it, because my own ass was pretty fucking great.

Marcel—and his ass—ignored my quip as he carried me up the stairs, down the hall, across his bedroom to the en suite. He plunked me on the bathroom counter, bent, and...pulled out a cast cover from the bottom drawer of the vanity.

I went all squishy inside...then squishier when he gently slipped it on.

But he was only gentle for a moment because then he was carrying me into the shower.

Which he turned on.

Making me squeal again.

But then his mouth was on mine, the water was getting warm, and I forgot about the shock of cold, the batter sliding down my skin.

Because I had his mouth, his hands, his *cock*.

And when I looked into his eyes as he thrust into me, I knew...that I might have his heart, too.

I PARKED Biscuit next to Marcel's sleek SUV.

The two vehicles were the hilarious juxtaposition of yin and yang.

One elegant, *well-planned*. The other—mine—a behemoth that didn't think about functionality. It was big, drove like a boat, and got horrible gas mileage.

Smirking, I got out of the car, started to head to my office. Marcel would be firmly in pregame mode—or he had been when we'd parted ways at his place two hours before.

His arrival time at the rink was earlier than mine, for obvious reasons like warm-ups, stretching, fueling, game prep (plays, roster adjustments, last-minute tape-watching), and though he'd offered to drive me, I hadn't wanted to get in the way of his routine.

Because routine was sacrosanct.

Players had lucky socks, certain meals, ice baths or hot tubs or special stretches. Changing their laces, getting a new stick, meeting with the masseuse. They all had their own thing or own combination of things.

I'd already trashed his kitchen; I didn't need to mess with his routine.

Not that it hadn't been fun to clean up together. I'd discovered that the way to get Marcel to talk was to argue with him about movies. He, no surprise, preferred a well-thought-out plot, and it wasn't like I *didn't* prefer that. I loved a movie that was plotted so well I took a moment to appreciate its greatness after the credits rolled. It was just...I didn't mind a *Snakes on the Plane* or *Sand Sharks* or *Howard the Duck*.

Not fine cinema.

Just something fun to get lost in.

And fun to argue the merits of their plots with Marcel.

Because *all* the words came. Camera types and plot threads, character motivation and cinematography. Why the director chose a particular camera angle, what it portrayed, and what it foreshadowed.

Shit I'd never *ever* considered.

No surprise, I liked to drop into a film, sit and enjoy the story, and then move on to the next thing.

But Marcel saw all the planning that went into them, and he was passionate about it, and...it was fun as hell to push his buttons about how none of that mattered. Until he stopped with *all* the words, got all growly, then realized I was teasing him and decided to punish me.

With orgasms.

My grin didn't fade, certainly wasn't going to, not when I could feel him between my thighs.

Not when he'd ordered me to bring him a key so he could meet me at my place after he was done with his post-game requirements. This being after I'd rebuffed the first order to stay at his place and watch the game with my ass parked on his couch, food ordered in ("Because I don't trust you with my stove"), chilling until he made it back.

I wasn't the chilling type.

And anyway, Walker was playing that night.

I wanted a glimpse of him from the owner's box, to see my hard work come to fruition—and his, I supposed, since he was actually the one playing (but...meh, small details).

Marcel's compromise had been to drive me—I wasn't there yet, and anyway, I needed to go get him that key.

Not that the orders had come in...well, that order.

But...I wasn't quite ready for the whole couple-to-the-rink together thing that Luc and Lexi, Hazel and Oliver had going.

We were new.

He was *in*.

I was just...still getting used to the sensation of my new skin settling.

And then there was the whole fact that if the team knew that Marcel and I were dating, the shit-giving and the interference and the betting and the gossiping and...hell. *All* the nosy nellies (and that meant the entire team, perhaps minus the exception of Walker since he was new to the team and maybe not yet up on the gossip skills of the other guys) would be in my business.

I wanted a little time with just me and Marcel.

Time to make sure I didn't fuck this up, to embrace the feeling, to blowtorch the remnants of those steel plates.

Because I was determined to be open to this, to keep Marcel.

To have another tie in my life.

And not just because he'd had to force his way in, a la Hazel style, but because I wanted him in.

And look at me go.

Being all mature and open and grown-up and shit.

Me patting myself on the back was probably why I missed it.

Missed Smitty watching me approach through the door to the rink, shit-eating grin in place, at least until I was right on top of him, my body awareness stopping me before I collided with the mountain of a man.

He didn't move out of my way.

Didn't speak.

Just stared at me with that smirk. Until it faded, and his face got uncharacteristically hard.

"Yeah?" I asked, my brows coming up.

"You gonna fuck around on him?" A growl. A rumble that vibrated through me. "Gonna hurt him?"

My brows pulled together.

Seriously, did the man have radar for this type of thing?

"Pru," he growled again when I didn't immediately answer. "*Are you going to hurt him?*"

Intense. Loud. Because Smitty was *always* loud.

But that loud snapped something inside me. Maybe it was because I'd been in a lust- and like-filled cloud, excited to keep a little piece of me and Marcel to ourselves. Maybe it was just because I was feeling *all* the things right then.

Either way, I snapped, jabbing a finger into his chest and moving close, rising on tiptoe. "I fucking *love* him," I said, or rather growled, taking a page out of Smitty's book, too on a roll to fully process the words and all they meant—especially for a woman who'd lived her life in a steel cage and underwater and so fucking numb. But *of course,* I loved him. It was new love, still fledgling, still unfurling before it developed into something weighty and heavy. But it was centering, a buoy in the ocean, a life jacket when I'd been drowning.

It was love, and it was the only thing strong enough to have pulled me from those crashing waves of my life.

I didn't process all of that until later, however.

Right then, I was mad as hell that Smitty would put me in the same category as Marissa.

Because fuck that bitch.

I kept on with the growling. "I would never hurt him intentionally, and if I do *unintentionally*—because that's life and shit happens—then how I make it up to him will be between him and me, not your big, dumb ass."

Smitty's glower faded, amusement sparking. "Pru—"

"And furthermore," I snapped, "Marcel is private and quiet, and so *you* won't hurt him by spreading this around and giving him a hard time. Got it?"

Conner's mouth twitched. "Pru."

"*Got. It?*" I snapped, jabbing him again, and getting in his face, even though he was nearly eight inches taller than me. "You will—"

Click.

I frowned, saw Smitty had snapped a picture, probably because he had plenty of space to do so—even with me getting in his face—because...circling back to that nearly eight inches of height separating us. "What the fuck?"

He spun away, held up his cell over his shoulder. "The group chat about you and Marcel is going to *love* this shit." He chuckled. "*You* threatening *me?*" Another chuckle. "Fuck, that's good," he said, now talking to himself, mainly because I'd gotten stymied at the whole *group chat about you and Marcel* thing.

"Group chat?" I asked.

He waved a hand, the one still holding up his cell. "Cat's long outta the bag, darlin'. But nice try."

And then he was gone.

But not before I heard his phone start chiming.

From a multitude of texts coming in.

Fucking hell.

NINETEEN

Marcel

"YOU GOT IN HIS FACE?" I asked.

She scowled.

"In *Smitty's* face?"

More scowling. "He was going to give you a hard time."

I smiled.

Her bottom lip stuck out, and it was so fucking cute, I had to curl up and slant my mouth across hers, to taste that pout on my tongue.

"Not fair," she muttered when I'd settled back against the pillows of her bed—pillows that were absolute shit, along with a mattress that wasn't much better...which meant that I was going to encourage sleepovers at my place.

Either that, or I'd use my newfound key to arrange a mattress delivery.

Hmm.

I didn't think she'd react well to that, considering she'd flipped out about me having dinner delivered to her office before she'd gone up to the owner's box to watch the game. That flipping out was why she was currently naked and on top of me, her chin pillowed on her uninjured arm. She wasn't used to someone spoiling her—if buying her one dinner could be considered spoiling. I'd pointed out that she'd brought me dinner the other night (getting a scowl in return—one that was rightfully earned since I was an idiot who'd then obliquely brought up the Carrie fiasco), so then I'd quickly changed tactics and pointed out that she'd kept the gift that came from dinner.

That gift being a gift certificate to a gift-wrapping service.

"I *needed* that," she'd muttered.

"You also need food," I'd said. "You know, to like, help your body function."

She'd grumbled, fought the caring—well, fought it this morning when we woke up, demanding I not do that again.

Something I'd blatantly refused to do.

Something I'd had to orgasm her into submission to stop whining about.

Now I was catching up on the group text—something I'd silenced after the pop-puck-head-video—or *had* been anyway.

Because then I'd come to the picture of her fiercely glaring into the camera.

Which had turned out to be her fiercely glaring at Smitty.

Who was a fucking giant.

Who could snap her like a twig.

Now would the man—even with all his loose cannon-ness—ever hurt a woman? Hell no.

That didn't mean I liked her getting in the face of someone who could hurt her, even if it was in defense of me.

"No more confronting six-foot-six-fuckers who can break you like a toothpick," I said, smoothing my thumb over her bottom lip.

Her eyes went warm...and then she nommed onto my thumb, her teeth gripping the pad. Not lightly. But not hard enough to actually hurt. Just a goofy, cute thing from Pru that I was going to cherish like the gift it was.

Because she was giving me her.

Wide open.

"I'll confront whoever I need—"

I dropped my hand to her ass, squeezed the rounded globe. "Do I need to orgasm you into submission again?"

She scowled.

I needed to orgasm her into submission again.

Fingers in her hair, mouth on hers, tongue stroking deep.

Then I flipped us and set about gaining that submission.

"HELL. FUCKING. YES!"

That was not the reaction I'd planned for.

It *should* have been, because this was Pru, and she was always up for an adventure...even, I was realizing, if it was of the smaller variety.

"I am *so* into this!"

This not being Wreck It, despite Hazel's recommendation.

This being an arcade.

"It's not going to be too much for your wrist?"

She shrugged. "It's feeling a lot better." Another lift and drop of her shoulders. "I'll probably suck with one and a half useful hands, but I'll still kick your ass in the one-handed ones." She turned, pressed her body to mine. "Or maybe I'll make you play one-handed, too."

I rubbed my nose along hers. "I can do that."

"Good." She pulled out of my hold, reached for her pocket, to the wallet I'd watched her stash there earlier (jealous of her hand being able to cup that lush ass when I couldn't, not if I wanted to take her out on a date), but—as always—I had planned ahead. It was Sunday. Early. The kids weren't out of church or bed yet. The arcade was mostly empty. It was me and Pru and a few stragglers.

We could game until we dropped.

Something I'd planned along with—

I cleared my throat, lightly snagged her shoulder, halting her as she moved toward the machines on the far wall to prepay for the games, and then held up a card, extended it out toward her. It was preloaded for several hours of game play.

Because we were both competitive, and it might take us several hours to feed that beast.

Even now, her lips curved, her eyes danced with challenge. "You can't orgasm me into submission here."

"I could—" I stepped close.

She shivered, lips parting on an exhale. "Marcel—"

I cupped her cheek, pressed my thumb into her bottom lip. She nibbled. And fuck. I'd just had her, but I wanted her again. "Why do I want to fuck you all the time?"

Her body drifted toward mine, a shudder wracking her frame. "Not fair," she whispered, leaning close. "Not when I can still feel you between my legs."

My cock twitched, and I extracted my thumb, pushed back her hair.

And stared at her.

Just gave myself that for a moment.

Brown eyes, high cheekbones, a bottom lip that was bigger than the top, which had a cupid's bow (something I'd had to look up to discover the term for) I liked to flick my tongue over. Freckles coating a pert nose. A scar near her jaw I found myself running my fingers along, as though I could erase it, knew instinctively it was from the same injuries that had nearly killed her, that had left thin white scars on her abdomen.

Scars I'd missed that first night because they were so faint, because they were mostly covered with a tattoo of irises.

And she'd given me *that,* too, when I'd brushed my fingers over the ink after she'd shared, after *we'd* shared, as I'd gently kissed the old hurts.

"My mom's favorite," she had whispered. "*My* favorite."

My heart had pulsed, fucking ached for her.

But I'd kept on with my gentle.

And, in the end, when I'd brought us both there, she'd held on extra tight.

"What's not fair," I said, stepping firmly back into the present, because I had to be on my toes with this woman, "is when you say shit like that in public where I can only orgasm you into submission by risking arrest." I tugged at the bang that always seemed to get in her face. "And we both have a season we worked hard for to get through, yeah?"

Her eyes narrowed, but she nodded after a moment. "Yeah, getting arrested for public indecency would suck," she agreed. Then reached for her pocket again. "But that doesn't mean I'm letting you pay for me—"

I knocked her hand away, snatched her wallet out of her pocket, and...shoved it down my pants.

Okay, the last wasn't well thought out.

Nor particularly comfortable.

But at least she'd agreed with me about the whole public decency thing.

And the arrest thing.

Though, her expression shifted quickly from aghast to outraged to amused.

She gave me more, gave me *everything,* bending at the waist, laughing loud and long. So long that by the time she straightened, her eyes were filled with tears of mirth, her cheeks were bright pink, and she was smiling.

And...I had to taste that smile.

So, I did.

Then nearly got us arrested for public indecency, if the throat clearing and subsequent disapproving look from the manager when I finally managed to pull away was any indication.

Pru laughed her ass off.

But didn't get us kicked out because she snatched the card from my hand, hauled ass to the machines, and...then proceeded to kick my ass.

We both played one-handed.

Because if I'd used both, I definitely would have kicked hers.

Definitely.

Definite—

TWENTY

Pru

I KNOCKED on Luc's door, a stack of folders he'd asked me to bring to this meeting tucked under my casted arm, my iPad stuck under the other.

He glanced up, phone to his ear, started to tell me to wait, but then seemed to get a good look at me because he said, "I'll call you back."

Click went the receiver.

Up went his feet.

Or rather, he went up *onto* his feet, rounding the desk and crossing toward me. "Shit, Pru," he said, "next time remind me that you have a broken arm before I request that you start schlepping files."

"It's fine," I told him. "I hardly feel it anyway."

Though that was a tiny lie.

I *was* a bit sore, probably from all the schmexy times—I wasn't the type of woman to lie back and think of England while Marcel did his business. I liked participating. Actively.

And despite his best efforts to do all the work, I had managed to ride my hockey player into submission the night before.

That thought had me smothering a smile.

Mostly because I'd extracted a promise from Marcel to let me have my way with him—which meant *him* lying back and thinking of England.

Or, I supposed, lying back and clenching his fists into the comforter, trying—and ultimately failing—at his endeavor to let me have my way.

The moment I'd started coming—the *moment!*—he'd flipped us, started pounding into me.

It had prolonged my orgasm in the best freaking way.

"Pru?"

I blinked, dropping out of my sex fog and feeling my cheeks heat.

Luc smiled in that slow—and objectively sexy way—and even though he was my boss's boss and in love and married to the totally awesome Lexi, I could appreciate the pretty that was Luc.

He was no Marcel.

But he was hot.

And he was currently tugging at the files, trying to take them from me.

"O-oh," I stammered, releasing them quickly. Which meant the whole pile dropped to the floor, papers scattering in all directions. "Shit," I muttered, bending and— "*Ow!*"

My forehead glanced off Luc's, who didn't quite *ow* as loudly as me, but he did curse softly, rub his head, and then gently grasp my shoulders, tugging me to my feet and guiding me over to one of the chairs at the conference table that took up a corner of his large office. "Sit," he ordered, pulling it out.

I sat.

"Sorry," I muttered.

He lightly squeezed my shoulder. "Been in the love fog before," he said, "nearly got my ass run over by a car."

I gaped.

He grinned. "I'll take a forehead bump any day of the week."

I nodded, but internally, I was wondering how in the fuck-all he'd been distracted enough to nearly get hit by a car. Well, wondering that and also wondering what *nearly got my ass run over* meant. How nearly?

Fruitless thoughts.

Distracting thoughts.

Because it was embarrassing as fuck that my boss was cleaning up my mess. Instead of focusing on that—and instead of going further down the nearly run over rabbit hole—I put my attention toward my tablet, pulling up the program that Oliver had commissioned the previous season.

It tracked stats, training schedules, injuries, what types of additional skill development our younger players might need. Well, not just the younger players. We had an entire separate database for the progress we hoped the rostered guys would make, along with tracking the usual stats, injuries, etc.

All together in one sleek program.

All easily accessible for trainers and coaches and support staff. Though, some stuff, including the specific areas of skill development for all the players was password-protected. We didn't need egos bruised or feelings hurt or confidence dinged because one of the guys saw a note. And we didn't need someone who didn't need to know the team's plan for our players having that information. Some of it was sensitive (think injuries), and some of it just wasn't anyone's business outside of the coaches and the players they were interacting with.

Luc, obviously, had full access. Oliver and I as well. The coaching staff also did.

But the trainers, the masseuse, Hazel as the team psychologist, others...they merely had bits and pieces.

Luc set the files on the table, and we spent the next few minutes organizing them.

Thankfully, I had footnotes in each and page numbers, making this easier.

But it took long enough that Luc decided to brave the love fog conversation topic again. "So, you and Marcel, huh?"

My fingers froze on the twelfth page of Walker's file, and I mentally cursed my only somewhat tech-happy brain. Because if I was *full* tech-happy like Oliver, then I would have been totally comfortable bringing up the profiles Luc wanted on my iPad and sharing it with his, thus not needing the paper files at all.

Thus, not having to have this conversation about my love life with my boss's boss.

"How's Noah?" I asked.

Going for distraction.

Which didn't work.

Luc just smiled, said, "For the record, I like you two together."

I cringed, barely resisting going full turtle. Which Luc, thankfully, seemed to realize. Because he picked up the file he'd fixed, flipped to the front. "Jackson Hunter. How do we think he's progressing with the Tide?" he asked. "When should we try to cycle him into the roster?"

"Thank fuck."

I didn't mean to say it out loud.

I did anyway.

Luc grinned. "Not big on the relationship talk?"

"Not unless that relationship talk is with Hazel." A beat. "Or the relationship a player has with the puck."

Luc's grin widened. "I can focus on puck relationships."

"You sure?"

His amusement didn't fade, despite me throwing attitude at my boss's boss. "For the record, *you* circled us back to this point."

I growled.

More grinning. "Another for the record?"

Boss. Boss. He was my boss. No, my boss's boss. I couldn't give him much more sass than I had already dished out.

A breath. My voice neutral. "Hit me."

"You know about the group text, right?"

I groaned, dropped my head to the table.

Luc chuckled.

Then, thankfully, the only relationships we discussed had to do with pucks.

———

"Hey, Trouble!"

I stopped, stifled my glare. I was heading up to the owner's box, trying to slip by the locker room, not wanting to mess with Marcel's pregame mojo.

I knew he'd struggled the season before, had needed a serious reset.

I didn't want to be the reason that he relapsed.

Any hope of sneaking was stalled by the annoying mountain standing in the doorway, yelling, apparently, my newly bestowed nickname.

"Conner," I said evenly, starting to brush by him.

He shifted, blocking my way. "Where you going, Trouble?"

And yup. Great. Apparently, he *was* bestowing me with a new nickname. Joy of joys.

"I'm going to do my job." I shoved at his chest. Not that I could *reach* his chest. The man was a mountain normally. Add in the extra couple of inches his skates gave him, and he absolutely towered over me. Which meant that I ended up shoving at his stomach. Which *meant* I was shoving at an area that was *way* too close to below the belt.

Literally.

Almost below the *garter* belt some of the guys used to hold up their socks—and Smitty, I'd unfortunately discovered during a drive through of the locker room, was one of the guys skipping the shorts with Velcro and going full garter to hold up his socks. Also, side note, apparently, I was lucky that I hadn't seen him (as in, *all* of him) because Smitty liked to be naked.

Like all the time.

So much that it was a team joke.

If only we could go back to focusing on Smitty and his nakedness, instead of me and Marcel and the fucking group chat.

Which I half wanted to demand to be added to. The other half of me, of course, was saying absolutely no fucking way to that—because *fuck* group chats.

"Trouble."

He stepped closer, and my palm went flat...and I felt muscle.

A *lot* of fucking muscle.

He had his gear on, but the front flap of his shoulder pads didn't come all the way down to the top of his hockey pants. There was a strip of exposed torso beneath his jersey, a strip that my palm was currently resting on.

I dropped my hand.

That just meant he came closer.

"How'd you do it?"

My brows pulled together. "What do you mean, Conner?"

"I—" Closer still, an earnestness in his deep brown eyes. "I mean, how the hell did you trust your instincts enough to *do* it. To jump in. To *love* him."

The last was said quietly.

Well, truthfully, *all* of it was said quietly.

And thank fuck for that.

Because, yeah, the cat was out of the bag, relationship-wise with the team, but it wasn't like I was ready to shout my emotions from the rooftops. Hell, I'd processed that I felt the L-word for Marcel, but I hadn't gone further than that, hadn't said it out loud—or at least not to anyone outside of Smitty, and in that one heat-of-the-moment instance.

When I told Marcel—because I wasn't numb any longer, wasn't beneath the surface—so it was a *when* and not a *hell no, not ever going to leave the twisted sanctity of my mind*. But anyway, *when* I told him, I was going to do it myself, not because Smitty ran his big, fat, loud mouth.

"Pru," he said, somehow still channeling that uncharacteristic non-Smitty quiet.

That finally snapped me out of my head.

And I remembered the breakup from last season.

I hadn't been around full-time yet, still playing in the women's league, only with the Breakers part-time. Just barely learning about the guys and their dynamics.

Smitty had joked about getting his heart stomped on.

He'd been loud and brash and self-deprecating.

But...maybe that had been a shield.

It wasn't like I didn't know *all* about shields, about hiding behind them.

Mine were quiet and steel, numb and shoving shit down.

What if Smitty's were jokes and brash loudness and generally being an annoying little—big—pest?

"I didn't," I said. "I didn't make the leap to trust my instincts. Marcel just made it so I didn't have to leap. He lined a staircase with red carpet, put a plate of strawberry waffles on a pedestal just beyond the bottom step, and waited—" I smiled. "And got mad about me falling down my stairs, and Biscuit, and the state of my mattress, and...he"—my voice went soft. I heard it. I *loved* it— "kisses me on the temple and brushes back my bangs and strokes my scars as though he wishes he could take away the pain."

That was...*so much.*

Too much to share.

But the steel had been blowtorched away and Smitty was asking, his eyes serious and sad and...I found that I wanted to give him a little of what I had, even though mine was new, even though we weren't particularly close.

Even though he was the annoying harbinger of the group chat.

"Pru," he whispered.

"Find a girl to give that to. Find one who will know exactly how much that means, honey."

He nodded. "Temple kisses, check."

I chuckled. "You know that *temple kisses* is a metaphor, right? One for the small gestures that this wonderful woman who will see you not for the pain in the ass, shit-stirrer you are, but the sweet, protective, caring man who will give her the affection she needs."

"He doesn't give you temple kisses?"

"He does, but—"

A firm nod. "Temple kisses."

"Smitty—"

He stepped away, placed a hand at my back, urged me toward the open door of the locker room. "Go," he said. "Get a kiss, on your temple or lips or wherever." I dug in my heels to the increasing pressure on my spine. "Let that man see you, know that he's playing for *you*." I clutched at his arm. "Trust me when I say *that's* the perfect red carpet-lined staircase for a man like him, like me, like *us*. That's the temple kiss equivalent for a man who's had his heart broken."

My breath caught. "Smitty," I began.

"Markie!" he yelled. "Get out here and kiss your girlfriend before *I* do."

Gasping, I jerked to the side...just in time to see Marcel come out of the locker room.

His gaze locked onto me before it slid to Conner. Conner, who was standing very close to me, his back now to my spine... while I was clutching at his arm.

And Marcel—Marcel, who'd been cheated on by his girlfriend and his former teammate. Marcel, who was staring at us with fury on his face.

Fury that disappeared behind steel, his expression going blank.

Oh...*shit*.

He had to play, to concentrate, and I was cuddled up to Smitty.

Never mind that I was giving him advice on how to find a girl of his own.

Marcel didn't know that.

Marcel...spun on his heel, took one step down the hall.

Away from us. Away from me.

My gut twisted itself into knots, I shifted my weight forward, ready to go after him, but then he whirled around.

"Mar—"

The distance between us disappeared, and he was in my face, his hands cupping my jaw, his body bending to take my mouth in a kiss that left my lungs burning, my head spinning.

"You're mine," he said, pulling away, the words whispered fiercely in my ear. "*Mine*."

"Yes," I said, winding my good hand into his hair. "Yours. *Only* yours."

He started to straighten, eyes dark and intense and turned toward Smitty, murder intent in those amber depths.

"Marcel," I whispered.

They flashed to mine.

"I love you."

Still.

Like a statue, his arms convulsing around me.

And then the fury left him, his gaze melted, trapping me in place, a fly to honey, quicksand trapping me in place.

"Fuck, princess," he whispered.

Fear crept in.

And then he kept talking. "Now Smitty is going to hear me tell you I love you for the first time."

"Fuck yes!" Smitty said, fist-pumping. His voice—all of the previous quiet totally gone—boomed down the hall. "They love each other, motherfuckers!"

I groaned and dropped my head to Marcel's chest when the cheers came from the locker room.

Marcel smoothed back my hair. "They'll find something else to be interested in soon."

"Not if you keep kissing me senseless in hallways."

The ghost of a smile. "Senseless?"

I scowled. "Senseless." A light shove to his chest. "I wasn't planning on telling you that *anytime* soon."

Fingers on my cheek, curling around my jaw. "Why not?"

"Why not?" I sputtered. "*Why* not?" A shake of my head. "We've had *one* date. *One.*"

"So?"

His question was so neutral that for one second, I didn't catch the teasing in his eyes.

"You're awful."

He bent, nipped my earlobe. "Tell me again." Soft words that made me shiver...and obey the whispered order.

"I love you."

Conner whooped again.

I sighed.

Marcel just held my eyes. "One date, or a million, I fucking love you."

Heart pounding, joy in every cell, I turned my head, pressed a kiss to his palm...and ignored the chimes of the group text going crazy.

TWENTY-ONE

Marcel

I SPENT the next two weeks—and eight games—flying.

Absolutely fucking flying.

My line had gelled on the ice. My game play was strong. My personal life was on point. Every single day with Pru was better than the last.

We didn't sleep apart—except for the nights I was traveling and she was home.

We didn't fight. She'd didn't give a shit that I planned my life and lived by a schedule. Because she was used to the same. Because she might be adventurous and have visited more countries than I could probably name, but she had been an athlete for years.

She knew when a routine was important, understood that I needed to follow a meal plan and work out on a schedule and that I had commitments after games, so I couldn't always rush home.

She *got* it.

So, life—*all* aspects of my life—were perfect.

What was *not* perfect?

The fucking mattress at Pru's place.

But I had a plan for that. I just needed to talk Pru around.

In the meantime, I needed to focus. The puck was getting ready to drop, my teammates were lining up, and I needed to get my ass ready for the face-off.

The whistle trilled.

The ref dropped the puck.

And the play began. Zero to a million in a fraction of a second. Sticks cracking together, skates grinding into the ice, players flying into motion.

Bodies crashed; curse words were exchanged.

The game sped forward in fits and bursts. So fast, so fucking fast when I was playing, digging the puck out of the boards, sprinting up the ice, fighting for position in front of the net, hauling ass to make sure Marty had numbers in front of our own goal.

Thirty, maybe forty-five seconds of intense, balls-out play.

Then slow...so *fucking* slow when I was on the bench, recovering, sucking in air until my pulse steadied, until my teammates finished their shifts on the ice and it was my turn to hop over the boards, to do it all over again.

Cool air drifted up from the ice, tightened my skin as I sat and waited.

Sweat dripped down my temples, burned like hell when it drifted into my eyes. But I was good at ignoring it, at blinking it away. And there were towels available when I sat my ass on the bench.

"I'm in love with your girl," Smitty said when the action on the ice paused and we waited for a commercial break.

Men and women skated across the rink, shovels scraping the surface as they moved, pushing the snow toward the Zam door where it was scooped into garbage cans and carried off the ice.

None of that helped me tamp down the urge to strangle Smitty.

"Like really love her." Smitty socked me in the shoulder. Hard. "Like really *really* love her."

"What the fuck, dude?" I snapped, shifting away (getting out of punching distance).

"She's awesome."

"Yeah." And she was mine. And I knew that I didn't have anything to be jealous about. But, fuck, *all* Smitty did was wax poetic and declare his undying love for Pru, for *my* girlfriend.

My. *My.*

Yeah, so I may have some leftover baggage about Marissa.

It was just...I never felt possessive about her, never went out of my way to claim her—or *wanted* to, really. Because I wasn't an alpha hole and didn't do that jealous bullshit.

But Pru meant more...meant *everything*.

And so, I had all the possessive, caveman energy flowing through me every second of every day.

Smitty bringing his love for her up every fucking moment didn't help.

"I'm *in love* with—"

I swiveled on the bench, tried to be conscious of the cameras—and the looks they might catch (and stifling the urge to throttle Smitty because they *definitely* would capture that, and me attempting to take down the Giant of the Breakers would make all the sport shows and blogs). I didn't want my legacy to be having started a brawl on my own bench.

So, I sucked in a breath through my nose, released it slowly.

Then said, cutting off Conner's soliloquy, "I need you to fucking *cool* it."

Smitty shut up, his eyes going wide, as though *just* coming to the realization that all his blabbering about Pru was making me lose my fucking mind. "Oh shit, man," he said quickly. "I would never—*she* would never do what Marissa—"

"Don't," I hissed, trying to control my breathing, trying to make sure I didn't start that brawl.

"She helped me, dude." God. Smitty could just never shut the *fuck* up. He slid close, and luckily I was gripping my stick so I didn't throttle my teammate. "No," he said, probably hearing the creaking of the fiberglass composite shaft. "I'm serious." His voice dropped, earnestness dripping with every syllable. "She...I'm—I...I—" Conner sucked in a breath, and the haze of anger finally faded from my mind.

Because Smitty didn't stammer. Or lose his train of thought. Or struggle for words.

And he didn't do quiet.

But...he'd done it with Pru in the hall. When I had nearly lost my shit seeing Smitty almost wrapped around her. Because caveman and alpha hole and Marissa baggage.

Pru had snapped me out of it with her declaration.

I now realized that I hadn't processed all that came before the best fucking moment of my life.

Smitty quiet, his expression falsely cheerful. His demeanor trending toward trying too hard instead of devil-may-care.

And he'd been that way a lot over the last few weeks.

Serious. Over the top effusive with his praise of Pru.

I had thought it was because he was trying to push my buttons. Now...now I wondered if it was something else.

Smitty answered that question before I could ask it out loud.

"She helped, man," I said quietly. "Helped me understand. I—I felt broken. Like she had been. We all saw it," I added. "Last season when she came to join the team, we all saw the walls, the barriers, and the barbed wire, and the Do Not Trespass signs. But you...one fucking plane ride I find out you like her, and the next she's *open*, she's declaring her love, and...I *wanted* that."

This was so not the time and place for this discussion.

It deserved more time.

The whistle was going to blow any second. We had to go out and do our jobs, to play hockey and win and—not talk about sappy love stuff.

But Smitty was broken.

Like I'd been. Like Pru had been.

"She's so fucking brave," I whispered. "So amazing that I feel lucky every moment of every single day."

Smitty's throat worked. "I'm happy for you. For her." The whistle blew, and he smiled—and thank fuck, it was the normal Smitty shit-stirring smirk. "And I'm glad she gave me what she gave me so that I can hopefully find that happy, too."

Coach called my line. I stood up, tapped my stick across Smitty's shin guards. "I want that for you, too."

I started to climb over the boards, stopped when Smitty called my name.

Or my awful nickname, anyway.

"Markie?"

I lifted a brow.

"Why does Pru blush when she mentions waffles?"

Fucking bastard.

I sighed, shook my head, and hopped onto the ice, flipping Smitty the bird when the fucker began cackling, called, "Oh man, I can't wait to find out the truth and get it in the group chat."

The ref blew the whistle.

I hauled ass to the face-off dot, took a breath and focused, not on caveman tendencies or jealousy or wanting to throttle my friend. I focused on hockey, on the puck drop.

And I did it while hating motherfucking group chats.

"So, where are you going over the holiday break?" I heard Samantha, the Breakers' head trainer, ask.

It was early in the season to ask that, but not too early, I supposed, considering it was nearing Halloween. But the planner in me appreciated the question. The team didn't have too much time off over Christmas, so travel needed to be thought out.

"Oh," Pru's voice made me speed up, her voice making me smile as I turned the corner toward the training suite. "I think I'm actually going to stay in town."

Silence.

"You?" Samantha asked, surprise in her tone. "*You're* going to stay in town?"

An uncomfortable chuckle. "Yeah," Pru said, something in *her* tone I couldn't pick up. Regret that she'd canceled her trip? No, she'd been all over giving Hazel those presents. So, it must be something else. Something—

"It's because of Marcel, isn't it?"

"I—"

Now my feet slowed, felt like they'd been coated with concrete, gluing me to the floor, fixing me in place, so I continued to eavesdrop, to listen to a conversation I had no business hearing.

"I'm not sure what you mean," Pru said, after a long moment.

"If I had him in my bed, I wouldn't be planning any extended vacations either. I'd keep him there and happy and reap the benefits every *single* night."

Pru chuckled. "Yes, Sam, it's because of Marcel."

Another laugh, and this one sounded forced, causing a trickle of discontent to flow through me. She'd said she'd canceled the trip because of Hazel, but what if that wasn't the real reason?

What if it was because of me?

No.

No.

That was ridiculous. First, we hadn't even been together when she'd done the shopping—and canceling—second, Pru was a straight shooter.

If she had an issue with me, she'd tell me.

Right?

She was happy. She loved me.

But...Marissa had been happy, too. She'd loved me once and—

Fuck, this was a stupid thought process to be having while eavesdropping and worrying about meaningless shop talk between two co-workers.

It meant nothing and—

"He's really great," Pru said. "I'm totally gone for him."

My hackles settled, and I told my inner worrywart—the one that liked to plan for every scenario, best to worst case—to cool it.

Gone for me was awesome.

Gone for me was *amazing.*

Samantha kept talking. "Okay, that's all well and good," she said dismissively. "We all know he's a good guy, but seriously, give the poor, single girl a bone! Please, tell me he's good in bed. With those amber eyes and all that *focus* just on you. It's gotta be good, right? *Right?*"

I saw Smitty round the corner ahead of me, didn't want to get caught eavesdropping and have my sexual prowess hit the group chat.

Shaking off the proverbial concrete, I started forward, slipping into the doorway.

Pru was sitting on a table. Sam was examining her wrist—or well, her fingers, since Pru's injured wrist was encased in gauze and fiberglass for a few more days—shifting them in different directions, massaging her palm. I remembered that Pru had mentioned Samantha teaching her some exercises that would help prevent muscle loss while she was healing.

Apparently, that was happening today.

Apparently, it meant girl talk.

I cleared my throat.

They both jerked, twin guilty expressions on their faces.

I crossed to them, sat on the edge of the table next to Pru, pushing back the piece of her bangs that always got in her eyes. "You good, princess?"

Sam sighed. "It's good," she breathed.

Pru brushed her fingers over my jaw, smiled at me, but her words were directed at Samantha. "It's good," she agreed, and Sam cackled.

I sighed.

Pru kissed me on the cheek, which was sweet, but not nearly enough.

Which *meant* that I had to wrap my arms around her and kiss her on the mouth...*and* make it count.

Which I did.

Because Pru kissed me back.

Which was probably why I was too busy kissing Pru to notice Sam pulling out her phone and snapping a picture.

A picture that hit the group chat.

Sigh.

A picture that had Smitty booming before I even made it into the training suite, "Now *that's* what I'm talking about!"

I lifted my head, saw Conner's cell in his hand, glanced at

Sam and saw hers in *her* hand, an expression on her face that was a cross between chagrined and gleeful. Pru sighed. I sighed. We both muttered begrudgingly, "Fucking group chat."

Which made our eyes lock, humor in Pru's. Which called humor in me.

Then we were both laughing.

This time I heard the *click* of Smitty's phone.

And I didn't even care that the next pic to hit the group was of us. Again.

Because when I saw the photo, saw Pru smiling up at me, me smiling down at her, our eyes only for each other, I saved that shit.

Set it as the background of my phone.

She was happy. *Really* happy with me.

But the picture, even as great as it was, it didn't completely erase that niggle my eavesdropping had dug free, that maybe... maybe someday that happy with me would fade.

TWENTY-TWO

Pru

"YOU *DIDN'T!*" Hazel exclaimed.

I shrugged. "Just a few—"

"Not a *few*. Not a fe-few. N-not a-a—"

Oh boy.

Here they went.

Tears and sobs and pregnancy hormones rearing their ugly head. *All* the baby things had hit my friend. Nausea. Boob growing. Crying at a tissue commercial.

If I had some of Marcel's planning skills, I would have anticipated this.

That had me smiling as I wrapped my arms around Hazel and held on tight. Or as tight as I could without bashing my friend with my cast.

Which was getting more annoying as the weeks went on.

It didn't hurt.

It still had to stay in place (probably thanks to my eager

participation in bedroom antics with Marcel), though thankfully, they *had* cut it down for the final two weeks of my life as a cast model (heh). Instead of wrapping around my elbow, it sat just below it. And the increased mobility? Chef's kiss.

Mainly because it was easier to hold on to Marcel's shoulders while he pounded into me.

Less resembling a chicken with its wing stuck out, more... human and less poultry.

Hazel got control of herself, sniffed a few times and said, "It's too much."

Maybe I should have parceled the gifts out, instead of getting Marcel to help me haul them all over to Hazel and Oliver's place. I'd been excited and glad that Haze was back from her honeymoon and finally feeling good enough to bully her into a double date—not to mention, she was beyond thrilled that her friends "who"—her exact words—"were perfect for each other in every conceivable way had finally got their heads out of their asses and did something about it."

Hazel was cute when she was telling it like it was.

Not that it wasn't true.

But...

Still cute.

"So, I went a little crazy," I said, shifting Hazel so she was facing the mountain of presents, "but my godchild deserves the best." A squeeze, my voice dropping as we headed over to the bags. "Plus, you're my best friend. *You* deserve the best."

Another sniff.

Thankfully, Oliver stepped in. "Presents now or dinner first?"

Hazel rolled her earring—a sure sign the psychologist was torn.

Thankfully, something Oliver also knew, that also had him

stepping in. "Okay, presents now. Dinner reservations pushed, and if that can't happen, it's a DoorDash and movies on the couch kind of night."

That sounded perfect to me.

Hazel had a huge couch, and cuddling up to Marcel, watching a bad movie (because Hazel was as much of a fan of poorly planned shoot-'em-ups and romcoms as I was) was something we hadn't done much.

We fucked. We went to dinner. We'd even gone back to the arcade and destroyed shit in a rage room—during which he'd told me that Hazel had given him a membership, helped him use it to manage the temper I'd gotten occasional glimpses of. The temper—that in small glimpses—I had to admit was sexy. But also, the temper I was glad he'd gotten a handle on.

Because I didn't need that shit in my life.

But that aside, all those activities in Marcel's flurry of date-planning plus the season starting up and road trips and home games meant we hadn't had any time to just...sit our asses on the couch and do nothing together.

That wasn't my typical.

Marcel probably knew that, was trying to plan and account for my adventure-seeking soul.

But when it came to him, I didn't want my typical.

I wanted the quiet and the loud, the standing still and the hauling ass. I wanted...everything.

Next date was mine.

Tonight belonged to Hazel, to our friendship, to the link we shared, fortified by steel that Hazel had honed, making it impossible for me to cut her loose.

So, I got out of my head, took Hazel's arm as Oliver pulled out his phone to call the restaurant. I sat my friend on the couch, plunked the first present into her lap.

Haze took one look at the flounced tissue paper and grinned. "Marcel wrapped these, didn't he?"

I burst out laughing, my gaze drifting to tall, dark, and pretty, who was looking at me with warm amber-brown eyes and a wide smile. Then I reached forward, picked up another bag—this one with decidedly un-flounced tissue paper—and said, "Not all of them."

Hazel laughed.

Marcel mouthed, "I love you."

My heart expanded, not a scrap of metal in sight.

Hazel began opening, pulled out the first present, a onesie that was printed with tiny electric guitars and emblazoned across the chest with, *My Mom Rocks.*

And then Hazel burst into tears again.

Oliver spun on his heel, lifting the phone to his ear. "You know what?" he said into the receiver, "You'd better just cancel that reservation altogether."

Smart man.

Because Hazel kept opening. The tears kept coming.

And no one cared.

I'D FIGURED out the waffle maker.

I'd whipped the cream.

Did I turn it into sweet butter the first go around? Yeah, so what? The second time turned out fluffy and perfect.

The strawberries in the store were shit, so I'd gotten some apples and cooked them on the stove with cinnamon and sugar, turning it into a compote.

Side note: compote had been a word that frightened me when I'd been looking up different types of waffle toppings in the middle of the grocery store.

It was now a fear I'd conquered.

And who said that adventures could only be found on the tops of mountains?

With me in the kitchen, using tools that weren't the microwave or boiling water on the stove, and it was the most adventurous adventure of all time.

"Losing it, Pru," I said lightly.

Not giving a damn that I was talking to myself. I was happy and *"in luuuuvvvvv,"* as Smitty had hollered from across the ice that morning at the rink.

Now, it was a week since we'd had the all-night cry and present fest with Hazel and Oliver. All the tissue paper had been recycled, the gift bags folded (and taken back to my place because Oliver had begged me to get the animal printed bags out of Hazel's sight when my friend had begun blubbering over how cute the baby giraffe on the front was).

A week since we'd finished with those presents, eaten the DoorDash, and then had vacated the premises.

Because all that crying and present opening had made Hazel tired.

She'd nearly nodded off over her udon.

Goodnights had been exchanged, Marcel and I had gone home. Me with the intention of coaxing him into movie time. Marcel...well, his intentions had leaned less toward movie, couch, and cuddles and more toward pleasuring me within an inch of my life.

I'd liked it.

I'd loved it.

But...I wanted domesticity, to slow down and be.

A scary concept—or it would have been a few months before. With Marcel? Perfect. It seemed perfect.

So, after a week of work and games and travel and a season that was going well, we finally had a free night. One I'd commandeered, demanding that I be the one to make the plans —the aforementioned food, couch, movie, and cuddles.

Then more pleasuring within an inch of my life.

Humming to myself, I dumped more batter into the waffle maker, knowing he would be home any minute and wanting his waffle to be absolutely perfect.

I had set the coffee table with plates and syrup and butter, not that we needed the last two with the delicious *compote* I'd mastered, but including them seemed to be the thing to do. Napkins were set with silverware. My plate already had a waffle sitting atop it. The compote was covered with foil. Candles were lit.

On the coffee table.

Maybe I should have set it up on the dining room table, but that was far away from the couch and cuddles, and anyway, I'd found the perfect movie for Marcel.

Fight Club.

He hadn't seen it, and it was manly. It was well-plotted. It had a twist that would blow his mind.

I couldn't wait to see his reaction.

The garage door hummed up, the vibration drifting through the walls of the kitchen.

And, perfect timing, the waffle maker dinged.

I flicked the lock, did the complicated twist maneuver and carried the hot, crispy deliciousness to Marcel's plate in the family room. Would it have been easier to have his plate next to me and to just dump it on there then walk it to the coffee table? Of course, it would. But I was new at this domesticity thing and so my method called for me to toss it from hand to hand while muttering, "Hot. *Hot!*"

The waffle hit the plate.

My ponytail holder slid out from my hair.

I didn't have an apron or heels. I was wearing a sweatshirt and T-shirt, but I could do my hair down. He liked my hair down, smoothing his fingers through it, twisting a lock this way and that as we talked, threading his hand into the strands and holding tight as he kissed me.

Yes. To all.

Smiling, I turned and—

Froze.

He'd slipped into the house sometime during my hair zhooshing, was leaning against the opening between the kitchen and the family room, shoulder casually resting against the frame, his ankles crossed, a bouquet of flowers resting at his side.

"Whatcha doing, princess?"

Teasing words that were filled with so much warmth, my blood vessels felt as though they'd expanded to ten times their size.

"Date night," I murmured.

"I see that." He walked toward me, coming in close, pressing his lips to mine in a kiss that wasn't deep and long, but was firm and intense enough to tell me that he liked what I'd done.

Really liked it.

He handed me the flowers. Irises.

And shit, Hazel wasn't the only one who was going to have issues with spontaneous tears. "Saw them," he murmured, "thought of you."

My lips parted; a shaky breath slid out. "Thank you, baby."

In response, he rubbed his nose to mine, kissed me lightly.

"Waffles?" he murmured, glancing over my shoulder when he'd pulled his mouth from mine.

I bent, set the flowers on the table, then gestured for him to sit on one of the cushions I'd positioned at either end. "Turns out I can learn how to use kitchen appliances."

A shadow of a grin.

"The kitchen wasn't a mess when I walked through." His fingers drifted over my cheek, along my jaw.

"I cleaned up as I cooked."

The shadow disappeared, and then I got a full grin.

"I don't think I've ever heard you say anything sexier."

I swatted at his chest. One, because the cheek on the man! Two, because his eyes were going all hot and I could read the intention in them, and that intention was less eat, couch, and cuddle during movie time, and more skip-straight-to-the-*post*-cuddle time.

"I made apple compote," I blurted, stepping back. "And whipped cream."

Not the right thing to say.

Because I didn't have to be a mind-reader to see that those two toppings gave the man ideas.

"Sit," I ordered. "Sit and—"

His arms wrapped around my waist, tugged me close. "I'd rather do this."

And then he was kissing me, deep and long and with tongue and one hand in my hair, tilting my head back, fingers pressed to my scalp in that way I *loved*.

But I'd busted my ass to get those waffles ready, and his was the perfect temperature.

Or it *had* been, and now it was getting colder by the second and—

His free hand slid down my side, dipped under the waistband of my sweats. Straight into my underwear, cupping my ass.

"Wait," I said, pushing lightly at his chest.

Those fingers slid forward, dipping in between my folds.

I moaned, breath hitching in my lungs. "Marc—*oh*."

Pleasure down my spine, a thick finger circling my entrance.

But waffles and whipped cream, apples peeled and diced into tiny, perfect cubes. Wrestling with the waffle maker and searching his kitchen drawers for a lighter for the candle.

"Wait," I said again, the words barely formed between our lips before he was kissing me harder.

The tide began tossing me this way and that, seaweed wrapping around my ankle, sucking me down.

Down.

Down.

I kicked. Hard. Abruptly.

Surfaced.

"No, Marcel," I said, shoving at his chest. He growled, leaned in. "*No*," I repeated forcefully enough that he stopped. Finally, he stopped.

I bent slightly, trying to catch my breath.

"What the fuck, princess?"

"I—" My gaze darted away from his, my body telling me to go back to kissing. But my brain, *that* was niggling, warning bells going off. "Sit, Marcel. Please, just sit."

His eyes clouded. His shoulders straightened. "Baby," he said. "Come here. Let me take care of you before—"

"I don't need a fucking orgasm!" I snapped.

Lies, my breasts said.

Bitch, please, my pussy yelled.

I ignored them. Because Marcel rocked back on his heels at my explosion, his eyes going dark. Not with fury. No...with resignation.

What the *fuck*?

"Please, sit down," I said.

"Just give it to me, Pru," he returned. Not cold. Just resigned. "Tell me."

Tell him what?

Silence fell as I tried to decipher that confusing statement.

"I wanted to plan tonight," I began, watching as his shoulders stiffened, "because," I pressed on, noting the clench of his jaw, the muscle ticking just beneath it. "I wanted a night in, just the two of us—"

He looked away.

What the fuck?

My throat was tight, but I was a badass motherfucker. I'd looked sharks in the eye, survived being shot, had climbed mountains, and jumped off bridges. I could tell my man that I wanted cuddle time.

But as I opened my mouth to do so, he shoved a hand through his hair, stalked away. "I don't understand women. I *don't*. I'm too boring. I try to be spontaneous. Hell, I *plan* on being spontaneous—"

If I wasn't so bewildered, that would have made me smile.

As it was, I was confused. Really confused.

Because I'd never said he was too boring.

I'd never said I didn't like anything about him. Because I liked *all* of him. But—

Ah.

Marissa. The fucking bitch with the gift that kept giving.

And maybe it made me a bad girlfriend for not realizing exactly how deeply Marcel had been wounded until that moment. He'd shared. I'd seen that glimpse of jealousy, of course. But he'd locked down *this*—the insecurities left behind. Hidden by anger and fury and possessiveness and caveman tendencies.

"Marcel," I began.

"I'm trying to give you what you want, and it's never enough—"

"*Marcel.*"

He continued pacing, not looking at me, furrows in his hair from his hands.

And I stopped thinking.

I picked up his plate—dumped his formerly perfect temperature waffle onto the napkin and chucked it at the wall.

TWENTY-THREE

Marcel

THE PLATE SHATTERING two inches from my shoulder made me jump.

Then spin to face Pru, who was standing next to the coffee table, another plate in her hand. "Do I need to throw another one?" she asked. "Or are you going to stop spiraling and *listen* to me?"

"What the fuck?" I whispered.

She threw the other plate. Picked up a glass. "It seems to work at the rage room," she said. "So maybe I need to break shit to get you to break shit, to break old habits."

A sinking feeling in my gut. "Pru."

"No." She pointed a finger at me, but thankfully set the glass down. "*No,*" she repeated. "I am *not* Marissa."

She let that sit there, heavy like a thundercloud, for several long moments.

And then she started moving toward me.

In socks.

With shattered plates on the floor.

Fuck.

I closed the distance between us, scooped her up and set her on one of the cushions she'd set out. "I know you're not," I began.

"No." A fierce refusal, starting to get to her feet, stopping me when I was turning for the kitchen, intent on getting the broom, the vacuum, on cleaning up those shards of porcelain so she didn't hurt herself. "*No,* you don't know that."

I sucked in a breath, held it.

And realized she was right.

I *didn't* know that. "You live a big, *big* life, princess," I said gently, willing her to understand. "I just want you to—"

"Stop."

She pushed my shoulder, and I let her press me down onto the cushion before clambering into my lap, her arms going around me, the cast catching on my shirt, her uninjured hand cupping my neck, her face getting close. "Just...*stop,*" she whispered. "Just stop and *think.*" That hand slid up into my hair, clenched tightly. "Have I asked you to change anything about yourself?"

I stopped. I thought.

She hadn't.

But Marissa hadn't at first, either.

Then look what had happened. How wrecked I'd been afterward. And what I'd felt for Marissa paled in comparison to what I felt for Pru.

Too big. Too much.

"I can't do this," I whispered. "I can't—"

I'd kept moving, kept planning, pushing forward. Because if I'd stopped to consider what would happen if Pru found me lacking. *When* she found me lacking...

Fuck.

I tried to shove her off my lap.

"Stop, baby," she whispered.

"Oh, fuck," I whispered back.

"I'm here."

I shook my head. "You're going to wake up one day. It might be months from now. It might be days. But you're going to look at me and realize that I'm boring, that I can't give you the adventures you seek. You're going to hate that I plan and want to think things out. Hate that I'm not spontaneous—"

Her hand came to my cheek. "Stop." An order, and coupled with her lips sliding against mine, one I obeyed. "You like order and planning," she said.

My gut twisted.

"I *like* you." Her lips brushed mine. "I *love* you."

Now.

She liked me *now.*

"Pru," I began. "You want—"

"No," she said, her lips still close, near enough that the word brushed my mouth as she spoke it. "Don't tell me what I want," she murmured, "not went it's *right* here." She straightened, backed up enough to meet my eyes. "I traveled the world. I lost myself in all sorts of adventures, but they were all just *that.* Getting lost. Hiding from my life, from what I didn't have." Her hand dropped to her belly. "To what I wouldn't ever have. So, I ran and I kept things free and loose because if I could get lost in the adventures, then I didn't have to think, to realize how empty I felt. How empty I *was.*" She sighed. "Hiding behind the adrenaline, going bigger and grander because if I just kept plowing forward with them, at least I was feeling something, even if it was just a moment of terror before I plunged back into all that numb."

I cupped her cheeks. "Princess—"

She shook her head, not dislodging my hold but cutting off

my words. "So don't tell me what I want, unless you're telling me I want you. Because *that's* the fucking truth. I want you. The moment I saw you walk into CeCe's months ago, I started to feel. You grabbed my arm—threw my fucking parachutes over the edge—and those feelings exploded through me." Her lips twitched then flattened, expression going serious. "At first, that was terrifying. But by then I'd gotten a taste of you, of the way you held me and how you looked at me, and I liked it. Enough that I knew it would be the best adrenaline rush of my life. Enough that I wanted to reinforce the tie between us when I'd spent a lifetime of *not* doing that."

I smoothed back her hair. "You lost a lot, princess. It makes sense that you'd keep distance between yourself and the rest of the world."

Half her mouth turned up. "Yeah, honey. It does. Just like it makes sense that your ex saying that shit about you, cheating on you, that relationship ending the way it did, would leave scars. Deep, painful scars you'd plaster over and try to forget—by planning to obsession, by trying to give me the stimulation you think I need."

Fuck.

Those words were arrows, sinking right into me, hitting home, making so much shit make sense.

"I *don't* need it," she said. "That day in the hall, what Smitty and I were talking about." Her hand slid down, rested on my chest, just above my heart, which was pounding like a motherfucker. "I told him about the temple kisses."

I frowned.

"That first night together, you treated me like...I don't know." She stopped, shook her head. "Okay, I *do* know. You treated me like I was precious. Like I was important and you weren't shy in showing me. You wanted me to stay and made that absolutely clear. It was just...all out there, no games, no strings, no barriers." She rested her forehead against mine. "You *never* gave me barriers. And you did that by brushing my bangs back, by kissing my temple gently, by cooking me breakfast for dinner, by worrying over my steps, grumbling about my mattress."

Her mattress was shit.

The rest of it...

Well, that was because I loved her.

"I never let myself have that, put up barriers to make sure it didn't find me, but you weaseled, or maybe *badgered*"—her lips quirked, but I didn't get the joke, probably because she was slaying me with her words—"your way in. Get this, baby, I spent a lifetime thinking I needed to keep living bigger and bigger, couldn't stop searching for the thing that would give it the right meaning, only to find you and realize that the thing I was missing was a person to call home."

"Pru," I whispered.

"Baby," she whispered back, her gaze holding mine. "It's true."

"Fuck."

I dropped my head to her shoulder.

Because my eyes were burning.

Because she'd laid it out there, clear and complete, making total sense, obliterating all the things I'd thought I knew, thought I needed to give her.

"For the record," she whispered. "That person is you."

"*Fuck*," I said again and felt a tear slide out from the corner of my eye. My arms convulsed, and I buried my face in her neck, the jasmine of her scent washing over me. "I need to talk to Hazel about this, don't I?"

Her hand came to my nape. "Probably," she whispered. "I can tell you that I like you as you are, over and over again, but Marissa sliced you deep." She lifted her head, gazed into my eyes. "I've had six years of Haze working me over, and it probably would have taken six more...if not for you."

"I love you, princess."

"I love you"—she smiled—"*and* when you call me *princess*."

"Because you deserve to be treated like one."

Fingers into my hair, lips coming close. "I know, because you *treat* me like one. Every day. Every second."

I wound my arms around her waist, tugged her close, gently smoothing back her hair. "Thank you."

A small smile, lightness counteracting the heavy. "For breaking shit and yelling at you?"

"Yeah." I smoothed back her hair when she laughed. "And for letting me plan..."

Her eyes narrowed, rightly reading the mischief in my words.

"...to buy a cheap set of dishes for you to throw when I get stupid."

A swat to my chest, a brush of her lips, clambering out of my lap. "Now," she said, "I know it's going to kill you to not clean up the mess I made, so I'll graciously make us fresh waffles while you run the vacuum, and then we'll get on with my date night."

"Which is food and more plate chucking?"

"Which *is* hot waffles, apple compote, whipped cream that is *not* butter, thank you very much, no more plate chucking, the best movie of all time, cuddling on the couch, and then finally, *fucking* on the couch where you will put your planning skills to perfect use with the leftover whipped cream and apple compote."

I grinned, swept her up over my shoulder, carried her into the kitchen, setting her on her feet by the waffle maker—and well away from the shards of plates.

"Now," she said, taking a bowl of batter from the fridge (it seemed like all my planning was rubbing off on her), "does that sound like a plan to you?"

"That sounds like the *perfect* plan."

I kissed her temple.

And knew as I moved to the hall closet—to where the vacuum was stored—that the smile she gave me was going to be imprinted on my soul forever.

Home.

I was home.

TWENTY-FOUR

Pru

I WAS GOING to kill the man.

Straight up take a skate blade to the man's carotid, watch him bleed out, and then bathe in his blood.

Okay.

I might be acting a tad dramatic. *A tad.*

But tell that to the girl who had just opened her door expecting to see her man, only to find six hockey players standing on my stoop. Two of them holding a mattress. Two of them on either end of my stairs, each holding one end of a new couch. The final two holding a box spring. And that didn't even mention the big bags stacked on the edge of my landing.

I glared at the man on the front end of the mattress.

The man I was ready to kill.

"Hey, princess," Marcel murmured.

"Want to tell me what the fuck this is?" I growled.

"Knock. Knock."

I narrowed my eyes.

"Who's there?" he said after a moment, in such a poor impersonation of my voice that I nearly laughed.

Which he knew.

The stink.

"Mattress delivery," he said.

"Mattress delivery, who?!"

The boom—from who else? Smitty—made me jump and whack my arm against the door.

Marcel shot him a glare, turned back to me. "Let us in. Please, baby?"

Not princess—which I loved—but baby. All husky and sweet with warm amber eyes and I was ready to cave.

Except the man had bought me a mattress.

And a fucking couch.

And I suspected several more (okay, *many* more) items that were going to make me want to go full carotid.

Grr.

So, I glared.

And made him wait.

He didn't speak again. Just stared at me with those damned amber eyes and made me want to give in.

Double *grr*.

Luckily, Oliver broke the stalemate—both the one in my mind and the one happening on my front stoop. "Umm, guy out here with one leg holding the heavy end of a couch. Am I putting it down or am I coming up these steps?"

I was tempted to tell him to put it down.

But I wasn't a jerk...or not too much of one, anyway.

I stepped back, waved a dismissive hand, and glared as the boys brought the stuff inside.

Well, glared at Marcel.

The others just got narrowed eyes because they'd gone

along with Marcel's scheme, but I reserved my glaring for the scheme-leader himself.

Who was utterly nonplussed.

The mattress and box spring disappeared down the hall.

The couch was deposited into the family room.

My old loveseat—which, look, had definitely seen better days—made its way outside, hefted on either end by Raph and Smitty. Oliver and Theo taking over positioning my apparently new (and bigger) sofa where my loveseat had once sat.

Since it *was* bigger, that meant it was a bit of a squeeze, during which I recalled a conversation a few days before, Marcel complaining about my mattress (whose better days had been seen well before the better days of my couch). I'd told him to man up and quit whining. But the next day, I'd gone online and ordered one of those fancy mattresses.

Which was vacuum-packed and rolled up, stashed in its box, and sitting in the corner of my family room.

Which meant I currently had six hockey players in my condo—which had *one* bedroom and now three mattresses.

Though, that thought had barely crossed my mind before Marcel and Walker (he'd recruited *my* Walker into his scheme!) came out, carrying my old, saggy mattress. They disappeared out the front door, Raph and Smitty coming back in, going down the hall. They reappeared a couple of moments later, hauling out my old box spring.

Meanwhile, Oliver and Theo were fluffing pillows.

Fluffing. *Pillows.*

Yup, that was happening in my one-bedroom condo. Two hockey players—and no, it didn't matter if one was retired due to a career-ending injury. Once a hockey player, always a hockey player. Once a Breaker, always a Breaker—were fluffing pillows.

Marcel came back in, dug right into the bags that Oliver had dragged in.

And pulled out...sheets, a comforter, blankets.

Then disappeared down the hall and into the bedroom.

Small victories that it was him making my bed.

Then again, I still had five other hockey players in my condo.

Speaking of which, Walker grabbed another bag and began unearthing a set of plates, tearing off the tissue paper that had been wrapped around them, balling it up, and shoving it back into the bag. He stacked the plates as he worked, then stood when he was done, carried them into the kitchen, and I heard the sink turn on.

Gaping, I turned and shot a glance over my shoulder, saw that he had begun washing them.

Fluffing pillows, washing dishes, making my bed.

And...hanging pictures.

"What the fuck?" I whispered.

They were...*oh, my God*...

"How?"

Smitty turned and grinned at me. "You may bitch about the group chat, but it has the perk of recruiting Hazel into our mischief."

Putting aside the fact that my best friend—*my best friend!*—was in on that mischief, I moved on numb feet across the room and got a closer look at what Smitty—and now Raph and Theo and Oliver were doing. On my naked wall, a huge empty space I'd never bothered to fill because I was never home, or when I *was* home, I was saving money for my adventures...on that naked wall, pictures were being hung. Of me and my travels—with a scuba mouthpiece between my lips, goggles over my eyes, a shark in the background. Another of me on top of Kilimanjaro. One with me and Hazel and Beth, arms around each other, OSU sweatshirts on, huge grins on our faces. Me on the ice with Oliver's team he was coaching, little arms wrapped around my waist. Me on the ice with the guys during training camp, them towering over me as I drew something on a whiteboard. Pictures of maps cropped to show the places I'd visited.

And the guys were putting those up on the wall in a pattern that I knew had Hazel's touch.

Because they had numbers on them, and Smitty had a piece of paper with a grid pattern on it.

Okay, so Hazel may have gotten the pictures to Marcel.

Because grid pattern? Numbered printout? Maps cropped to just the right location? Pictures all sized and framed and prepped with those sticky strip things that the guys only had to peel the backs off and stick to the wall.

That was *all* Marcel.

Prepped. Planned. Executed to perfection.

By hockey players.

And...I stood behind them, watching them work, staring at each picture as they were hung. Smitty had glanced at me when I first approached, his gaze going gentle, his hand dropping to my shoulder, squeezing lightly.

But he hadn't said anything.

Because he'd known.

Temple kisses.

That was when my urge to go full carotid faded.

The pictures went up. The sink turned off. The pillows were fluffed. The throw blankets were folded and draped across the couch.

But I barely noticed any of that, not when I was watching the final photo being hung.

Me and Marcel.

Arms around each other, smiles locked, laughter on our faces.

Home.

Smitty squeezed my shoulder again, and I tore my eyes from the collage and watched him walk toward the door. It was only then that I realized the other guys had gone, taking the trash with them.

And Marcel was leaning against the wall by the door, watching me.

"You still mad?" he asked.

Touched down to the very marrow of my bones, I just shook my head.

"Good," he whispered.

I stared at him, *all* the thoughts spinning through my head, emotions swirling, heart swollen to the point that it felt like it might burst. "Come here," I said softly.

He moved toward me, long strides eating up the space, his arms coming around me without hesitation. "I probably should ask *how*," I whispered, leaning into him, inhaling deeply, feeling his warmth, the spicy scent of him in my nose, "but it's just *you*. Wonderful, amazing, Marcel."

His arms squeezed, and he held me tight.

Words weren't needed, not when I had those pictures on the wall. Not when I had *him*.

But I gave it to him, anyway.

"Home."

A kiss to my temple, warm arms holding tight.

"Home," he whispered back.

———

"THE LEAST YOU CAN DO," I muttered, dragging the box down

the hall toward the spare bedroom at Marcel's place, "is to help me with this."

"Oh, you mean, help you on a game day when you said I shouldn't exert myself?"

I turned, narrowed my eyes, then turned back, still wrestling the stupid box, made all the more difficult because of the freaking cast. If it didn't come off the next week, I was going to saw it off myself. "Well, yes. And because you *already* exerted yourself this morning," I grumbled (not really a grumble, because all that *exerting* had been awesome). "Twice."

A hand in my hair, tilting my head up, his lips finding mine. "I thought it was *three* times."

I glared.

He lifted a brow.

A stomp of my foot. "Fine. It was *three.*"

"Sure, it wasn't four?"

"Mar—"

Another kiss. Then the box was out of my hands, and he'd hefted it over his shoulder, and...then I was jealous of a damned box. Because I knew what it was to be carried like it was effortless, to have all that strength holding me, surrounding me.

"Stop looking over my ass," he called, turning the corner.

"No," I called back, "it's my ass, and I can stare all I want."

His chuckle reached my ears, but it was the sense of home that reached my heart.

I JABBED a finger in his direction. "This is *not* a signal for you to buy me a new car," I muttered, slamming Biscuit's door and trying not to feel like this was the end of the line for my precious sedan.

I couldn't get sparkly gold paint standard nowadays.

Nor a door that threatened to amputate my fingers if I accidentally slammed them in the metal panel.

Or a steering wheel with leather so old it crumbled beneath my fingers.

"I'm not saying a word."

But his eyes had an edge of mischief.

"I *mean* it, Marcel. Not renting me a car. Not buying. Not leasing." I held his gaze. "Promise me that you'll let me sort out my car on my own." I'd already arranged for Biscuit to be towed to a repair shop.

"Nope."

I'd expected him to agree easily, to not say a word about it. I'd expected to have to fend off a sneak attack at a later date.

I'd *hadn't* expected him to outright deny my request.

He stepped close. "Not promising that, princess." His hands came to my cheeks. "I'm driving your ass to dealerships. You're picking out something that is safe, reliable, and will get you through the winter."

"Marcel—"

"No fucking excuses, baby"—and *God*, he had to break out the *baby*—"we're *going*. New car. *Safe* car. And I'm not going to bitch about not paying for it, even though I could easily buy it for you." He cupped my cheek. "You're not dropping another penny into this clunker, baby. We're gonna find you Biscuit 2.0, and we're gonna do it tomorrow."

"But—"

Here was the hard part. The part I hadn't told *anyone*.

"My godmother had this car." My voice broke. "I mean, this wasn't *her* car. But she had one like it, and when I needed to buy my own car, I-I saw this one, and...it's been with me ever since and—"

"Tow it to the shop, pay through the nose to get it back up

and running. Give it the works. New transmission or engine or whatever the fuck it needs. Get it pristine." Fingers on my jaw, gentle, *gentle* over that scar. "Then park it at my place, drive it in the summer. But, princess"—he shifted his hand, cupped my jaw—"tomorrow I'm gonna get you an SUV, something safe that you can drive in the winter, and you're not going to fight me on it, okay?"

"I—"

He pushed back my hair. "You take care of Biscuit, I take care of you, okay?"

I blew out a breath, couldn't quite believe that I was agreeing to allow him to buy me a car. "Okay."

"Good, baby."

My heart melted. "But—"

"Oh shit," he muttered, "here we go."

Rolling my eyes, I sidled closer. "Hush you. My *but* is that, when the time comes, you'll promise to let me take care of you back."

Clearly, that was not what he'd expected me to say.

Because *he* melted.

A big, burly—okay, somewhat lean, but big and strong with a yummy ass and killer thighs—hockey player melted.

For *me*.

"Home, princess," he said softly, sliding his hand down my throat, resting it on my chest, just above my heart. "We're home."

More melting.

But I didn't miss that he didn't promise.

Which is why I sidled close, rose on tiptoe, and whispered in his ear, "I'm not getting into your car until you promise that you'll let me take care of you back."

A grin.

A chuckle that slid down my spine.

Then...he leaned close and whispered in *my* ear. "Okay, princess, I promise."

My lips turned up. "Just that easy?"

"Just that easy." A swat to my ass. "Now, get this pretty thing in my car while we wait for the tow truck."

TWENTY-FIVE

Marcel

"SHE'S WONDERFUL, ISN'T SHE?" Lexi murmured.

I was standing on the periphery of the get-together at Luc's place, watching Hazel and Pru fuss over Luc and Lexi's baby, Noah.

The little guy had just started walking, and Pru and Hazel were taking turns holding their hands out and calling Noah's name. The toddler would grin and giggle and then take shaky steps from one woman to the other.

It was adorable.

It was bittersweet.

Because Pru would never have that.

Because once she'd told me what had happened, I'd got the excess of baby presents for Hazel. I got her ditching me for the one-year-old the moment we'd arrived for dinner and found that Noah had rebuffed sleep in order to party.

I didn't blame the kid.

We weren't getting plastered, and there were more board games and charcuterie than alcohol and wild times.

Hell, Octonauts was playing on the TV.

It wasn't like there were strippers showing up on the porch, ringing the doorbell, and coming in to perform lap dances.

Instead, it was the team's equivalent of family dinner at Luc and Lexi's place.

And it was fun as hell.

Once a month, we tried to all get together, to eat good food, shoot the shit, get the families all in the same place, and just strengthen the ties that linked us. No hockey talk. No drama. Just a team getting stronger because we came from a place of genuine caring.

Pru gave a little cheer when Noah had toddled to Hazel, making the little boy jump and fall onto his diaper-clad butt.

It was big and padded and couldn't hurt him.

But clearly, it startled him.

Because his bottom lip shot out, trembled, and tears began pouring down his cheeks.

Lexi started to take a step forward, mother's instinct taking over.

"Wait," I murmured, "Just...one second."

It ended up being more than a second, but Lexi stilled anyway, staying next to me as Pru scooped up Noah and began rocking the little boy, murmuring...no *singing*, I realized, as she started to make her slow, swaying, rocking way over to them. She was singing a little nursery rhyme that had Noah's tears drying up, his bottom lip stop quivering.

Noah lifted a palm, smacked it against Pru's throat, as though surprised that the gentle sound was coming from her.

"That's it, little one," she whispered, coming to stand by us. "Here's, Mama."

Except Noah burrowed into Pru's chest, yawned big and wide, and closed his eyes.

"You're a miracle worker," Lexi said softly, smoothing Noah's hair down.

Noah stilled, lips parting, breath slowing.

Lexi smiled. "He's always like that," she murmured. "Fights and fights and *fights* sleep...and then crash, he's *way* out."

The noise in the room increased—mainly because Smitty started booming, telling some story about what happened at the last game. To which Raph yelled, "No hockey at Family Night!"

To which, Smitty roared back. "It's not fucking hockey. It's a *fucking* hockey story."

Lexi glanced at me, lips twitching. "Does any of that make sense to you?"

Pru trailed a finger down Noah's nose. "Allow me to translate," she teased. "Smitty thinks that making fun of his teammate's foibles on the ice without discussing strategy means he's gotten away from the no hockey mandate."

"Ah," Lexi said. "Smitty Logic."

Pru grinned, agreed, "Smitty Logic."

Noah sighed, burrowed into Pru's hold a little deeper, and Lexi smoothed his hair back again. "You're so good with him." She smiled up at Pru. "I hope that you want kids someday because you'd make a great mom."

Pru went stiff.

And I knew that stillness, that motionless was a moment of shock, of her not in the here and now, and opened my mouth to say something to gently coax her back into the present.

Then Pru blinked, and she was back. Slowly swaying again, her hold softening, her eyes drifting to Noah sleeping in her arms. "I think I'll stick to being a godmother," she said quietly.

The words so hushed that they were nearly inaudible, especially over the noise of Smitty and Raph's hockey-not-hockey argument rising in volume.

Lexi went still herself.

Just for a moment, seeming to realize that she'd treaded on the edge of something painful. "You'll be a kickass one," she said gently.

I held my words and we stood, watching the scene, the argument, the good-natured and semi-hilarious back and forth for several minutes.

Then the volume got to the point that Noah, even as dead to the world as he was, startled in Pru's hold. Lexi leaned in and scooped him up. "I should get this guy to his crib." She smiled at us, tilted her head toward Raph and Smitty. "His room is soundproofed and well away from those two. And," she leaned in and added conspiratorially, "I recruited the night nurse who helped us last year to come tonight. Which means," she said as she hefted Noah against her shoulder, "that Mommy gets to be *wild* tonight and have that second glass of wine."

Pru chuckled.

I wished her goodnight.

Then Lexi disappeared, and I didn't miss that Pru's gaze followed them the entire way out of the room.

———

LATER THAT NIGHT IN BED, she gave it to me.

Without prompting.

No barriers, no steel.

Just opened up and let me take care of her.

"It's been so long, I thought I'd made my peace with it," she whispered, her arms around my waist, her face in my throat.

"Thought because I always knew it was off the table that I didn't want it."

I smoothed my hand down her hair, just let her have the space to process, to talk.

"But tonight, with Noah...I think I was okay until he put his hand on my throat. Then—" Her voice broke. "Then I felt his little fingers, and he smiled up at me, and..."

My throat grew wet from her tears.

"I wanted that," she whispered.

"I know, princess," I said. "I'm so sorry you won't have that."

"How am I supposed to be a godmother when I want... something more?"

"You are not supposed to be *anything*. You will be an awesome godmother because you love Hazel, and"—I held her tight—"because you have so much love to give, baby. It won't be hard. It'll come naturally because you're you." She released a shuddering breath. "And then when it's too much, I'll be there. I'll help you. I'll love you."

Quiet.

For a long, long time.

Then she sniffed softly, and I knew it took a shit-ton of courage for her to say, "But what if you want what I can't give you?"

I threaded my hand into her hair, tilted her head back so she could meet my eyes. "Lotta ways to make a family, princess."

I meant it.

She heard that.

Because she relaxed in my hold, every bit of tension leaving her frame.

"Okay, princess?"

Her lips brushed my throat. "Okay, baby."

She meant it.

I heard that.

And kept on lightly massaging her scalp.

"Home," she whispered long moments later.

"Home, baby," I agreed.

It took a long time, but eventually she fell asleep.

I didn't, holding her tight, staying awake. Making sure the nightmares from her past didn't resurface.

Making sure she found some peace in my arms.

"Tuck your chin down for me." A *flash.* "Okay, now a bit more." *Flash.* "That's it. Just like that. You look hot as hell, Marcel." *Flash. Flash. Flash.* "One more. Okay. I need my other lens and more oil!"

I heard a giggle.

Then Pru was at my side, a bottle in her hands.

"I knew this was the best idea *ever*," she whispered, squirting some oil in her palms and rubbing them together.

If there weren't twenty people around, this would be right out of my fantasy playbook.

But there *were* twenty people on this photo shoot for a very famous underwear brand that Pru would absolutely *not* hear the end of. Not when she'd seen the written offer my agent had sent over—this being after I had ignored the voicemails and the emails, because there was no way (no *fucking* way!) I was modeling underwear.

Pru, on the other hand, had other ideas.

And since the woman could pretty much convince me to do *anything*...I was now modeling underwear for a very popular brand and my abs (which I'd cut out carbs for the last three weeks for, along with drinking some foul-tasting tea that supposedly made my muscles look...extra *muscle-y*) were going to be plastered on fucking billboards.

The shit that was coming my way in the next few months was going to be astronomical.

But with Pru smoothing oil on my body, her smile so fucking gleeful, I didn't give one damn.

"I think you've oiled me enough, princess," I said when her hand drifted toward the waistband of the fancy, expensive underwear one too many times.

Mischievous eyes hit mine. "There's no such thing as too much oil."

"There is," I said dryly. "There definitely is."

A scowl. The bottle hitting a nearby stool. A glance over her shoulder, taking in the director of the shoot and the photographer deep in conversation. "You need anything?" she asked.

"For this to be over?" Another dry question.

Her lips twitched. "Besides that."

I shook my head. "No, princess. What about you? *You* need anything?"

"For this to be over so I can take your oily body back to the hotel and have my wild way with you?" she asked, waggling her brows.

"Fuck, princess," I groaned.

"What?" Innocence mingled with concern.

"Now I'm going to have to buy a bottle of oil, aren't I?"

Pru leaned close, rose on tiptoe, resting her palm on my chest as she whispered in my ear, "I already have."

My cock twitched.

There were about twenty flashes.

"That's it!" the photographer, Mick, yelled. "That's *fucking* it!"

Pru jumped, leaning away from me, her gaze going back over her shoulder. I got a whiff of jasmine, felt the silk of her hair slide across my chest. Hair which the hairstylist had spent the last hour curling and putting product in because Pru had, of course, charmed her. Joking and laughing and discussing our plans for a very fancy dinner that evening (this shoot conveniently being scheduled for an off day after playing the Rangers the night before).

The moment Rhonda had heard the name of the restaurant (a place it had taken a miracle to get a reservation at), she promptly guided Pru to her chair.

As planned.

Because...*planning.*

Same as the makeup artist dipping in and offering her services because she was "bored."

Now Pru had been pampered, her hair hung in shining curls down her back, her eyes had shit on them that I knew she dug (because she'd exclaimed excitedly about the lashes and so-called smokey eyes and how she could never do them at home herself).

She was happy and looked beautiful (as always, though I preferred her without the shit on her eyes).

What I *hadn't* planned?

The flashes. The photographer seeing Pru cuddled up close to me and yelling about it being *fucking it!*

The flashes cut off; Mick walked forward.

Held up the camera so we could see the image previewed on the back of it.

Pru's breath caught.

My entire body went still.

She was curled into me, our heads bent, our bodies in sync. Silken curls sliding forward, tumbling over her shoulders. A hand over my heart. Our lips a millimeter apart.

Eyes only for each other.

It was...*fucking it.*

It was—

"Home," Pru whispered.

I smiled, pushed back those curls, pressed a kiss to her temple. "Home," I agreed.

Then she turned to Mick, smiled wide, and said, "That's *fucking it.*"

TWENTY-SIX

Pru

I WAS HEADING to the bathroom to touch up my lipstick.

And seriously, *who* was I? Touching up my *lipstick?* That was a statement I'd never imagined crossing my mind.

But I was embracing my inner model that evening—and seriously, *how* in the hell had *that* happened?

But I'd seen the image on the back of the camera, the larger one on the director's monitor.

I'd seen the contract I'd signed...with a number for payment that was...

Well, suffice to say, all of Biscuit's innards could be replaced *and* I could afford to pay back Marcel for the mid-sized SUV he'd purchased for me.

Not that he would accept it.

The car was in my name, he'd paid cash, and he didn't want to hear any lip about it.

He'd actually said the last.

Any lip about it.

God, the man was trouble.

So *much* trouble.

And wonderful. So *much* wonderful.

Thinking about all that wonderful and trouble, I missed it.

Strong fingers were gripping my arm before I realized what was happening, digging in sharply, yanking me roughly to the side.

"Where you going, baby?"

Not said in Marcel's velvet rasp.

Instead, it was a drunken slur, those fingers tightening painfully.

I glanced back and to the side, saw the man in a business suit, clearly three sheets to the wind, and tried to yank my arm free. "Let me go, asshole."

The grip tightened. "Now, baby," he began, his leering eyes sliding down and then back up.

I shoved him away from me, succeeded in getting my arm free. "Back off," I muttered when he reached for me again.

"Pretty thing like you," he slurred, and he surprised me. Because instead of reaching for my arm again, he reached for my leg. Those sweaty, bruising fingers reaching for my thigh.

That was exposed in a short dress.

Because I'd wanted to tease Marcel all night.

Now, it just meant that the man got his hand on my skin, and because of the lack of material, had no trouble starting to slide that hand up.

"Don't," I gasped, trying to skitter back.

He stepped forward, forcing me against the wall, the narrow hall that led to the bathrooms not leaving me much room to maneuver. "All that skin," the drunk said, rancid breath in my nose, mouth coming *way* too fucking close.

I shoved his hand away.

But that just meant that his mouth came closer.

And then...he was kissing me.

It was...fucking awful. My hands came up to his chest, and I tried to shove him back, but it was like trying to move a brick wall.

He was heavy, immobile, and he was crushing me, making it fucking hard to breathe. And then...

Then he was gone.

Air rushed back into my lungs, and I retched, wiping my mouth with the back of my hand.

I sucked in a breath, tried desperately to center myself, and focused.

On the arms holding me. On Marcel tucking me close to his warm, strong body.

I saw the man on the ground, clutching his face, blood gushing out of his nose, dripping down his throat, staining his suit. Another man stood by him, shaking out his fist, wearing a white button-down and black slacks.

Our server, I realized.

Somehow, Marcel had gotten there, gotten help, and ensured that the team wouldn't get any blowback.

Planning. Always.

Thinking. Always.

"You brought help," I whispered.

He nodded, held me closer to him. "You were gone too long. I asked the server to show me where the bathrooms were. He walked me and we saw—"

My gaze drifted to the side. "Marcel, I'm—"

I felt gentle fingers on my jaw, looked up, and my heart clenched. Hard.

Because...Marissa cheating.

Because of his obvious jealousy (though he'd controlled it) in the hall when Smitty was close weeks before.

Because of the hurt he'd shared over Marissa's betrayal, the hurt that was still cutting deep...only weeks before.

And now, he'd seen me kissing some guy when we were supposed to be having a romantic dinner together.

"Don't," he said, turning me so I couldn't see the man. His tone was sharp and abrupt and...paired with gentle fingers on my jaw, my cheek, pushing back my tangled hair. "Are you okay, princess?"

"I—" My eyes filled with tears. "I didn't want him to do that."

A kiss to my temple, his arms wrapping tightly around me. "I know, baby. I *know*." A squeeze. "I'm sorry I wasn't here before he—" A soft curse. "It wasn't your fault. I'm not upset."

"Okay," I whispered.

"Now," he said. "You still want to fix your lipstick?"

"I—"

What *did* I want to do? It only took a second to come up with several things: get the taste of that man off my tongue, forget that it happened altogether, make sure Marcel was okay.

Yup. All of the above.

A trio of people entered the hall, obviously management, and behind them, a security guard.

Marcel saw them, too. "Go fix your lipstick, princess," he said, pressing a pack of gum into my hand. "And use that if you want."

"I should—"

"Go, baby."

I went, slipping into the stall, wetting a paper towel and wiping my lipstick that had gone askew, dabbing lightly at the skin beneath my eyes, wiping a few tears without messing up my smokey eye that would never again be replicated without the help of Jessie, the makeup artist from the shoot.

And just thinking about the shoot, doing something inane,

popping a piece of gum in my mouth...all of those simple, normal, small things meant that I grew more centered.

Felt more like myself.

Which Marcel no doubt knew it would.

Much more balanced and the memory of the drunk's touches washed (and gummed) away, I stepped out into the hall, and like he had some sixth sense, even though he was deep in conversation with a pair of police officers, Marcel immediately lifted his arm, curled me into his side, and held me tight.

They asked me a couple of questions, mentioned they'd get the security footage from the restaurant, and then gave us their card and told me they be in touch.

The man who'd accosted me had already been hauled away.

Thank God, I thought with a shiver.

Marcel's arm tightened. "Something else to give you nightmares," he murmured, holding me close, fury in the quiet words.

And I realized I wasn't the only one who might have bad dreams because of that evening.

Not because of Marissa and the feelings it must have no doubt conjured up, seeing his woman in another man's arms might bring.

But because he loved me, and it couldn't have been easy turning the corner and seeing that man assaulting me, couldn't have been easy controlling that temper of his—not when the past had to make his knee-jerk reaction come fast and furious. But he hadn't gone fast, and though the furious had been there, that rage came from wanting to protect, from witnessing someone he loved being hurt.

It came from Marcel being Marcel, and planning and thinking definitely didn't include his girlfriend being assaulted in the hallway on the way to fix her lipstick.

Hell, if the tables had turned and someone was hurting *him?* I would have lost my shit.

Even without the history of cheating and ex-slicing-him-open.

Because we were supposed to look out for each other, no matter what.

And that didn't even take into account the manly, kick-ass hockey player testosterone that had to be flowing heavy through him, the adrenaline.

I shivered again, my adrenaline having faded into pure exhaustion.

Marcel shifted, tucked his suit jacket around me. "I don't have nightmares," I whispered, as he adjusted the lapels. Protecting him by being open, by giving him the truth. "Because I know when I go to bed with your arms around me, you'll keep them at bay."

He stilled, fingers clenching on the lapels. "Princess," he whispered.

I reached up a hand, cupped his jaw. "And I'll do my best to keep yours away too."

His arms wrapped tight; his face was buried in my hair.

And he gave it to me. "I wasn't there."

"You were," I said back. "Exactly when I needed you."

Stillness as he no doubt processed my words, heard the truth in them. That there was nothing on my side, no regret or what if. Bad shit happened. He recognized something was wrong, moved to action, and he stopped it.

I'd learned long ago that I couldn't control the bad people in the world.

They did things without thought of the frightening and painful consequences for others.

But good—like Hazel, like Marcel, like Smitty with his

booming voice, a server who'd read the situation right and stepped in—kept the dark away.

"I saw you in his arms," he said softly. "Saw him kissing you." I went still, and he leaned back enough for me to see his eyes. "And I never even considered that you might be there of your own choice. I didn't look at body language, didn't think or plan. I just *knew* that you wouldn't."

My heart squeezed. "Baby," I whispered.

He brushed his lips to my temple. "Yeah." Then lifted. "Ready to go home?"

I gripped his jacket, let my body rest against his. "I'm already there."

A bop to my nose, his hold shifting so he had one arm wrapped around my shoulders and I was tucked into his side. "Sap," he said lightly.

I grinned. "Your fault."

Lips on the top of my head, a deep inhale. "I'll happily take the blame for that one."

"It was good you didn't hit him," I whispered, later that night, wrapped in his hold again, only this time I was naked. Well, we both were naked.

After a long bath, during which I'd washed off the smokey eye and the lipstick, twisted my hair up into a messy bun on the top of my head. Marcel had sat on the closed toilet, despite my best efforts to coax him into the tub with me.

It was probably a good thing he hadn't joined me.

The tub was small and if we'd been naked and pressed together...well, I didn't want to be responsible for the water flowing over and flooding the room below us.

Now we were in bed, pressed together...which had led to things.

Yummy, pleasurable things that had involved the bottle of oil I'd smuggled in and Marcel's glorious abs. Pleasurable things that had morphed into gentle, worshiping things. Soft brush of his mouth over the finger-shaped bruises on my arm. A barely-there skate of his palm over the scratches on my inner thigh.

Gentle. So damned gentle, even though fury had coated his amber eyes.

"I'm okay," I'd whispered, pressing him to his back when his desire had faded, holding him close until that rage had faded, until he'd kissed me, until I kissed every inch of him, until his cock got hard and he'd coaxed me down on top of him.

Slow. Oh, so *slow*.

Grinding and coaxing and pushing me over the edge with a feather-like touch.

The gentlest orgasm I'd ever had, the strongest arms catching me when I fell.

The events in the hallway might still mark my skin, but Marcel had erased them from my mind, my tongue, my body.

Just him. Just home.

"Hmm?" he asked drowsily—and just to say, I might have been in the midst of my gentlest orgasm ever (not that gentle meant bad...in fact it had meant good, *very* good), but I hadn't missed that *his* orgasm hadn't been gentle.

He hadn't pounded into me, but he'd come and done it hard before collapsing onto the mattress and tugging me down onto his chest.

Hence the drowsy.

I smiled. "I was just saying that I'm glad you didn't hit him...hit the guy who...you know..."

His eyes had been closed. Now one of them slit open as he said, conversationally, "Oh, I *hit* the fucker."

I blinked, pushed up slightly on his chest. "What?"

No remorse in that amber eye—not that the bastard from the hall deserved it—before the lid closed.

But...he'd hit him?

I didn't remember that. One second, I'd been pinned to the wall, punishing, rancid lips on mine, a disgusting tongue in my mouth, and the next, the man had been gone, Marcel holding me.

He absently rubbed his right fist, and I saw the beginnings of a bruise forming there.

Oh.

"Got him off you. Got one good hit in to make sure the fucker wasn't getting up anytime soon, and then I did the most important thing"—fingers in my hair, pushing back the locks that always escaped as he coaxed me back down onto his chest—"looked out for you."

Aw.

But...

I'd been worried earlier because I was thinking about the team, about *him*. About what (if any) disciplinary action he might face from the league, the Breakers. They all had honor clauses in their contracts. Beating up someone—even if it was definitely warranted—might trigger one. And that wasn't even considering what might happen if the media got wind of the story—if the new brand ambassador for that fancy undergarment brand (cough, underwear company) heard what happened. Would Marcel get in trouble? Maybe not criminally. But he was a well-known athlete. The guy who'd assaulted me could sue, could make his life miserable.

Which was what I told him.

To which he responded by shrugging and saying, "I don't care."

I pressed up on his chest. "You don't care?"

Fingers on my jaw trailing down my throat. "Nope." A shrug. "If it comes to pass, I'll talk to my lawyers, come up with a plan"—he traced the smile my lips made at his words—"and we'll deal."

Oh.

Okay then.

"Now," he said. "You good? Like actually really, no bull-shitting me good?"

I snuggled back down. "You got a plan to keep my nightmares away?"

His fingers slid through my hair. "Yup."

An arm around my waist, my body snug against his. "Then I'm good."

A squeeze.

"Good." Another. "Now, be good going to sleep."

"I will obey that order," I said, closing my eyes, "but only because *I* have plans for you in Boston tomorrow."

Quiet. Then a chuckle, a gentle stroke through my hair.

And I was out.

TWENTY-SEVEN

Marcel

"IF I'D KNOWN that your *plans* would mean that I had to walk for miles and miles," I grumbled, "I would have coaxed you into staying in the hotel room."

A glance over her shoulder, her ponytail bouncing along the collar of her peacoat—a coat that fluttered at the edge of her jean-clad ass and had me planning. It was never ending when it came to Pru and all the things I wanted to do with her—*to* her. "How exactly would you have coaxed me into staying in the room when there's all this history around?"

She waved an arm, gesturing to the *history* surrounding us.

Look. Boston was a cool city.

But I wasn't much for looking back. Lock that shit up. Move forward. Forget about dumping tea in the harbor.

No, those things didn't go together.

Yes, I knew that burying things down and never dealing with them—or only dealing with them when they exploded out of their carefully crafted box and began poisoning the other aspects of my life—wasn't the right move.

That still didn't make me give one flying fuck about the church Pru had spent the last half hour exclaiming over.

Now, thankfully, we were back on the street and not appreciating stained glass and carved wood.

"It's the Freedom Trail," she said, practically skipping next to me as we walked hand-in-hand through the streets of Boston. "It's ah-may-zing!"

"Is it, though?"

She wove her arm through mine, glanced up. "Are you really tired, baby?" she asked.

I wasn't.

And I *was*.

I hadn't slept well the night before, and then we'd taken an early train up to Boston so we could have some time away from the guys. The team had a game tonight, and then I'd fly on without Pru, who was going to watch some of the Tide's games and check up on her prospects.

We'd meet back up at my place in a week.

Or maybe hers.

Or maybe I'd convince her to move in.

Because I was tired of the back and forth shit, tired of planning ahead with games and travel schedules and clothes and workouts, trying to think about what we both might need to make sure our days went smoothly.

I was tired of planning.

Yes, *I* was tired of planning.

"Marcel?" she asked, her smile fading, her skip faltering.

I tugged her hand, spinning her back into my chest. "I'm not tired, princess."

Her eyes searched mine. "Really?" she asked softly. "Because I know when I get the travel bug, I can be a little..."

"Enthusiastic?"

"Pain in the ass."

I chuckled.

"It's true. I took Beth"—her and Hazel's friend—"with me the last time I went to Europe, and she nearly went home early."

"I heard that was because you tried to get her to go paragliding in Austria."

Her lips twitched. "Turns out Beth was more interested in touring the Swarovski showroom."

"Did you buy anything good?"

That lip twitch went full smile. "Of course, I did."

"Earrings?"

"A bracelet."

"You'll model it for me?"

She glanced up at me, brows dragging together. "It's a bracelet."

"Yeah."

The V between her eyes deepened. Then relaxed, going flat, clarity dawning on her face. "You mean model it naked, don't you?"

I brushed my lips over her temple, smiled deeply into her eyes. "I mean naked."

Laughter joined that clarity. Then she stepped out of my hold, took my hand again. "Okay," she agreed readily.

My cock twitched, and I was so down with the naked modeling that I hardly noticed when she led me into...

Another church.

Sweet Jesus.

More stained glass.

"I would have thought she'd take you bungee jumping or something," Smitty said, yanking at his laces before tightly tying his skates.

I was working on my own skates, adjusting the tongue and tautness of the laces until they were just right. Too tight and my feet would ache. Too loose and my ankles wouldn't have the support I needed.

Raph chuckled. "You ready for that?"

I shrugged. "I'm ready for anything."

Fuck no, I wasn't ready for it.

"Plus, she said she'd save that for the off-season. Doesn't want me to get injured when I have to carry your asses through all these games."

That got me hisses and boos, a balled-up sock tossed in my direction.

"I hope she takes you base jumping," Theo grumbled.

"No," Raph said, "she needs to lock his ass in that shark cage. Did you see the picture on her wall? That thing was fucking *huge*. I would love to see the color the ocean is gonna turn when Markie shits himself because one of those fuckers gets too close."

"Ew," Theo muttered.

There were more boos and hisses. A flurry of balled-up socks launched toward Raph, bouncing off his head, his neck, his chest.

"Seriously," Smitty agreed.

"Too far, man," I said.

But probably not *far* from the truth. If Pru got me in a shark cage—and she probably could, considering that one could talk me into anything—I'd be shitting myself...even as I didn't have any doubt it was going to happen. Well, maybe not the sharks. I believed her when she said that a lot of her adrenaline seeking was about self-medicating her pain, about trying to feel big when everything felt numb and shut down. I was down with traveling, and I was down with most adventures.

Sharks?

That'd be a stretch.

But I was down.

For whatever Pru planned...in the off-season. Yup. *Planned.* Because she'd told me she was planning ahead for next summer —and that was *all* she was telling me.

"I've got a plan, baby," she'd said, patting my chest. *"Next summer, you're all mine."*

"You're planning that far ahead?" I'd asked, flipping her onto her back, nuzzling at her throat.

She'd flipped us again, sprawling on top of me, leaned close, her tits mere millimeters from my mouth, and then she'd told me that she...was speaking my erotic love language.

Her words.

Not mine.

Her words that were *true.*

I smirked, thinking about what had happened after, when I'd flipped us again, taken my mouth to those naked breasts, her nipples hard against my tongue, and forced myself to breathe. To take a breath. Then I went to work on my other skate, ignoring the discussion that Smitty had taken over, pointing out all the different ways Raph could have taken it *too far.*

All of which were disgusting and in poor taste.

Ah, Smitty.

My teammate had never met a line he didn't ache to cross.

"Enough," Martin called, kneeling on his pads, leaning back to do up the straps. "If I let in a goal because I'm imagining Marcel shitting himself in the ocean, surrounded by sharks, I'm holding you all responsible."

"Man," Smitty boomed, "If you *don't* imagine Marcel shitting himself—"

"Can we seriously stop talking about me shitting myself?"

"Nope," Raph chimed in.

I shrugged into my jersey.

"Base jumping might be cool." Walker.

The kid had maybe said two words the entire time I'd been in the locker room so far—which had *so far* been the entire season. The rookie was a good fit with our game play, albeit quiet. But since I understood quiet—and because Pru had scouted the kid—I was inclined to like Walker.

Now I was inclined to like Walker even more.

Because he single-handedly redirected Smitty...and that wasn't easy to do.

"I can't *wait* for the pictures from base jumping," he said (yelled...said, same difference). "I guarantee Marcel will scream like a baby on the way down."

I tugged on my helmet, decided to do some redirecting of my own. "Pru told me she'd scheduled the two of you for a night out—"

Smitty grinned wide. "Now *that's* what I'm talking about."

"—to help feed a baby wombat at the animal sanctuary."

Smitty went pale.

I bit back a grin and did up the straps on my helmet. Apparently, Pru's research was correct.

Fuck, I loved my woman.

"Cool, man," Smitty said, snagging his jersey...and then promptly dropping it. Then picking it up again. Then dropping it. Again.

Raph, like any good teammate, picked up on that insecurity immediately. "What's up, butterfingers?"

"Nothing," Smitty said quickly, winning the battle and snagging the jersey, yanking it over his head. "My hands are just a little sore, that's all."

"Why are your hands sore, dude?" Walker—originally from

California, if the use of dude didn't make that immediately obvious—called.

The locker room roared with laughter.

Walker shot me a mischievous look.

Yeah, the kid was good people.

And knew how to handle Smitty—who slapped his helmet on his head, leaned close to me, and pointed his finger in my face. "There's no way I'm doing that."

"What do you have against poor, innocent little wombats?"

Smitty shuddered. "They're creepy as fuck. Giant rodents and teeth that wanna bite you."

"I think," Raph said, "they're technically marsupials."

"Yup," Theo—who was getting his bachelor's in zoology— said. "And herbivores, so while they *can* bite you. They're not really into eating humans for sport."

This didn't appease Smitty.

He shuddered again, grabbed his gloves, and shoved his hands in them. "Fuck you," he said to Theo. "And you." To Raph. "And you, too, kid." To Walker. "But most of all, *you.*" He scowled at me.

Then he stomped toward the locker room door.

"You gonna go with Pru?" I called.

He skidded to a halt, giant shoulders sinking as his head dropped forward. "Fuck, man."

I waited—hell, the *whole* locker room waited—even though we all knew what Smitty's answer was going to be.

Because Pru had them all wrapped around her very capable fingers.

"Yeah," he muttered. "I'm going."

Then he was gone.

Then I was pulling out my phone.

Not to add to the group chat...but rather, to invest in some serious wombat merch.

TWENTY-EIGHT

Pru

WALKER WOUND UP, let it loose.

Hot damn, the man could shoot.

It zipped through the air, rocketed right into the upper corner.

Pretty.

"Okay," I said, "now do it with your eyes closed."

One brow came up, a smirk that belied the man he was going to become. "'Cause I'm going to have my eyes closed in the game?"

"'*Cause* I want to see if you can do it with your eyes closed."

"Player development at its finest," he teased. But before I could mentally fist-pump about the teasing—okay, I did have time to fist-pump, at least mentally...so I did—he closed his eyes.

Shot.

And it hit the corner.

I whooped.

He grinned.

"Again," I demanded.

"Nope," he said. "Now it's your turn. One foot off the ground, far side post."

I had skates on, of course. We were on the ice. And I held a stick, though I'd done little except use it to shag pucks and pass them to Walker. I'd scheduled this time with him, not because he needed the practice, but because I'd wanted to check in, in a way that made it seem as though I wasn't checking in.

Light. Casual. Make sure all was good.

It *seemed* good.

Walker was playing phenomenally. He and Marcel had chemistry, and they'd put more than a few points on the board.

But I was protective of my guy. I wanted to make sure he really *was* good.

And it appeared that he was.

"I'm on the hot seat now?" I asked.

"Damn right," he said. "You've put me through my paces for months now." A nudge of his stick against my leg. "You need to show me your chops."

"My—" I started chuckling. "*Chops?*"

"Too scared?"

I rolled my eyes, wound up, and shot.

Ping!

"Now, with your eyes closed."

Grinning, I closed my eyes, shot.

Ping!

Now, it was Walker's turn to whoop, though he nudged me with his stick again, teased, "I think that was technically *seven* inches off the ground."

I snorted. "Ass."

A grin. "You picked me."

I had, and I was glad that he'd finally relaxed enough to see that. "Ugh," I teased when he passed me another puck, called out another shot. "Remind me why I took the trouble to do that?"

Proving he *had* actually seen it, Walker said, "Because I'm awesome?"

I wrinkled my nose.

Then I shot, hit what he'd called out, called out a challenge of my own. Which he hit because he was talented as fuck. He reciprocated with another challenge, and we went back and forth like that for a while—well, until my arms were tired because I wasn't in hockey shape, because I'd just gotten my cast off and hadn't fully built my strength back up...and because I wasn't nineteen any longer.

I didn't often spend hours shooting just for fun, talking about nothing, teasing each other, staying on the ice for no reason except I was on the ice and hanging with someone I liked.

I had other things going.

But today, I stayed and shot and *had* a shit-ton of fun.

(Despite the ache in my arms.)

Because the ache in my heart, the one that told me Walker was firmly making a place for himself in my heart, was bigger.

THE MAN HAD A SPREADSHEET.

And a PowerPoint presentation.

He had a list of top ten reasons why it made sense for us to move in together.

But all he'd had to do was say, "Pru, I love you. Move in?"

And I would have agreed. Immediately.

Not that I wasn't enjoying the presentation—which was a phrase I never thought (*never!*) that I would ever utter.

But the man had slides detailing the possible adventures I might be able to do, just by pooling our income and expenses. He'd created a chart tracking something called the happiness quotient, a suggested list of chores, had even included several bullet points of cleaning services with quotes for weekly and bi-weekly visits so we didn't have to worry about that "with our busy schedules."

He didn't get that the best adventure I'd ever had was our time together.

Literally the best adrenaline high of my life was seeing him waiting for me at the rink, knocking on my office door, letting himself into my condo (because we'd gone the exchanging keys route several weeks ago).

Or maybe he did understand that our relationship was the best adventure ever. Because he felt it. Because I'd told him.

But maybe, he just didn't quite believe it.

Maybe he had a tendril of doubt, that persistent niggle that made it so he needed the reassurance. Which was easy to give. Because the man gave so much to me. Visiting churches and temple kisses. A freaking SUV and the space to park Biscuit, who was now purring like a kitten. The day-to-day was the best adventure.

Something I never would have believed.

But...spreadsheets.

Marcel clicking through to the last slide (a Venn diagram of our compatible traits) and finishing his obviously rehearsed presentation with, "And that's why I think that we'll be happier together."

He closed his laptop, sat down next to me, and...waited.

I didn't make him wait long, just took his hands, sidled close, and said, "Okay."

He blinked, those amber eyes reading shock. "Okay?"

"My lease is up in six weeks"—which I had no doubt the man knew—"we sleep together practically every night, anyway. I love you. You own this place. My condo is a shithole. It makes sense for me to come here."

He shifted, lacing our fingers together. "You're going to give it to me? Just that easily?"

"When *haven't* I given it to you easily?" I teased, because, seriously, so much for my steel walls. The man had worn me down, barreled in, and I was gone for him.

That made the shock disappear. The self-satisfaction creep in.

"True," he murmured, leaning back on the couch, tugging me on top of him. His hand slid beneath the waistband of my sweats, cupped my ass, nuzzled my neck. "You're moving in, princess?" he murmured against my skin.

"You'd better make room for all my heels."

Which were three pairs.

Which he knew.

Which meant he chuckled. "Deal."

"That was too easy," I teased. "I'd better make you work harder for it."

His hand slid down. "You can buy more heels, princess."

"What if I don't want to make you work for more closet space?" I nipped at his bottom lip, arched against him. "What if I want you to work hard for something else?"

"Then"—that hand inched lower, found that *something else* as he always unerringly seemed to be able to do—"I'd say that I guess I'd better get to—"

The doorbell rang.

His lips were a hairsbreadth from mine.

His hand was curved between my spread legs, most of his fingers occupied, two curling deep, another circling my clit.

"Ignore it," he murmured, slipping a third finger in deep, causing a moan to drift from my lips, my hips to buck against his, which—thank you Jesus—reminded me that *he* was wearing sweatpants, that *I* had easy access too.

I was *so* down with ignoring the doorbell.

Shifting slightly, I managed to get my hand between our bodies—no easy feat when Marcel didn't move his hand, just kept circling my clit, kept curling those fingers deep.

I squirmed and wrestled my way into accessing his hard cock, palmed it, and—

A flicker of movement to my right.

At the windows that lined the whole front of Marcel's house.

Which didn't have curtains, because he didn't have neighbors on this side of the property, but they *did* have a hedge in front of them. Trimmed neatly, along with the lawn that surrounded that part of the yard.

A lawn that a cluster of people were now standing on.

Staring *into* the window nearest the television.

And his fingers were inside me, my hand was wrapped around his cock, and—

I screamed.

His fingers jerked.

I moaned—was only sidetracked for a second (really, only a second...okay maybe, two)—and then I was tugging my hand out of his pants, he was tugging *his* hand out of *my* pants...

"What, princess?"

I pointed...with the same hand that hand been on his cock —a sad turn of events that it was no longer gripping and stroking the hard length—though...creepy peeping toms were certainly more of a priority than orgasms, right? (Right. Maybe. *No.* Right.) "The window—" I began, still pointing. "There are—"

The curse words that came out of Marcel's mouth made even *my* used-to-hockey-cursing ears blister.

Then he was up on his feet and storming toward the door and throwing it open.

Exclaiming, "Mom, Dad. What the *hell* are you doing here?"

THIS WAS my definition of hell.

Or maybe payback for all my adventures I'd been able to take without parental oversight.

I'd never had to deal with surprise visits or my parents seeing me *in dishabille.*

So much joy that I was having my first experience with it tonight.

The adventure of a lifetime!

"Fuck," I whispered, smoothing back my hair as I stared at my reflection in the mirror. Should I try to do something with it aside from my standard messy ponytail?

Put on some makeup?

Try to look like the kind of woman they'd probably expect to be matched up with Marcel—someone girly and feminine, who knew how to do smokey eyes?

All I'd done so far after having heard Marcel exclaiming over his parents' surprise appearance was dart into his bathroom to fix my pants—well, more to fix my underwear since that had been sitting uncomfortably askew from Marcel's handiwork (literally).

Should I swap my sweats for jeans? I thought I had a nice blouse hanging somewhere in Marcel's closet.

But would that be weird?

Making a complete wardrobe change?

"Ugh," I whispered, dropping my head into my hands. I needed someone who knew what it was like to charm parents. I *needed* someone who *had* parents. I needed someone who knew me inside and out and—

I needed Hazel.

Reaching my hand into my pocket, I pulled out my cell, grateful for the fact that I was wearing men's sweatpants and because of that, the sewn-in pouch was actually big enough to hold my phone.

Then I stopped thinking about pockets, jabbed at the screen, and dialed my best friend.

Hazel picked up on the second ring. "Hey, Pru, how are—"

"I'm freaking the fuck out, Haze," I hissed, probably ruining my friend's just-back-from-her-honeymoon glow, turning on the faucet to drown out the sound of my conversation, before quickly shutting it off again. Not only was that wasteful, but would Marcel's parents think it was weird if I washed my hands for minutes on end?

Either weird or really hygienic?

Oh God, what was I *doing*?

I turned the water back on, sank onto the plush rug in front of the sinks, and focused. Well, I'd certainly gone big with my first foray into parental disappointment.

"Pru?" Hazel asked. "*Pru?* What's the matter, honey?"

"Marcel's parents showed up unannounced."

A small hitch of my breath.

"They rang the bell and we ignored it because—" Heat rushed to my cheeks, and I cleared my throat. "Because we were..."

"I get it, honey."

"No," I muttered, "you *don't* get it. Marcel had his hand in my pants, his fingers—" I broke off, voice dropping. "*Inside* me, and I had my hand on his—"

"Oh shit."

"Yeah, Haze. *Oh shit.*"

"But they were just at the door, right? I've been to Marcel's place. You can't see anything from the front porch."

I groaned.

"What happened?"

"The bell rang a couple of times. We were busy and ignored it and"—the rest of my words came fast and furious, embarrassment coiling through me—"then I was jerking him, and his fingers were inside me, and I looked up..."

"Oh no," Hazel breathed.

"And I saw people staring in through the window. Staring at *us* with our hands—"

Horror in my friend's voice. "Oh, *shit.*"

"He freaked, jumped up, ran to the door, and when I realized who was outside the window...I freaked. I panicked."

"Where are you now?" Hazel asked, horror firmly gone. Calm was front and center, and I felt some of my terror fade.

"I'm hiding in his bathroom trying to decide if I should attempt to curl my hair."

"Pru."

"Or change my clothes."

"Pru—"

"Or maybe I should put on some makeup. I can't meet his parents for the first time without makeup. But...I don't really *have* makeup aside from some lip gloss and mascara and samples from the photo shoot and—"

"*Pru.*"

"I don't have heels. I should put on heels, right? They'd expect the woman Marcel is seeing to know how to do those fancy, wavy curls, and smokey eyes, and heels. Definitely, they would expect her to be in heels."

"Pru, honey," Hazel snapped. "Shut the fuck up and listen to me."

I startled, the sharp words jerking me out of my brain, my downward spiral.

"They're going to *love* you," she said firmly.

"How do you know? My parents—"

"Because you're fucking lovable. Because you love Marcel and he loves you and it's a beautiful thing to witness. Just be you, be yourself with him, and they won't miss that, honey. They'll get it and get on board."

"But—"

"And aside from being lovable," Hazel went on, "you're fucking cool and amazing and people respect you. *And* I'm not just saying that because you're my friend. I'm saying it because you're all those things. My parents see it, which is why they're always hounding you to come over for dinner. The guys see it, Oliver sees it, Luc and Samantha and Lexi and the entire organization sees it. You're special, baby, don't you forget it."

I took my first full breath in what felt like ten minutes.

Damn.

Hazel gave a good pep talk.

"Really?" I asked softly.

"Really." A beat. "Now you're going to get your ass up. You're not going to change a damn thing about yourself— whether it's your hair or your makeup or your clothes. You're going to be *you*."

"Shit," I whispered. "Now you're going to make me cry."

"Nah," Hazel said dryly. "You're a badass motherfucker. You only give your tears on very special occasions."

"Does that include when your boyfriend's parents see you in *flagrante delicto*?"

"No. They're reserved for your man, for godmother duties,

and for sappy romance novels that strike the perfect balance between cheesy and schmexy."

"I think schmexy is the technical term," I said dryly. Delaying.

Which Hazel knew. Because she ordered, "Go, Pru. Take a deep breath, hang up the phone, and don't worry about anything except showing Marcel's parents how much you love him."

I took that breath. "I can do that."

"I know."

I hung up the phone.

I shoved it in my pocket.

Then I took another breath, didn't fix my hair, didn't search out my fancy blouse.

I just turned off the faucet, walked out of the bathroom, and set about showing Marcel's parents how much I loved him.

TWENTY-NINE

Marcel

I'D EXPECTED her to run.

No, to *flee*

We hadn't even been able to celebrate her agreeing to move in with me.

I'd just had to deal with my parents randomly showing up, worrying about my girl hiding in the bathroom, trying to surreptitiously wash my hands because one of them had been in Pru's pants and I couldn't hug my mother with a hand that had been finger-fucking my woman...

I'd done the last—well, avoided the finger-fucked hug by telling them to sit on the couch while I got them something to drink, thus allowing me to get my hands washed, coffee on, a beer out of the fridge for my dad.

Only *then* had I greeted my mother as she deserved.

With a tight squeeze. A kiss to her cheek.

"My baby," she murmured, wrapping her arms tightly around me. She gave the best hugs, and though I'd spent close to a decade avoiding them—because I was a tough hockey player and we hit shit and shot shit (well, shot *pucks*)—I'd finally gotten my head out of my ass in my early twenties.

Because she'd gotten sick.

"How are you feeling?" I asked.

"Fine, honey," she said, pulling back. "But because I know you'll worry until I tell you, I just had scans and they're clear, so I'm *fine, honey*."

Relief slid through me. "Good, Mom."

"Now," she whispered, following me into the kitchen so I could pour her a mug of coffee, "why didn't you mention that you have a *girlfriend?*"

The last was said with the expectation that I'd better not have been finger fucking a girl on my couch without her being at least my girlfriend, if not my fiancé, but preferably, that woman would be my surprise-we'd-just-popped-over-to-Vegas *wife.*

It would also help if that wife was pregnant with a grand-baby on the way.

A pulse through my heart, a moment of grief for what Pru and I would never have. She would never grow heavy with my child in her belly, would never cradle our infant in her arms. I'd never hold her hand in the delivery room, wouldn't put my palm on her belly and feel our baby kicking inside.

Losses.

A lot of them.

But I almost meant it when I'd told her that there was more than one way to make a family.

Because the only one I could foresee making was one with her at the center of it.

I dumped two sugars and a dash of milk into my mom's coffee, stirred it, and then passed the mug over. "I should go check on my *girlfriend*."

My mom grinned, rightly picking up on the unspoken confirmation that I'd heard *her* unspoken request for a daughter-in-law and grandbabies. "I can't wait to meet her."

"Me either."

My mom and I froze, turned toward the entrance to the kitchen.

Pru was standing there smiling, though I didn't miss the uncertainty in her eyes as she came forward and put out her hand. "Hi," she said, "I'm Pru…Prudence Hansley."

"Cathy," my mom said, clasping Pru's hand. "Cathy Aubert." A smile. "Though I suppose you already knew that was my last name." She didn't let go of Pru's hand, just held tight and said, "You have the prettiest hazel eyes I've ever seen."

"I—" Pru blinked those pretty hazel eyes. "Thanks," she whispered. A beat before she was talking again, chin coming up, voice growing stronger. "I often think that Marcel has the prettiest eyes *I've* ever seen, so I'm in good company I suppose." Another pause, her throat working, probably because my mom's brows had drawn together, confusion on her face. "Because I'm in the presence of the person responsible for making them," Pru finished quietly.

And just like that, Pru had her.

That confusion disappeared.

Pleasure infused her expression.

My mom tugged at Pru's hand, drawing my woman close, and then slid an arm around her waist, guiding her into my family room as though this was my mom's place and Pru was a first-time guest there. "Come in here and meet my husband, Leo. Leo. *Leo!* Turn off that game and meet your son's wonderful girlfriend—"

Pru glanced over her shoulder, eyes wide.

"And no grumbling! For God's sake. You can have five minutes in your life without sports."

"Just saying, Mom," I called, following them into my family room, "part of the reason I'm where I'm at is because Dad is a sports freak."

My mom whirled around (which meant that Pru was whirled with her). "No lip, mister."

I grinned.

On a huff, she whirled back (taking Pru with her again).

My dad, not a stupid man—and smart enough to recognize that my mom was in one of her *moods* (meaning she was emotional, excited, and wanting things to go perfectly, even though they were already going fine)—was already on his feet, game on mute, but not off (his way of communicating to my mom that he got this was important and that she was excited but she needed to take it down about one hundred and fifty notches). "Leo," he said, extending his hand.

Pru took it. "Pru."

"Nice to meet you." He sat down, picked up his beer, and his eyes went to the silent—but still playing a football game—TV.

"Leo!" my mom hissed.

"There's thirty seconds left," he countered. "You made me take a flight that had me missing the majority of this game. I'm watching the last thirty seconds."

"Record it."

His eyes didn't move. "I'm watching it *live*."

"Leo," she hissed again, like Pru and I weren't in the room. But then again, when my parents got on one of their tears, they didn't pay attention to anyone but each other...and it usually ended with them making out.

My parents fought hard...and loved hard.

I loved them.

But growing up, it had been tough to get a word in edgewise.

Pru had slipped out of my mom's hold. Probably because my mom had reached for the TV remote, and my dad had pushed it away...then reached for her, tugging her down into his lap and wrapping his arms around his wife.

"No wonder you ended up quiet," Pru murmured, sidling close, nudging my arm with her shoulder. I picked up on the message and lifted it, wrapped it around her.

"You okay?" I whispered.

Pru's lips twitched. "Before or after my freak-out in the bathroom?"

I smoothed her hair back. "After."

A nod. "I'm fine, honey." Her lip twitch expanded into a smile. "Mostly because Hazel set me straight."

"She's good at that."

Another nod, her hand coming to my chest, resting lightly over my heart. "*You* okay?"

I shrugged. "I'll survive the tornado that is my parents. The question is whether my relationship will." I nuzzled at her throat, inhaled woman and jasmine. "You still moving in?"

"Did I or did I not say that Hazel set me straight?"

My mouth curved. "You're moving in."

"Yes, baby." She stretched up, brushed her mouth over mine, whispered, "You'd better make room in your..."

I expected her to say closet, or bathroom, or hell, maybe even on my bookshelves.

"...garage."

That I didn't expect.

That was trademark Pru.

"I have a lot of sporting equipment."

I busted out laughing, her quiet chuckles joining in.

The volume kicked on the TV.

"Leo!"

Somehow forgetting that my parents were there for a few

seconds, my mother's exclamation snapped us out of each other. We turned.

"Give the kids their moment, Cathy," my dad muttered, eyes on the television.

"*You* ruined their moment."

"Then let the kids watch the final...now *twenty* seconds of the game with me."

A sigh. "We're here to visit our son."

The volume went up a couple of clicks. "We will."

My mom tried a different tactic. "Pru doesn't like sports."

My dad's gaze slid from the TV to Pru. Mine did, too.

"Mom—" I began.

"Umm," Pru said, "sorry to disappoint you, but I'm kind of a sports fanatic, too."

My mom groaned.

My dad perked up, full attention diverted from the game (probably because of the commercial break, but still). "Yeah? What sports?"

"Well, I like football—American—and I haven't missed a women's soccer game in years. I follow a little bit of college basketball, but, mainly, hockey."

"She played college and professional hockey, Dad."

Now my dad *really* perked up...and he clicked off the TV, set my mom aside, and began peppering Pru with questions.

My mom, over her huff (as was her way...and because the game was off). "Now you've done it," she said to me. "You'll never get her back."

Pru glanced over at me, smiled softly.

"She hasn't gone anywhere, Mom."

THIRTY

Pru

THE DOORBELL RANG ABOUT thirty minutes after Leo had begun interrogating me over my opinions of the Jets' chances at taking it all, the equal pay lawsuit the women's soccer team had been fighting, what it was like to play at OSU, how many seasons I'd been a professional hockey player, and what I was doing now.

When I'd mentioned my position in the player development department and we'd gotten into the nitty-gritty of my job —complete with stat and milestone tracking—he'd gotten so excited that I'd busted out my tablet.

With names covered, I showed him the program Kailey had created.

Which he'd fawned over.

Literally *fawned*.

Turned out Marcel's dad was into tech—like literally *into* tech. He worked at one of the big companies Congress was always threatening to break up.

"This is good," he was saying as Cathy moved to the door, boxing Marcel out of the way in her haste—and I had the notion that Leo might have given Marcel his organization abilities, but Cathy had given him his on-ice skills. That was seriously a good hip check.

"And this right here," Leo said, pointing at something on the screen. "She really thought through the user dynamics and—"

"You have *got* to be fucking kidding me," Marcel snapped.

I immediately glanced up, saw a slender woman walk through the door, carrying several brown paper bags. Even from a distance, it was easy to see that she was related to the Aubert crew. Same dark hair. Same narrow build as Cathy. Same facial features.

But that wasn't what had Marcel upset, what had Cathy wringing her hands.

Because he wasn't glaring at his sister.

He was glaring...at the woman walking in behind her.

Tall and blond. Tits and ass. Makeup on her face (smokey eyes), shining hair. Heels. Tight sweater. Jeans that encased long, long legs.

She was beautiful.

"Kylee," his mom whispered, "what are you doing?"

Kylee, apparently, set the bags on the kitchen counter. "You asked me to pick up groceries." She shrugged. "I picked up groceries."

And an ex.

Because that was Marissa.

I hadn't seen a single picture of the other woman. Marcel didn't have any in his house, and I hadn't gone trolling on his social media for them. I hadn't wanted to know. It wasn't that I was insecure and felt unworthy (or at least I was trying to get to the point that it didn't bother me). It was just...I knew that Marissa and I were very different women.

Marissa was beautiful. I was...sporty.

Marissa wore heels like they were surgically attached to her feet. The last time I had worn anything other than sneakers, sweats, or jeans, I'd been assaulted in a hallway.

Marissa had decimated Marcel's confidence and cheated on him.

That thought had me jumping out of my own brain and finding my feet, moving toward Marcel and getting myself positioned in front of him two heartbeats before Marissa reached him.

"Baby," she said, arms out, boobs on display in a shirt that was cut down to *there*.

I put *my* arm out, palm flat, elbow locked.

Marissa only had eyes for Marcel (and fuck, even their names went together), so she missed my extended hand, my palm.

Or maybe just didn't care.

Either way, I didn't move. But Marissa *kept* moving.

And I got to cop a feel, my palm pressing against Marissa's breasts, because I refused to give an inch, refused to let that snake get close to him.

Beady—and one might say *snake-like*—eyes locked onto mine.

There was hatred in them. *Hatred.*

"What the fuck, Kylee?" Marcel asked again, not even looking at Marissa. He slid an arm around my waist, tugged me back against him, and spun us both so we were out of the splash —*er* Marissa hug—zone.

Kylee, I was surprised to see, had all the Aubert physical traits but appeared to have none of the emotional ones. "I ran into Marissa at the grocery store."

Marcel snorted.

"We got to talking, and she wanted to come and see Mom and Dad."

"It's been a long time," Marissa said. "When I heard they were in town, I wanted to catch up."

"Since when do you grocery shop?" Marcel asked coolly.

"I—"

"No one important *grocery shops*," he said, the words deadly cold. "Those were your words when you didn't want to go, didn't want to schedule a delivery. Important people have *people for that*. Or am I remembering incorrectly?"

"I—"

He was stiff as a board, his arm so tight that I was having a hard time drawing in a full breath. "Or maybe you don't have someone to shop for you anymore...or rather, to pay for you to do that?"

"That's not—"

The words slipped out. I shouldn't have let them, but they did and then they were out there and I couldn't bring myself to wish they weren't because Marissa was a bitch. "Or maybe the person who used to do that for her is in jail." I shrugged. "Just saying."

Marissa's snake-like eyes cut back to me, murderous intent in those cold, blue depths. Then she sniffed. "I don't even *know* you."

"Thank God for *that*," I muttered.

Marcel's arm relaxed, a soft chuckle in my ear. But his voice was hard when he addressed Marissa. "There is nothing we have to say to each other. Not now. Not *ever*." Marissa opened her mouth, started to say something, but Marcel had already turned to his sister. "And *you*," he said. "You know what she did."

The first glimmer of discomfort in his sister's eyes. "I... She made a mistake."

"And what?" Marcel said. "Tripped and fell on his dick?"

Kylee's cheeks went pink. "That's not—"

"Multiple times, apparently," Cathy said.

I felt a curl of amusement glide through me.

"You know that's not what happened," Marissa said. "I—"

"Didn't like the life we were building so thought that you would fuck one of my teammates and make me change?" Marcel asked. "And then when that got you *nowhere* except with an asshole, you doubled down and moved with him when he was traded." He tapped a finger across his lips. "But he's an asshole—"

"And a felon."

More words slipping out.

Whoops.

Marcel's arm tightened again, but this time it wasn't from rage. I knew this because he kissed my nape before continuing. "We were young when we got together," he said. "So, I could have maybe understood the cheating."

I stiffened.

"*Maybe*," he repeated, smoothing a hand down my spine. "But I could never forget the poison. You shot that shit so deep that it festered and I barely managed to get it out." He leaned forward, kissed my temple, whispered. "Because of you."

A sniff. "And I'm supposed to believe that *she*"—God, Marissa had disdain down pat—"was the one who cured you?"

Me. *Me.*

With sweatpants, no makeup, and bare feet. With a ponytail, more T-shirts than blouses, and preferring sneakers to heels.

Yeah, I wasn't Marissa.

Something Marissa obviously wanted me to know.

Something—which would probably surprise the bitch to know—was something that I got.

Something...I didn't give a fuck about.

Because Marcel didn't want Marissa. He wanted *me*.

"I don't give a fuck *what* you believe," Marcel said, and I felt his body shift, saw the glint when he dug out his cell. "Now, am I calling the cops? Or are you showing yourself the door?"

Marissa stood there with her perfect hair, in her perfect heels, with her perfect makeup and gorgeous body clad in gorgeous clothes.

And I had never felt more beautiful.

Because Marcel's arm was around me and he was holding me close and...he wanted *me*. Not Marissa and her smokey eyes.

But me, with my messy ponytail, the bangs always in my eyes, my strong legs and small boobs. My broken body. My slowly healing heart and mind.

Me.

Just me.

I spun in his hold, cupped his face with my palms. "I love you."

No hesitation. "I love you, too."

Easy. Simple.

Us.

"Home," I whispered against his lips, rising onto tiptoe and kissing him deeply.

When we broke apart, he smoothed back my hair, pressed his mouth to my temple, and whispered, "Home."

No one acknowledged when Marissa turned on her heel and left.

Well, no one except for Kylee.

But no one cared when she followed her friend out that front door.

"I'll talk to her later," Leo promised...himself or Marcel or me or Cathy...or maybe just made that promise to the universe, to promise to straighten out his daughter, who clearly wasn't thinking straight when it came to the poison that was Marissa.

Or maybe I was infected, too.

Either way, Marissa the bitch was gone. An awkward scene had been had. A scene I didn't give a shit about. I just wanted to make sure my man was fine, his parents were fine, and then I wanted to eat, sleep, and have a series of orgasms courtesy of my man (and I'd be charitable and throw an orgasm or two in for him as well).

Of course, orgasms would have to be had quietly.

But I was creative. And a hard worker. I could make it happen.

Cathy rubbed her hands together, sighed. "We both will. Gotta get that girl's head straight. You think she'd grow out of picking toxic friends."

"How old is Kylee?" I whispered.

"Just turned eighteen."

"Young."

A nod. "A surprise baby."

"Impressionable."

Another nod. "And Marissa is good at making an impression."

"Thought it was strange she insisted on tagging along last minute," Leo muttered, moving to the door, closing and locking it. "Though it was even stranger she insisted on being the one to get the groceries before we'd even walked through the front door. Must have planned this with Marissa, saw Pru, and decided to go to the Bitch Queen."

"Leo!"

"What?" he asked, moving toward us. "That one was always that way." He clapped Marcel on the arm. "Glad to see you traded up."

Marcel chuckled.

My mouth had fallen open, and I was hardly aware of it because...I was processing.

The manipulation of his sister. Marcel's parents hating the *Bitch Queen*.

Leo looked at his wife. "I'll get her straightened out."

Cathy nodded. "I'll give you first crack. Then I'm jumping in."

Another chuckle from Marcel, but when I looked up at him in question, he just kissed the tip of my nose. "You've met my mom, even if it's barely been an hour. How intense do you think her *jumping in* will be?"

Big.

I knew it would be *big*.

Yikes.

"Exactly," he murmured, then lifted his voice. "Food, Mom."

"I can cook—" I began.

Marcel glanced down at me, ran his thumb along my bottom lip. "You're not a bad cook"—which said quite clearly what he thought of my cooking, *hmph*—"but even if you were Gordon Ramsey, my mom would still be cooking for us. Let her, okay?"

"I—" Shouldn't I be playing hostess, or at least offer, or—

"She needs it, princess."

I relaxed, clamped down my protests, of the thoughts of what I *should* be doing. "Right."

Cathy was already bustling into the kitchen, buzzing like a busy bee. Leo was heading back to the couch, remote in hand, a new game already blaring.

I thought of the drama of the last few minutes.

Of Snake Eyes Bitch Queen. Of Kylee taking her side and leaving.

Of bickering parents and surprise visits.

"This is what having a family is like?"

Marcel stared down at me cautiously. "With my family," he said slowly, "it is."

My hand smoothed over the bristles on his cheek. "Good," I whispered, "because it's fucking awesome."

He smiled, and it was the most beautiful thing I had ever seen.

But I saw it for only a second.

Because Cathy demanded my help in the kitchen, and then Leo wanted my opinion on the game...and I spent the next hour trying my best to please them both, with Marcel running interference, and then eventually ending my dashing between rooms by catching me around the waist, tugging me into his lap, and kissing me senseless.

Then he set my tablet on the side table, cleared off the remotes, tugged the coffee table away from the couch (and out from beneath his dad's feet), and ignored his mother's protests, bringing the food—pasta, bread, salad—to the squat wooden table, positioning plates and napkins and utensils, grabbing wine and glasses, dropping cushions onto the floor.

"It's movie night, Mom."

"But I set the table—"

"It's Pru's and my thing. I'm letting you be in on the Thing," he said. "So, movie night, picnic-style, and then if you're not too tired, we're taking you down in UNO."

"I—"

He lifted a brow, waited.

She glanced from the table to me, and her face grew soft.

"Movie night," she agreed.

Marcel turned on the movie.

And then we all sat down and ate and bickered and talked over the movie (which was one of my favorites...namely because it lacked plot).

And it was perfect.

It was...home.

THIRTY-ONE

Marcel

I WAS surprised that my sister had shown back up.

Well, not surprised. She'd taken the rental car, much to our parents' displeasure, but she didn't have a place to stay, couldn't book a hotel.

I *was* surprised, however, that she'd shown up, her sour mood gone, an apology for Pru, my parents, me, and had asked to join in during the next round of UNO.

Probably, she'd gone back to wherever the fuck Marissa was hiding and Marissa being Marissa (aka Bitch Queen), had been unhappy that Kylee hadn't facilitated a happy (for Marissa, for me...miserable) reunion. Marissa had probably taken it out on her and done it harshly, done it in a way that she'd been sliced deep. And that probably was *probably* a certainty because until I'd had this easy, this happy, this *home* with Pru, I'd become very familiar with Marissa's various forms of unhappiness.

She lashed out, cut to the quick. Made me feel stupid and

unworthy and had fueled the imposter syndrome Hazel had helped me get in check last season.

I'd told Marissa she was poison.

I meant it.

Luckily, Kylee wasn't stupid.

Or it appeared that she'd gotten smarter much faster than I had.

Because she'd come back subdued, but with those apologies.

No sulking in her room, just remorse in her eyes and a quiet request to join in.

And then asking Pru questions about herself, seeming genuinely interested when she heard about her travels.

"I've always wanted to study abroad," she said, drawing a card from the stack.

"You should do it," Pru said, sending a teasing smile my way. "While you're young and single and don't have to bring an expensive, needy boyfriend along." She skipped me.

I mock glared and waited for my dad to take my turn. My stack was getting low and I had to plan ahead. "Just because I have no interest in shark diving—"

Kylee's eyes went wide. "Shark diving? You've gone shark diving?"

"Cage diving," Pru said, waiting for my mom to put down her card then playing...right into my hands (muahaha!). "I wasn't in the water with sharks. Okay, I was, but I was in a cage and it was safe and amazing and—"

"UNO!" I called.

She narrowed her eyes.

Kylee put down a card, yelled, "UNO!"

"This is your fault," she pointed at me. Then Kylee. "And yours. Asking me questions," she grumbled, "then coming out with all your *UNOs*. It's terrible."

"Where else have you gone, honey?" my mom asked, drawing from the deck, same as my dad had done.

Exactly as I had planned.

Double muahaha.

"Where *hasn't* she been might be a better question," I said, watching as Pru waffled between two cards and then finally set down a Wild.

Come on. No whammies. Big money—

"Blue," she called.

I slammed down my final card, much to the groans and glares and boos and hisses of my family.

Pru, however, smiled. "You'd planned that, hadn't you?"

Calmly stacking the cards, I paused to blow on my nails, to buff them on my shoulder.

And there, right in front of my family, she leaned across the table and kissed me senseless.

"Love you," she whispered against my lips, and since that was my favorite thing ever, I wasn't expecting it.

"Fifty-two card pick up!" she yelled, and then dumped the stack of cards over me like very large confetti.

"Are there fifty-two cards in UNO?" my dad asked.

"Don't care," Kylee said, grinning as she scooped up a handful and dumped them on me.

"Me neither," my mom agreed, throwing hers across the table.

The rectangular pieces of paper bounced off my face.

"This is a model's face," I said. "I have to—"

A card landed in my mouth.

In my *mouth*.

Coasting between my lips, stuck between my top and bottom jaw. I spat it out. "What the fuck, Dad?"

My dad just flexed his fingers. "I was the champion card thrower in college."

"In one bar. One night," my mom said. "For *one* game."

My dad turned and shot her a look...and then showed off his champion card thrower skills by tagging my mom in the shoulder.

And then...it was war.

Turned out there were a lot more than fifty-two cards in an UNO deck.

And I would swear that between Pru and my family— and, not to forget, my dad's champion card throwing skills— that every single one of them ended up beaning me in my head.

We'd cleaned up the cards.

My mom had made her kick-ass sundaes (though Pru had helped by whipping the cream...and sending me a proud look when my mom had exclaimed over its perfect, fluffy consistency).

We'd eaten them in front of the TV, re-watched the movie we'd talked over earlier.

And had talked over it again because my dad wanted to know more about the scouting program, because Kylee had wanted to know more about Pru's travels, and my mom had wanted to know more about Pru's family.

She'd discussed them quietly, but in a way that didn't bring down the mood, in a way that comforted my mom when tears filled her eyes and guilt slid across her face. Pru had seen that, too. Had put my mom to ease, okaying the questions, giving gentle answers, and when the topic was settled then had turned to Kylee and asked what were the top places she'd like to study abroad.

We'd discussed the merits of a few different locations.

What might be a good jumping-off point for a home base so that Kylee could visit other spots easily.

Then Pru had effortlessly transitioned to my dad.

Giving him Kailey's name and contact info, answering more questions about the program, discussing the merits of a three-five-two versus a four-four-two formation for soccer.

And all the while, she sat next to me and held my hand or brushed her head against my shoulder or nuzzled at my cheek.

My family was charmed.

I was more in love than ever.

She cuddled up to me in bed. "Your family is..."

I braced, but I shouldn't have, not when it was Pru.

"Wonderful."

"*You're* wonderful." I kissed the top of her head.

She giggled. "Your mom is going to take me and Kylee shopping tomorrow, any idea what that'll be like?"

"Torture."

She giggled again. "I was being serious."

"I was, too."

"Well, I guess I'd better get used to the torture since you're stuck with me."

I held her tighter, buried my face in her hair. "Damn right I am."

She sighed, and I knew it was a happy one when she burrowed into me and yawned quietly. It had been quite an eventful day, and it was late, and I had to play the next night. I should be asleep, or at least, on the way there.

Instead, I was wide awake and content to just have Pru in my arms.

Everyone was tucked into bed, I'd given Pru—and myself— a very quiet orgasm, and I was feeling all that contentment because everything with Pru had just been so easy.

Well, not *everything*.

The beginning had been a little rough.

But from the moment she'd opened herself up to me, it had been easy.

She gave. Gave and didn't take, and after Marissa, I knew exactly how big of a deal that was, how *lucky* I was.

Which is why I was awake and holding her, smoothing my hand down her hair and thinking, "I'm going to marry you."

Then I realized I was more tired than I'd thought because I promptly fell asleep.

And missed completely that Pru had gone totally stiff in my arms.

Because I hadn't just thought it.

I'd said it aloud.

THIRTY-TWO

Pru

I'M GOING *to marry you.*

The words had shocked me, stunned me from my drowsy state, even as my man's arms had loosened and he'd drifted headlong into sleep.

But I'd gone from drowsily drifting off to...*holy fucking shit.*

In a good way.

In the *best* way.

Was there a bit of panic inside me?

Yes.

But the bigger part of me was doing a happy dance, or maybe a really, *really* good goal celebration, riding my stick like a pony as I skated down the ice.

What I wasn't—or at least not any longer—was ready to sleep.

So, I slipped out of Marcel's arms, pulled on my jammies that the man had oh so pleasurably (and quietly, because the man had skills...and was good at muffling my moans with his mouth) removed. I shoved my phone into my pocket because I might as well get a few rounds in with my word search game while I was up...

Then I tiptoed from the room.

There was some whipped cream left and I was going to get a spoon and *treat yo self.*

Then I'd crawl back into bed, enjoy my man, and sleep until whenever Cathy began bellowing to Leo to turn off the game because she had made breakfast.

I just knew it would involve bellowing...and certainly something delicious.

I couldn't wait.

Quietly, I made it to the bottom of the stairs and started to turn toward the kitchen, but then stopped...because there was someone in the family room.

Bent over the side table.

"What are you doing?" I asked, thinking it was Kylee.

The shadow jumped at the sound of my voice, skidded back a step, and then the shadow wasn't a shadow anymore. It was a person drifting into the sliver of illumination the hall's plug-in nightlight created.

And that slice of light showed me that I was wrong.

So wrong.

Instead, it was...Marissa, her hair shining silver in the moonlight, her hands holding—

I frowned. "Are you really that hard-up for money that you're going to go to jail for stealing an iPad?" I took a step toward the woman. "What's next? Are you going to take the TV, too?"

Marissa scowled. "Fuck you, bitch."

Original.

Maybe she *wanted* to get caught because she'd been denied

conjugal visits and she wanted to join her sleazebag of a fuck buddy.

Marissa's arm fell to her side.

And I got it.

It wasn't about conjugal visits or about joining her sleazebag in the clink.

It was about making me and Marcel pay.

"He wouldn't believe it," I said, "you know that."

Even from a distance, I recognized the Breakers tracking program was open to its login screen, its distinctive colors and format obvious. The program I'd spent the night talking to Leo about. The one I'd—a flash of movement at my side—the one that *Kylee* had overheard me discussing.

I turned, watched Marcel's sister slide out of the shadows behind Marissa and flick on the light.

"You let her in?" A gentle question, one I already knew the answer to based on the fact that guilt was written into the lines of Kylee's face.

Kylee bit her lip. "I—"

"What are you doing, honey?" I asked. "She's not a good person. Doesn't care about you."

"She said—" Teeth still nibbling. "I wanted—" A shake of her head. "I told her about the program. It was stupid. *I* was stupid. I shouldn't have. She just... She thought that—"

"*Kylee*," Marissa hissed.

"She's going to try to put notes into there, notes that Marcel will see and make him break up with you and—"

"Shut up," Marissa snapped.

"I texted her earlier," Kylee said, closing the distance between us, clutching my hands. "I know it was stupid. But she was mad at me for earlier, and I don't like it when people are mad at me, so I texted her to apologize, and she said that the only way she'd allow me to make it up to her would be if I called her before I went to sleep."

Young.

Kylee was *so* young.

"And then she wasn't just on the phone, she was here, so I went outside to talk to her. I should have just ignored her, but then *she* apologized and said she was wrong, that she just wanted to make things right and..." Kylee pushed her hair back off her face. "I'm so stupid. I didn't realize what she was doing until I mentioned your job and how Dad was so impressed by the program, and I knew—I *knew* she was playing me."

I shook my head. "Oh, honey."

"They weren't like the questions you asked," Kylee whispered. "She was searching for what she wanted, and she didn't give a damn about me—*doesn't* give a damn about me."

"It's okay, honey," I began. "We'll get this sorted and—"

"It's not okay." Kylee pulled back, shook her head. "I let her in, and I shouldn't have, and Marcel is going to be furious and... she's trying to break you two up." Tears trickled down her cheeks. "You two are perfect for each other. I don't want you to break up."

I reached for her, tugged her close. "We won't, honey. I promise we won't."

"But what if she—"

"He wouldn't believe it," I murmured, "even if she *could* get my login and password. Which I won't give her."

Relief on Kylee's face. "Really?"

"Really," I said. "Now, we need to talk about picking better friends later," I whispered. "Okay?" A nod in response. "But, for now, I've got to get Marissa out of here and then go back up to bed—"

I hadn't forgotten about Marissa.

Who'd obviously been listening because she set the tablet on the coffee table and was inching toward the front door.

"Are you going to tell him?" Kylee asked.

"Of—" Fear on the girl's face had me changing my answer from *of course* to, "No, I won't. This will be between you and me."

Relief, a squeeze of my hands. A whispered, "Thank you."

"Bed, sweetheart. I want to get back to my man—"

I hadn't forgotten about Marissa.

But I *had* underestimated her.

"Bitch!"

A flicker out of the corner of my eye.

And the world went black.

THE IRONY of this situation was not lost on me.

Wind whipped around us, cutting through my pajamas like knife strikes. The barrel of a gun pressed to my throat.

And I was on the same bridge I had been on months before, no parachute strapped to my back this time, but with bruising fingers guiding me forward, shoving me toward the metal railing.

I was alone—well, alone with Marissa.

And the gorgeous, model-like blonde had clearly lost her mind.

My phone was in my pocket—somehow it was still in my pocket—but it was also in the pocket closest to Marissa, who was doing all the shoving and gripping and propelling me forward.

So, I hadn't had a chance to use it yet.

It was the middle of the night, freezing, and the metal gun barrel was frigid against my skin.

But the railing was getting closer, and I had a feeling what Marissa was planning on doing, and...I had to do something.

Luckily, the dark provided me with some cover...or at least made it so that she couldn't see clearly.

I tripped over some debris, arm torn from Marissa's grip, landing on the concrete and asphalt surface hard.

My skin flayed open, the cotton of my pajamas providing little to no protection and none to my palms.

Pain sliced through me, hot blood trickling down my arms.

I rubbed my hands on my pajama pants...and grabbed my phone.

"Get up!"

"What are you doing, Marissa?" I asked quietly, inputting the code into the screen, hoping I was hitting the right numbers and then relieved when I saw a flicker of light that said I had. A thumb to the bottom left, then quickly tapping the top of the screen, hoping that I was hitting the right spot.

A soft ringing told me that I had.

But it was loud, *too* loud.

I had to get Marissa talking. "Why are you doing this?" I asked loudly, not listening to the answer, completely in tune with the ringing, with Marcel's frantic voice coming on the line. "Why would you take me to this bridge, Marissa? It's too dark to jump off it. It's too dark to *base jump* off it."

Oh God, please let him understand.

"*Get up!*"

"I'm sure I can get Marcel to talk to you," I tried. "I'm sure I could get him to stop for a second and listen. I'm sure he'd take you back and—"

Anything.

I'd say anything to delay, to buy time, to—

"I don't *want* you to do anything, you bitch. Except to. Get. The. Fuck. Up!"

A hand on my arm, fingers gripping hard, yanking me to my feet.

I was barely able to get my cell back in my pocket before Marissa was dragging me forward.

"Marissa," I began, trying to move as slowly as possible, because the fucking railing was growing closer and for the first time in my life, I didn't want to be on the opposite side of it. I didn't want to jump, didn't want an adventure.

I wanted to be home in bed and—

The barrel of the gun dug into my neck. "Move, bitch."

I moved, still slowly, trying to stay away from the middle of the bridge. If we could stay by the edge, then maybe the fall wouldn't be so—

But that staying away lasted for only a few heartbeats.

Because then Marissa's hand was wrapped in my ponytail, and between the gun and the grip, I had no hope of controlling any of this.

And *then* I was back on the edge of that narrow dusty road, in a different time, with a different gun.

Only this time, I was alone.

"No," I whispered. "*No.*"

"Shut up."

It wasn't in Spanish.

This wasn't the past.

But it didn't matter. The past had firmly resurrected itself, wrapped its talons around me, and had sucked me under.

I yanked herself out of Marissa's grip and started running.

The gun went off.

A hot, burning pain sliced through my middle, but I didn't stop. Not when the gun went off again, not when footsteps echoed behind me.

I just *ran.*

Straight toward the end of the bridge.

Straight toward the headlights coming my way.

THIRTY-THREE

Marcel

I THREW OPEN MY DOOR, leaving my sister in the passenger seat of my car, and sprinted across the narrow strip of steel and asphalt and concrete. "Pru!" I yelled. "*Pru!*"

Flashing lights were everywhere, the bridge was lit up like it was daytime.

And Pru was nowhere to be found.

"Pru!" I yelled again, running forward, tearing through the police tape like it was tissue paper, shrugging off the hands that tried to stop me. "Pru," I said, grunting as they tried to drag me to a halt. "Where is she?"

"Here, baby."

The best sound I'd ever heard.

I'd missed the ambulance, nearly missed her getting put into the back of it. Gauze was strapped to her side, and she was pale as hell. I moved toward her, ignored the hands grabbing at me again.

"It's okay," Pru said. "He's my boyfriend."

At that, they let me go, and I climbed in after the gurney.

Just before they closed the door, I saw Kylee through the back window of the ambulance, standing on the bridge, her arms wrapped around herself and terror on her face. A face that was already black and blue, covered with dried blood, and terror written into every inch of her expression. She was the reason I was here, why the cops had come, why Pru was still breathing. She'd barreled into my bedroom, yelling at me to wake up, that Marissa had come to the house, that she'd let Marissa in.

Stupid.

But a stupid kid who'd been manipulated.

One who'd been knocked unconscious by my ex.

One who had been freaked the fuck out not only because Marissa had knocked her unconscious, but because she'd done that *after* knocking Pru out.

All because Kylee had second thoughts about her involvement and had tried to stop the plan Marissa had concocted to get me back.

Marissa had snapped when it became clear that plan was fucked, and had done so while brandishing a gun, demanding that Kylee help her carry Pru to her car, all while muttering about a bridge with a deep river beneath where they'd never find Pru, never in a million years find her body...and as soon as Kylee had told me that, I had known—I *known*—exactly where Pru was.

Even before Pru's call. Even before the desperate words and clues she'd tried to give me.

A sixth sense in my gut.

And some common sense, I guessed, because none of the nearby bridges were isolated enough. It would have to be that one, *had* to be.

So, I'd called the police, gotten in my car, told them where to go—and thank fuck, they'd agreed to send a unit without hesitation.

And I'd been right.

Thank *God,* I'd been right.

But the call from Pru, her frightened words as she'd clearly tried to buy time while giving me information. And then the gunshots. Her cry of pain.

And now she was strapped to a stretcher, pale and bleeding, and not in the least bit worried about herself, apparently.

"I called," she said softly. So pale. So *fucking* pale. "I tried to tell—"

"I know, princess," I told her. "You did good, baby. I heard you, and I was already on my way."

Confusion on her face.

"Kylee told me."

Relief in Pru's eyes, her fingers spasming, her face contorting with pain. "She's—she's...okay?"

"She's fine."

"Good." Her throat worked. "You shouldn't be mad at her," Pru whispered, reaching for my hand. "She's just a baby, didn't get it."

"She's an adult," I said quietly.

Her brows drew together, skin so fucking pale. "She tried... tried to...stop it."

"I'm not mad," I added quickly, not wanting to upset her, not when the paramedics were hanging bags from her body, not when that gauze at her side was getting redder by the moment.

Something that had the paramedics worried, if their hurried words were any indication.

More gauze went on.

One of the medics got out of the back, hopped in the front, and the rig started up, pulled away.

"Promise me," Pru said, her fingers loosening from mine,

hand slipping free. I grabbed her wrist, held tight when she murmured, barely audibly, "Promise me you won't be mad."

"I won't be mad."

"No matter what happens."

Fuck. But I gave her that. "No matter what happens," I promised.

Her eyes slid closed. "Thank you, baby," she whispered. "You know..." I leaned forward to hear her. "I would have been so happy to...marry...you."

I clutched her hand. "Stay with me, princess. Stay with me."

"Right...here..."

"Tell me about where you want to go on our honey—"

I didn't finish the question.

Because her heart stopped beating.

THIRTY-FOUR

Pru

"HOSPITAL JELL-O IS THE *SHIT!*"

"Shut up," someone hissed. "He's finally sleeping."

"Shouldn't we be worried about *her* sleeping?"

"Give me the green one," someone else said. "I want to try lime."

I tried to open my eyes, but they felt crusted shut, as though there were concrete blocks attached to my lashes.

"No, I want the green one—"

Smitty.

That was Smitty talking...or rumbling, rather, his big voice booming around the room and hitting me in the stomach.

"Seriously, though, shut up." And Oliver.

"Pru looks pale. Should we get a doctor?" Hazel.

"You're right, Smitty, this *is* good. *Really* good." Raph.

"We should be quiet. She needs rest." Walker.

Fingers on my head, pushing back my bangs. "Hey, honey."

I managed to peel open my eyes, saw Cathy standing over me. "Hi," I whispered...or more like, rasped.

Cathy smiled. "Hi. You need some water?"

I nodded. Water sounded amazing right then.

No sooner had my chin dipped then a straw (and a cup) appeared. I tried to sit up to drink, but even the slightest bit of movement had my side screaming in agony.

"Don't move, honey," Cathy said. "Just drink up, and I'll get the doctor, let her know that you're awake."

I drank. I didn't move.

Once I'd drained the whole glass, Cathy quietly set the cup on the side table and then slipped from the room. Meanwhile, the hockey players who'd apparently taken over my room, crowded around my bed.

"How ya doing, sweetheart?" Conner rumbled.

I smiled when he reached out to touch me then halted as though afraid he might hurt me with his big ol' mitts. "I'm okay," I said.

His brows came up.

"Been better. Been worse."

Those brows came down, dragged together. "You've been shot."

I smiled. "Like I said. I've been better. I've been worse."

Smitty glanced at Raph, who shrugged. "Total badass."

Walker nodded in agreement.

"What time is it?" I rasped.

"Four," Smitty said.

I frowned. I'd slept the entire day away?

"On Wednesday," he finished.

I jerked. Which was a very bad idea. But the shock of sleeping an entire day away had given way to the shock of sleeping *five* days away.

His parents had come on Friday.

It was Wednesday.

I jerked again. "You all have a game—"

Smitty nodded. "We're taking off in a few minutes." He smiled, dropped a hand to my ankle (somehow gently, even with those big mitts). "Glad we got to see those pretty eyes of yours." A nod to my side, and belatedly, I realized that Marcel was curled up next me. "He was worried about you."

I knew he had been, even without seeing the dark, bruised circles beneath his eyes, the pale skin, the rumpled hair, and the half-grown stubble.

Because if the tables had been turned, I would have been beside myself with worry.

I lifted my arm, pushed back the hair lying across his forehead. "Did he get any sleep at all?" I asked when he didn't so much as stir.

Raph glanced at his phone. "Yeah. About fifteen minutes."

Shit.

No wonder he was so out of it that we were having a full-blown conversation and he wasn't stirring.

"We should let you both get some rest," Hazel said softly, moving in and giving me a gentle hug. "I'm glad you're okay," she whispered.

"I love you," I whispered back.

Hazel jerked, leaned back. "Pru." Tears in her eyes. "I love you, too, honey."

"I shouldn't have waited so long to tell you that," I said softly.

"No, *we* shouldn't have," Hazel said.

A touch to my cheek, tears in my friend's eyes, and then Haze was leaning against Oliver as they slipped out the door.

"You guys should get ready for the game," I told Smitty, Walker, and Raph. "Thank you for coming, but I don't want your routine to be—"

"Fuck the routine," Smitty rumbled. "There are more important things than hockey." He squeezed my ankle, glanced up when the doctor stepped into the room, Cathy on her heels. "But I'm guessing the doctor needs to examine you, so we'll get out of your hair." He cut his eyes to Marcel. "Try to do it without waking that one."

I smiled gently. "Okay."

Walker patted my hand. "Glad you're okay, Pru."

I nodded, then accepted Raph's kiss on the cheek, his whispered assurance that everything was going to be okay.

Because it was.

It was going to be okay.

Cathy slipped out while the doctor examined my wound.

Marcel slept on.

And, it was a good thing, because being poked and prodded —even just for a couple of minutes—had exhaustion flooding my veins, dragging me back under.

Wrapped in Marcel's arms, I let it.

IT WASN'T until a week later that I finally got the details of everything that had happened.

Well, I remembered the bridge part and Marissa going insane at the house.

But what came after, and what happened at the hospital. That was kind of sketchy.

"Scared the shit out of me," Marcel murmured. "You went so pale, and then you coded. The medics worked on you the entire way to the hospital. Then they took you straight to surgery and..." His voice cracked.

"I'm sorry, baby," I whispered.

"Luckily, I was only in the waiting room by myself for a few minutes. Then the guys showed up. Every one of them. The support staff, too. We filled that room with the Breakers, until every single one of your family members was there watching and praying and sending good thoughts."

And looking out for him.

Because he was family, too.

"And in my room, too."

He nodded. "They'd only let them in one at a time at first, then a few at a time," Marcel said. "They all wanted to see you, so the guys took up a rotation."

"Really?"

He smiled. "Really," he said, pushing my bangs back. "Lucky, it happened during a home stand. Otherwise, I don't think that Luc would have been able to roster a team."

"Crazy boys," I whispered, shifting slightly in Marcel's bed.

"They love you."

"*I* love *you*."

I knew he did. But he had also been by my side for the last week. I'd needed him, too. I'd felt like...well, like I'd gotten shot. It was brutal and scary and brought up old shit, and full recovery was going to take a while.

And I was lucky.

The bullet had missed everything critical...well, everything except the vessels that had caused me to nearly bleed out.

But I didn't lose any organs.

I hadn't lost my life.

And...Marissa.

Well, Marissa had.

She'd fired at the headlights, the ones that I remembered running to. The ones that turned out to be a police car...a police car followed by several others because Kylee had told Marcel enough details that he knew where Marissa had taken me. And it turned out that police officers didn't like it when you turn a gun on them.

They fired back.

Marissa was alive, but it wasn't looking good that she'd wake up.

And maybe it made me a bad person, but I didn't give a shit if Marissa *ever* woke up.

Marcel settled the pillows behind me, tucked the blankets up to my chin, and I could say, having a man who never left my side was a good thing for my recovery.

And it was.

It just...wasn't a good thing for *his*.

I waited until he finished with his fussing, then took his hand and drew him onto the bed next to me. "You need to go back to work."

His eyes clouded. "Princess."

"No excuses, honey. You need to get back to your routine. *I* need to get back to my routine."

"You were *shot* a week ago."

"And I can't do anything but lie in this bed."

"And I should be—"

"Here?" I asked. "Fluffing my pillows?"

He scowled.

I cupped his cheek. "I love you. I so appreciate that you were here, but we're both okay. We need to...I need us to start to try to get back to normal. And that means hockey." My lips curved. "I need you to get on the ice, so I have some stats to track."

His scowl didn't dissipate, but it did soften slightly, his hand coming up to cover mine. "You don't even track my stats," he murmured.

"If you play, I *can*," I countered.

"Princess."

"Baby."

He sighed. "I don't know how to go back to normal. I lost you in that ambulance. You were gone, your heart stopped, your blood—"

He cut himself off.

But I knew, just knew that it would take time for us to get that normal.

But I also had backup.

A knock at the bedroom door, just on time.

Exactly as planned.

Cathy walked in, followed by Hazel, Leo, and...slowly, her expression wan and full of regret, Kylee followed them.

And behind *her?*

Smitty.

Holding up a set of keys, rattling them slightly in his palm.

Hazel wriggled herself onto the bed, held up two DVDs. "Sappy or sappier?"

"Sappier, obvs," I told her. "Except, we'll need to stream it. No DVD players in *this* house."

"I know." She opened the case of sappier, pulled out a paper with a download code. "Your man isn't the only one who can plan ahead."

"Come on, Markie," Smitty said, when Marcel just sat by my hip. "Gotta go before we hit traffic."

Marcel's indecision was as clear as day, but when Cathy snuggled in near Hazel and when Kylee sat at the foot of the bed and when Leo took a seat in the chair by the window, he allowed me to shove him lightly and found his feet.

"Princess," he said softly.

"I'll be okay," I said. "I've got our family," I whispered. "Now you've got to let them take care of you, too."

He brushed his lips over my temple, whispered back. "I'm freaked the fuck out."

My hands found his hair, and I admitted, "I am, too." I knew it was the right thing, that we couldn't hole up in this bedroom and live on DoorDash forever. "But," I added when he jerked in response to my words. "You broke through steel, baby. I know if I need you, you have me."

Still.

He was so still.

Then he smiled.

It was small.

There were still shadows under his eyes, his hair was in disarray, his yummy jaw coated in stubble. "I'd have you," he whispered.

"I know."

"You have *me*."

Now he was getting it.

"Yes." A beat. "Now *please*, baby, go play some fucking hockey."

EPILOGUE

Marcel

"THERE," she murmured, hanging the last picture.

I watched her climb down the ladder, and it had been long enough that I didn't immediately move to steady her.

One, because she'd quickly lost patience with my fussing.

And two, because she'd been given the all-clear from the doctor for normal activities.

It was Christmas Eve, and we'd just finished moving her stuff in.

She'd spent the last hour trying to recreate the mosaic of pictures I'd put together for her place, something that was made more difficult by the fact that I didn't have the same empty walls...and because we'd bought a *giant*—and I meant *giant*—Christmas tree two weeks before.

It took up most of my living room and blocked any of the decent wall space for mosaic hanging.

But Pru had been determined.

She had wriggled her way behind the tree and been 3M-stripping it for close to an hour now.

And from what I could see of the photos, they looked amazing.

"All done?" I murmured.

"All done," she agreed, shifting to my side and wrapping an arm around my waist. "What do you think?"

"It looks amazing."

"Yeah?"

I nodded. It did look amazing. She'd added a few more pictures from our time together, sprinkling in shots of us and the team and several photos from my parents' various visits during her recovery.

She glanced up at me.

"Do you like the new photos I added?" she asked.

My gaze darted over a group shot of me, Pru, Smitty, and Raph, at CeCe's, all with huge smiles on our faces.

We'd been celebrating Pru putting on real pants for the first time since she'd gotten out of the hospital (real pants meaning jeans). That had also been the first night we'd had sex again, and when I'd been determined to go gentle and easy, Pru had taken things into her own hands.

I was thinking about that night and how fucking good it had been, which was probably why I missed the hint in that statement.

"But do you *really* like them?" she asked.

I'd liked her breasts in my mouth that night. Her pussy clamping down around my cock. I'd loved...every single second of it.

"Marcel?"

Maybe I could talk her into riding me again...or maybe, I could coax her higher, put my hands on that lush ass and bring her up so that she rode my mouth. "Hmm?"

"Marcel!"

I blinked—and truly, I swallowed the drool that was forming. "Yeah, princess?"

"I *asked* if you liked the pictures."

"Baby, I said—" I cut himself off, focused on her face. Or more realistically, I focused on her gaze...and how it kept darting to one particular part of the wall.

Frowning, I looked where she was looking.

And then...I struggled.

For one long moment, I struggled to see what I was...well, *seeing*.

The mosaic was there. The new pictures of the guys and my family were there. But there was more. Interspersed throughout the wall were photos of words, and when I read left to right, top to bottom, I saw that those words formed a sentence.

No.

A question.

"Pru?" I whispered.

"You didn't see that coming, now, did you?" she murmured.

I hadn't.

I had a plan for this.

That plan didn't involve Pru doing the asking.

Because the question was:

Will. You. Marry. Me?

Scraped into the ice, shot from up close.

On my wall.

Her hand rested on my chest; her body was pressed tight. "Do you need me to get down on one knee?" she whispered.

My heart pounded. "Princess."

"I'm guessing you had a plan for this," she said softly, eyes gentle.

I nodded.

"I'm guessing that I threw it *all* out of whack."

I nodded again.

She grinned. "So, baby, my next question for you is..."

I lifted a brow.

"Are you ready to sign up for a lifetime of me ruining your plans?"

A lifetime sounded good, sounded fucking *great*.

"Pru?"

"Yeah?"

I reached into my pocket, tugged out the ring I'd stashed there just that morning. The ring I'd planned on presenting to her over waffles and strawberries and whipped cream. The ring I'd imagined her showing off to our family the next day.

"Yes."

"Yes, what?"

I stepped close and kissed her temple.

Because she melted every single time I did it.

Because I knew that it made her feel special, so I loved giving her that.

"Yes, to the lifetime of messed up plans," I said. "Yes, to the photos on the walls and the woman who hogs my blanket at night. Yes, to your laughter and your smile and"—I rested my palm on her chest—"your heart."

She sniffed.

"But I have to ask, princess..."

Her hand lifted, rested on the side of my neck. "Yeah, baby?"

"Are you ready for a lifetime of spreadsheets?"

Her smile was huge, her eyes dancing, and then her other hand joined the first, lacing into my hair, pulling my mouth down to hers. "Fuck, yes, I am."

Then, sealed with a kiss that stole my breath and packed

my heart carefully in Pru's special brand of cotton wool, I slid the ring onto her finger.

And I knew that my future was just beginning.

I couldn't fucking wait to see what adventures we'd have together.

And I couldn't wait until we found our way back home.

Pru, Three Years Later

"See that, baby?" I whispered to my wide-eyed daughter. "That's why we allow Daddy to have extra time in the gym."

Because the man's abs were glorious spread out over a fourteen-foot tall and forty-eight-foot wide billboard.

Why the specific size?

Because I'd planned ahead...or at least asked ahead.

Before I'd brought Marcel out here.

We were on the road, joining the team for their game against the Rangers, getting a babysitter so we could eat at a fancy restaurant, sans the hallway accosting. But mostly, it was because I'd heard from our favorite photographer, Mick, that Marcel's new campaign was going live.

I loved seeing my man on a billboard.

Hence the trip.

Plus, it meant that I got to impart some New York City love onto my travel bug of a six-month-old daughter, who'd been to more states and on more plane rides than most adults.

Because she was precious and wonderful and a gift that I had never expected to receive.

So Catherine Hazelbeth Aubert traveled with me whenever possible.

Marcel groaned as he took in himself in just a pair of tight black boxer briefs on the billboard. "Fuck, princess. They *just* stopped giving me shit for the last campaign."

I grinned. "Don't listen to Daddy," I whispered, smoothing down Catherine's peach fuzz turning into sort of hair. "He *loves* it."

Marcel, handsome, wonderful, an amazing husband and a father any kid would dream about, scowled and smoothed *his* hand down our son's hair as he cradled Leonardo Oliver (our kids had mouthfuls of names, but no one gave us shit about bestowing those mouthfuls—they'd been too touched and happy for me and Marcel).

Because it turned out that having one ovary meant having eggs.

As Beth had pointed out when she'd come down for my wedding, encouraging me to meet with a fertility doctor when I was ready.

It had taken me a bit to be ready.

But Beth had been ready all along. My friend, my best friend who'd lived so far away for so long, who'd come back after I had found Marcel, taking a job in Baltimore...and had offered to be a surrogate for me and Marcel.

I had been shocked, freaked out by how the surrogate process would work.

But Beth had calmed that freak-out.

She'd offered but hadn't pushed.

And, eventually, Marcel and I had taken her up on her offer.

Beth had encouraged us to implant all three of the embryos we'd managed to make into *her* uterus, and Beth carried my babies for me, protected the two embryos that took, and was never upset that she'd signed up for single-baby-carrying-duty and had ended up carting around twins for thirty-six weeks.

She'd cooked our babies to full-term, done it with a grin on her face, and a casual, "The uterus was primed and ready to go. We might as well have made it count."

And she had.

Because Marcel and I now had our family.

Catherine Hazelbeth (mouthful one) and Leonardo Oliver (mouthful two).

Wonderful, amazing, soul-fulfilling gifts...

"Mom?"

"Hmm?" I asked, absently stroking my free hand over my other daughter's head. Seven and with type one diabetes, Mila Rose had been an orphan, in state care, lost and sad, and I...I knew what it was like to be lost and sad. I *didn't* know what it was like to have diabetes, but we had good health insurance, great friends, and a willingness to learn.

So we'd adopted Mila, and we hadn't regretted it, not one time in the last ten months.

Not knowing that we had twins on the way and sleepless nights in our future and it might be overwhelming.

Not knowing the health challenges were going to be intense.

Not knowing that we'd had seven years without her, so we might never be *Mom* and *Dad* to our Mila (thus making the gift of Mila giving that to us a few months ago all that much sweeter).

Not knowing that we were going from two to five in the blink of an eye and were going to be over our heads and outnumbered.

Because my man was a fabulous planner and we had everything from field trips to school lunch to diaper and formula runs sorted.

Because we had love in o hearts and a legion of hockey players at our backs.

And because...there was more than one way to make a family.

"Yeah, baby?" I asked, wrapping my arm around Mila,

holding both my daughters tight like the precious gifts they were, leaning my head against Marcel's shoulder when he drifted close, bringing himself and Little Leo into our huddle.

"I think Uncle Smitty is going to tease Dad about this."

Laughter bubbled up in my chest, overflowed, loud and light...and no trace of steel in sight.

I pulled out my cell, handed it to Mila, and said, "Take a picture, baby, and put it in the group text, would you?"

Smitty

I'd found her.

One look and I'd known.

Quiet where I was loud. Smart when I wasn't.

Pretty...well, I'd never been and would never be considered pretty.

She was walking down the halls of the practice facility, earbuds in, eyes on the tablet in front of her, totally oblivious to anything except what she was concentrating on.

Certainly, she was oblivious that she was...*mine.*

But I'd known.

Just like Pru had said.

I'd seen the slender column of her throat, the narrow shoulders, and long, long legs, and my heart had kicked.

Hard.

Hard enough that even a big brute like me had paid attention.

Stopped me dead in my tracks, sweat dripping down my spine, my temples, my beard.

And she?

She'd walked by without noticing me. *Me.* A man of my size didn't get missed. *Everyone* knew that I was there. Because if my size didn't get their attention, then certainly my voice would.

But...I hadn't talked when she'd walked by.

Because of that heart kicking, and I'd also had some lung squeezing action happening. Which meant that any hope of talking to her—*her!*—had disappeared.

I'd been reduced to a quiet sort of gurgling sound, and that had, luckily, been missed by *her* because of the earbuds she'd been wearing.

And now, still sweating, I was following her.

Trying to think of something charming and witty that would get her to realize that I was hers and then we'd have our happy ending and everything would be fucking cool.

Like Pru and Marcel.

Like Hazel and Oliver.

Like Luc and Lexi.

She'd paused outside an office—empty, I knew. Or maybe not empty any longer, I realized, seeing the new nameplate attached to the wall.

Kailey Henderson.

One piece of the puzzle solved.

Next, convincing her that she was my soul mate.

I walked up behind her, stood close as she pushed open the office door, caught the wooden panel before it shut. She didn't seem to notice that it didn't close, that I'd followed her inside.

Earbuds. Dangerous.

But I'd discuss that with her later.

I moved to the desk, leaned a hip against it, and waited until she noticed me. Maybe she'd missed me in the hall. But in an enclosed space, this close to her person and eventually she would spot me.

And she did.

Five minutes later.

Probably because impatience had gotten the better of me and I was rocking my leg back and forth, shaking her desk.

She stood up, pulled out her earbuds.

I opened my mouth.

"Not interested," she said.

And then she spun on her heel, pushed out through her office door, and disappeared down the hall.

Thank you for reading! I hope you loved meeting Pru and Marcel! The next book in the Breakers Hockey series is BALLSY. Kailey Henderson dealt in code. Well, code, social anxiety, and online gaming. What I didn't deal in was sexy hockey players. But Smitty had decided differently...

CLICK HERE TO READ BALLSY NOW >

ARE you ready to meet Lake Jordan, star forward for the Sierra, underwear model, vodka proprietor, and the man everyone hates to play against? Lake's book, OVER THE LINE, is coming this November!

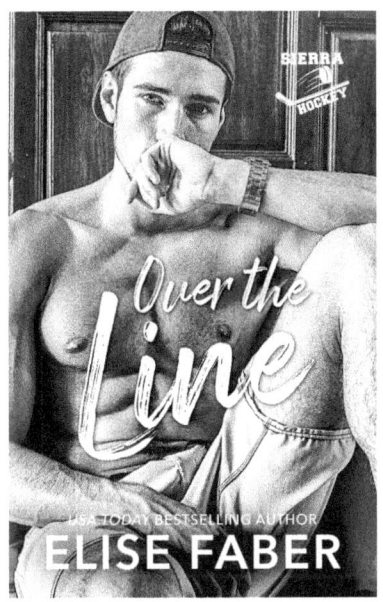

CLICK HERE TO GET OVER THE LINE NOW>

IF YOU ENJOY MY SERIES, considering supporting me on PATREON! Get access to early releases, bonus content, character art, audiobooks, special edition covers, swag, and much more!

CLICK HERE TO SUPPORT ME>

Hate missing Elise's new releases? Love contests, exclusive excerpts and giveaways?
Then signup for Elise's newsletter here!

www.elisefaber.com/newsletter

And join Elise's fan group, the Fabinators (https://www.facebook.com/groups/fabinators) for insider information, sneak peaks at new releases, and fun freebies! Hope to see you there!

If you enjoy my series, considering supporting me on PATREON! Get access to early releases, bonus content, character art, audiobooks, special edition covers, swag, and much more!

CLICK HERE TO SUPPORT ME>

I so appreciate your help in spreading the word about my books, including sharing with friends! Please leave a review on your favorite book site!

BREAKERS HOCKEY SERIES

ALSO BY ELISE FABER

Broken

Boldly

Breathless

Ballsy

Bewitched

Blowout

Breathe

Blazed

Sierra Hockey Series

Over the Line

Caught from Behind

The Big Skate

On the Fly

Eagles Hockey Series (all stand alone)

Broken Laces

Lace 'em Up

Knotted Laces

Loaded Laces

Lucky Laces

Oak Ridge Vineyards

Bottles & Blades

Beauty & the Boardroom

Rush Hockey Trilogy #1

Big Puck Energy

Filthy Puckboy

So Pucking Over It

Rush Hockey Trilogy #2

Love, Pucks, and Other Stories

All's Fair in Pucks and War

No Pucks Lost Between Us

Rush Hockey Novellas

Puck and Make Up

Billionaire's Club (all stand alone)

Bad Night Stand

Bad Breakup

Bad Husband

Bad Hookup

Bad Divorce

Bad Fiancé

Bad Boyfriend

Bad Blind Date

Bad Wedding

Bad Engagement

Bad Bridesmaid

Bad Swipe

Bad Girlfriend

Bad Best Friend

Bad Rebound

Bad Romance

Bad Business

Bad Billionaire's Quickies

Love, Action, Camera (all stand alone)

Dotted Line

Action Shot

Close-Up

End Scene

Meet Cute

Love After Midnight (**all stand alone**)

Rum And Notes

Virgin Daiquiri

On The Rocks

Sex On The Seats

Life Sucks Series

Train Wreck

Hot Mess

Dumpster Fire

Clusterf*@k

FUBAR

Perfect Storm

Free Fall

Lost Cause

Roosevelt Ranch Series (**all stand alone, series complete**)

Disaster at Roosevelt Ranch

Heartbreak at Roosevelt Ranch

Collision at Roosevelt Ranch

Regret at Roosevelt Ranch

Desire at Roosevelt Ranch

***Phoenix Series* (read in order)**

Phoenix Rising

Dark Phoenix

Phoenix Freed

***Phoenix: LexTal Chronicles* (rereleasing soon, stand alone, Phoenix world)**

From Ashes

In Flames

To Smoke

KTS Series (all stand alone, series complete)

Riding The Edge

Crossing The Line

Leveling The Field

Scorching The Earth

Cocky Heroes World

Tattooed Troublemaker

ABOUT THE AUTHOR

USA Today bestselling author, Elise Faber, loves chocolate, Star Wars, Harry Potter, and hockey (the order depending on the day and how well her team -- the Sharks! -- are playing). She and her husband also play as much hockey as they can squeeze into their schedules, so much so that their typical date night is spent on the ice. Elise is the mom to two exuberant boys and lives in Northern California. Connect with her in her Facebook group, the Fabinators or find more information about her books at www.elisefaber.com.

facebook.com/elisefaberauthor

amazon.com/author/elisefaber

bookbub.com/profile/elise-faber

instagram.com/elisefaber

tiktok.com/@elisefaberauthor

goodreads.com/elisefaber